Land *for* Fatimah

Essential Prose Series 152

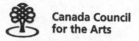

Canada Council
for the Arts

Conseil des Arts
du Canada

ONTARIO ARTS COUNCIL
CONSEIL DES ARTS DE L'ONTARIO

an Ontario government agency
un organisme du gouvernement de l'Ontario

Canadä

Guernica Editions Inc. acknowledges the support of the Canada Council
for the Arts and the Ontario Arts Council. The Ontario Arts Council
is an agency of the Government of Ontario.

We acknowledge the financial support of the Government of Canada.

Land
for
Fatimah

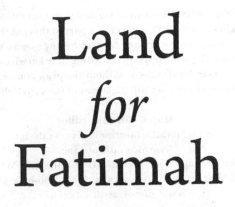

VEENA GOKHALE

GUERNICA
EDITIONS
TORONTO • BUFFALO • LANCASTER (U.K.)
2018

Michael Mirolla, editor
David Moratto, interior and cover design
Guernica Editions Inc.
1569 Heritage Way, Oakville, (ON), Canada L6M 2Z7
2250 Military Road, Tonawanda, N.Y. 14150-6000 U.S.A.
www.guernicaeditions.com

Distributors:
University of Toronto Press Distribution,
5201 Dufferin Street, Toronto (ON), Canada M3H 5T8
Gazelle Book Services, White Cross Mills
High Town, Lancaster LA1 4XS U.K.

First edition.
Printed in Canada.

Legal Deposit — First Quarter
Library of Congress Catalog Card Number: 2017955481
Library and Archives Canada Cataloguing in Publication

Gokhale, Veena, author
Land for Fatimah / Veena Gokhale. -- First edition.

(Essential prose series ; 152)
Issued in print and electronic formats.
ISBN 978-1-77183-269-4 (softcover).--ISBN 978-1-77183-270-0 (EPUB).
--ISBN 978-1-77183-271-7 (Kindle)

I. Title. II. Series: Essential prose series ; 152

PS8613.O42L36 2018   C813'.6   C2017-906407-X   C2017-906408-8

*Could a greater miracle take place than for us
to look through each other's eyes for an instant?
We should live in all the ages of the world
in an hour; ay, in all worlds of the ages.*
—**Henry David Thoreau**

*All I know is that every time
I go to Africa, I am shaken to my core.*
—**Stephen Lewis**

*Dedicated to all the idealists
and activists out there*

The Characters

ANJALI BHAVE BHAGAT: an international development worker at Health, Education & Livelihood Skills Partnership (HELP)
RAHUL: her son
INDUMATI: her mother
VANDANA: her sister
JEREMY: her boyfriend

FATIMAH DITTA: an Aanke farmer
AMADU: Fatimah's brother
KASI UMAR KAARYA / BAABA KAARYA: Fatimah's father
MASUMI KASI DITTA: Fatimah's mother
LAHMEY: Fatimah's husband
HAWA AND JELANI: their twin daughter and son
ABUBAKAR: Fatimah's brother-in-law
EBUN: Abubakar's daughter

GRACE MADAKI: Chairperson of HELP
PETER DIA: Grace's brother
HASSAN: A consultant

ELIZABETH: Anjali's assistant
KAMAU: Elizabeth's husband
DR. NATHAN KALISH: Anjali's colleague
JULIE: Nathan's wife
ANNE: Anjali's colleague
MATHEW: Anjali's boss

MARY IWU: Anjali's maid
GABRIEL: her son
EDITH: Mary's cousin
AISSA: Edith's daughter
JOHN: Edith's son
OTIENO: Mary's brother
FATHER EMMANUEL: Gabriel's benefactor

FUDU: Anjali's gardener
KIBWE: Anjali's driver
JOHN: The night watchman

MARTHA HINES: Anjali's American expat friend
RICHARD: her husband
JERRY: her son
DANA: her daughter

Contents

Land
for
Fatimah

The Demolition

I T STARTED AS a normal day at Vishwas Bhau Colony, a small slum in Andheri. Then the men came from the Bombay Municipal Corporation to take it all down.

On that normal day toddlers with distended bellies and large, appealing eyes, clad in stained half-pants, entertained themselves with discoloured, wooden blocks and discarded plastic containers. One dragged an armless doll; another squeezed a cheerful, rubber monkey. Others crawled in the dust, content amidst the fallen leaves of a spindly *Neem* tree that arched overhead.

Nearby a handful of goats nibbled at the edge of a large rubbish heap, while a brood of hens kept a respectful distance, waiting their turn at the trash. Smoke from charcoal kitchen fires lingered in the morning air.

Some of the older children who did not go to school, or had skipped school, started a game of hopscotch. Others jumped energetically over a length of rope held taut by two docile playmates.

Old man Vishnu, squatting outside his lopsided shack, relishing his first smoke of the day, surveyed the scene with a benevolent smile. The hour when he would turn tyrant had not yet arrived.

Later, as the sun rose high to roast the corrugated tin roofs of the one-room shacks, ingeniously put together from plywood, plastic sheets, sticks, stones, rags and whatever else had been at hand, the adults would make for the shade. But the children, the children would suddenly run wild, as if directly charged by the ball of fire up in the sky. As they chased each other through the little alleys that separated the rows of shanties, screaming, an excited dog or two would follow them. Other dogs kept wisely to the shade, cocking half an ear at the kids gone berserk.

The toddlers would be safely out of the way by then, snoozing inside their homes, lying on mats, half covered with soft, old *sarees,* flinching yet continuing to slumber as flies and mosquitoes settled on their exposed limbs.

Vishnu, still at his perch, also slumbering, his head jerking this way and that—he refused an official siesta —would suddenly come awake. Rising unsteadily to his feet, he would start chasing the children, displaying surprising agility, letting out a string of colourful curses. After all, his namesake, Lord Vishnu, was the keeper of order and preserver of the world.

The kids, an unruly bunch at the best of times, would slow down. Now a couple of mothers would emerge in brilliant nylon *sarees*, working their arms in many directions, shouting, reminiscent of Indian goddesses brandishing weapons and sacred objects in their multiple hands. In short order, the adults would prevail upon the gang; and the children, their faces shining with sweat and happiness, would turn to a quieter game.

That day the role of the gods was taken over by a dozen men, armed with sticks and axes, accompanied by four policemen. They arrived at mid-morning, in a whirl of dust, in two vans and a jeep. Jumping out, they took their positions at the entrance.

The events that followed were muddled and mottled like a gruesome nightmare; the many witnesses bore various versions of "the truth." But there are some indisputable facts. A few hours later, the 40 huts that formed Vishwas Bhau Colony had been reduced to rubble. And this was in 1971, before the time when slum demolition squads would employ bulldozers.

The demolition was not covered by media. There were no outside witnesses.

We can only speculate that there were bruises, blood, and even some broken bones. Cries of horror, shrieks of pain; people grabbing what they could of their possessions; gathering close their children, watching hypnotized as the municipal axe fell remorselessly on their lives. People must have questioned the men and beseeched them to stop. Perhaps a couple of young men had thrown themselves at the demolishers. Some of the women, virtual Amazons, must have stood resolutely at their door, daring the men to hack them to pieces along with their homes. The cops who accompanied the men from the municipality must have swung into action, meting out punishment.

Bruises, blood, broken bones. Cries of horror. Shrieks of pain.

How do you monitor what happens in slum demolitions in Bombay? Demolitions the media ignore, that lack external witnesses? How do you keep track of the human story while urban planning twists and turns, piling high turgid reports and policy papers on dusty, office shelves? One hand giveth, the other taketh away. The office that implements pro-poor schemes also sends out troops to level slums. Oh, the impenetrability of municipal politics! It has baffled even the most determined and outraged activists.

A few hours later, as Vishnu sat with his back against a collapsed wall, vacant eyed, shirt half undone, flecks of dust in his wild hair, a young girl, neatly dressed in a blue-and-white school uniform—long, straight braids, polished black shoes—bent over him. The girl—an outsider, thrust suddenly into a brutality that had been distant, until then—and the old man, looked for a moment into each other's eyes. He, slowly emerging from his stupor, gave her a twisted smile. All she could do was stare, continuing her descent into shock and distress.

For Vishnu that moment was no different from the others that made up his rough and ready existence, but the girl carried it within her, always. She never forgot that ambiguous smile.

CHAPTER 1

Dust Tracks

ANJALI LOOKED OUT of the car window at a landscape painted in multiple shades of ochre and brown. There was land, land and more land, empty, under a blank, blue sky, with a scattering of small, thorny plants. There were no trees here, certainly no baobabs—those magnificent, African giants that so become such a landscape. They had left them behind to traverse through this minimalist scene, rich in nuance only for those with knowing eyes.

This was a stretch of the road that brought dread, made her tongue stick to the roof of her mouth, even though she had made this journey from Venimeli to Makaenga many times in the past few months, without incident. But ... but what if something happened? What if the car broke down right here?

Africa will clear your mind of everything but itself.
Leave you breathless, beached, on an island,
somewhere within its immensity. Emptiness echoing
emptiness. In the middle of a scorched, arid plain,
not a tree in sight, not a drop of water to be had,
an unrelenting sun beating down on baked earth;

a dust track so faint that you wonder if it's real.
After some considerable time, a lone hut,
shimmering in the distance ... a vision that turns
out to be a mirage ...

The car lurched as Kibwe, the driver, swerved to avoid a rough patch. Don't be hysterical, Anjali told herself. This was not AFRICA. There was no such thing, really, except that it loomed large in the minds of foreigners. Scores of countries, a thriving diversity, collapsed into AFRICA. And they were actually driving through a rather civilized section of Kamorga.

Her skin was stretched taut by the desiccated air; her lips felt brittle, the physical discomfort exaggerating her emotional distress. Taking a sip from her water bottle, she glanced at Elizabeth. Her young assistant sat erect beside her, immobile, her hands folded on her lap, looking at the broad dust track that served as their road. She had hardly spoken since they had left Venimeli, two hours ago. Neither had Kibwe. Anjali marvelled at this capacity for silence, not unfriendliness but an enviable self-containment that she dared not breach.

She wondered how Elizabeth felt about the landscape. She was not originally from the small but influential state of Ampaler, which housed both Venimeli, the capital, from where they had come, and Makaenga, the town where they were headed. It was unlikely, though, that this journey made Elizabeth uneasy. In all likelihood she barely noticed the landscape, her thoughts taken up with other things.

Elizabeth had been educated in Kamorga, in a private, English-medium school, which Anjali imagined was not so very different from the one she had attended, in Bombay.

Both of them had grown up in young nations: former British colonies. But here the resemblance ended. Kamorga was home to Elizabeth, while Anjali was living in Africa for the very first time, replacing her colleague Anne, who had gone back to Toronto to tend to her dying mother.

Anjali wished that the dread that claimed her would evaporate. Why couldn't she just get over it? She had never felt apprehensive when she had traversed comparable desolation elsewhere. Born in India, it was understándable that she had been at home in Pakistan and Bangladesh, when she had gone there for work. Both the countries had felt familiar. The wide, open spaces in Canada, her adopted country, had not threatened either. Rather, they had delighted. All those landscapes had somehow been domesticated, but not this one. This one released an ancient, nameless fear.

She slumped into the lumpy, old seat, the belt straining against her body. She was the only one wearing one. She had stopped telling people to wear seat belts. Closing her eyes, she pictured Jeremy, a nourishing oasis in this wilderness.

Jeremy had come to visit them two months ago. He had been keen to learn as much as he could about Health, Education & Livelihood Skills Partnership (HELP), the organization where Anjali worked. And so she had taken him to HELP's field office in Makaenga.

They had held hands under the folds of Anjali's blue-green *chunni*, an Indian stole, falling gracefully from her shoulders onto the smooth, ivory-coloured upholstery. They had travelled in the sturdy office van that time, not in this old car. Now Anjali inclined her head slightly so that it rested on Jeremy's shoulder, narrow and bony, yet comforting. She could still sense the warmth of his body through his short-sleeved shirt, but his scent, mixed with sweat and aftershave, was waning in her memory, drifting away.

Grace, the Board Chair of HELP, had let Anjali have the van for a change. The van had been bought for field trips, and Anjali, as Acting Executive Director of the Africa Regional Office, was supposed to have as much access to it as she needed. But Grace kept it mostly for herself. This was one more thing that Anjali had stopped protesting.

"You want to take your fiancé to Makaenga? Why not?" Grace had said. They had decided on the phone, in advance, to play the "fiancé" game when he came to visit. It had included Jeremy finding his discarded, wedding ring and putting it on. Anjali always wore the gold ring with a single ruby that had once belonged to her grandmother.

There was another passenger with them that day— Rahul, sitting beside Jeremy and looking dreamily out of the window. They had let him miss school. His Game Boy was not in his hand, but tucked away in his pocket. A miracle! Earlier, Kibwe had loaded Rahul's bike on the top of the van and secured it to the rack with solicitous care. It rattled against the metal frame every time they hit a bump.

Rahul! His mobile face, like her own, had delicate features. The expression she envisioned on it was guarded; his eyes were remote. Anjali shoulders sagged as she thought of her son. His grades, never good in Kamorga, had hit a new low after Jeremy had gone back to Canada.

It had been wonderful going to Makaenga with both of them, she thought, sitting up straighter. Usually she travelled there with Elizabeth and Kibwe. She had also done this route with colleagues from abroad: a South African journalist, an official from the British Department for International

Development and a Canadian, a provincial politician. But on that day, shiny with promise, she had gone with Jeremy and Rahul, sharing not just a workday, but also this compelling journey from city to countryside.

They had set out from the HELP office in Lekme, Venimeli's city centre, where dingy glass fronts impartially reflected beggars, hawkers—wheeling crude handcarts, carrying wares on their head or setting up shop at street corners —and street kids rubbing shoulders with well-heeled professionals exiting from parked cars; shops, modest and upwardly mobile, jostling for customers; office buildings, some showing their age, others spruced up with a coat of paint.

And the roads! Such roads they were! The city centre and only the city centre had dream roads that wore a thick pelt of asphalt.

The riches of the core were not to be squandered on the periphery, and they soon dissipated, melting away into indistinguishable neighbourhoods, congested and alien, which Anjali scarcely knew.

As they moved into the suburbs they saw rickety, greyish shacks, lean-tos and low buildings, and little workshops where all kinds of products, used by the city dwellers, were made from scratch, or assembled. There were vendors with pushcarts piled with bunches of bananas or hardy vegetables—potatoes, onions, yams and carrots. Now and then a little market bloomed with eye-catching displays of food and clothes and chickens and household goods. Scruffy, inadequate patches of land, attached to small, dilapidated buildings, claimed attention.

In contrast stood proud little churches and mosques, their paint proper, the little piece of ground around them well tended. They always passed an untidy cluster of buildings in a huge compound; encircled by a twisted wire fence that Anjali knew to be Venimeli's biggest public hospital.

Soon the preponderance of urban life frayed, and little roadside villages straggled into view. A wind-worn, wooden shack here, an unpainted, brick enclosure there; and every so often, a small, half-completed, single-storey structure, sometimes with steel rods sticking out at threatening angles.

She admired these brave, little constructions that fronted the highway. Someone had got the money together to build them, even if they had run out of it mid-way. In Venimeli too she had seen abandoned half-constructed buildings, sometimes as high as three or four storeys.

Already in the distance she would see mud huts. Compared to India they had very few cattle here, though goats were common. It wasn't as if Anjali liked cows, but she experienced a little thrill every time she spotted one.

Amid the dust and plants and trees and hens were half-naked, pot-bellied children, and adults who looked a little poorer and thinner than their city cousins.

Then there were all those objects that the city had junked, which the villagers reclaimed: discarded car tires given a plastic base and turned into water containers; reused plastic bags filled with lurid-coloured drinks, sealed, and hawked for a couple of shillings; coke cans beaten flat to fortify and decorate rickety wooden food stalls; metal bicycle hubs pushed around gleefully with sticks by energetic boys. The flotsam and jetsam of the city acquired a new life in the countryside.

A circular mud hut with a thatched conical roof caught Anjali's eye, and her thoughts turned to the upcoming visit with Fatimah. She would be waiting for them under the ragged blue plastic awning, dressed in a rough cotton, off-white skirt—long and flowing—worn with a loose blouse of the same colour and material, a long, wide, patterned scarf casually draped around her head and shoulders. Metallic bracelets ringed her strong wrists, and she wore metal ear studs. A simple *Tawiz*, a sacred amulet, nestled at the base of her neck. How dignified she always looked!

It was at HELP's field office in Makaenga that Anjali had met Fatimah. An Aanke farmer, she lived in Madafi, the Aanke settlement not very far from HELP's compound. Fatimah had brought her great aunt, Bisa, to the HELP Clinic for a check-up. Bisa had swollen feet, a precursor to debilitating gout. They had run into them on Anjali's very first day at the field office, as Nathan, the young Canadian doctor who headed HELP Venimeli, was taking her around. He had introduced them, and Fatimah had invited her to visit Madafi. Anjali had enthusiastically accepted and gone there on her subsequent visit.

Soon Kibwe turned off the broad dust track into a narrower one that would get them, after a bumpy, thirty minute ride, to Madafi. Fatimah's story unspooled yet again in Anjali's mind. She had heard it directly from Fatimah, from Fatimah with Elizabeth translating, from Amadu, Fatimah's brother, who had a bit of English, from Nathan, and also from HELP project reports.

The tale had come to her without flourishes, but for Anjali the events were high drama. This story had gored its way into her soul.

Some stories cannot be contained. They refuse to remain confined to a particular place, whispered by a select group of people. These stories must get out and wander, make themselves known, grab this ear and that. Such was the story of Fatimah, and the Aanke from Ferun.

CHAPTER 2

Land Lost

I T IS UNCLEAR when or why the Aanke left West Africa to come to Kamorga, but there is consensus among anthropologists that their ancestry can be traced to the Mande people who inhabited that region. The Aanke themselves have a thriving lore about their long journey east; their songs date their migration to the late 1700s. They settled at first in Kamorga's Northwestern Highlands, and most of the Aanke still live and farm there. During a severe drought, some families ventured further inland and settled in two main areas, around Makaenga, in what became their settlement Madafi, and in Ferun, in south-eastern Kamorga. The fertile delta of the Feruni River was home to Fatimah.

Anjali started reading up on African history as she prepared to leave Toronto, in January 1991. What surprised her was the number of ethnic groups who had migrated, sometimes over long distances, on that vast continent. For some reason she had thought that most of the people here lived largely on their original lands. Yet another urban fantasy about rural people, she discovered. It was in north-eastern Africa, after all, that Homo sapiens had first emerged, fanning out, gradually populating the entire planet.

More than a year ago, two officials from the Central Government had come to the little village of Ferun. Fatimah's father, Kasi Umar Kaarya, was the chief there, so the officials came directly to their compound. Fatimah lived in the same compound with her husband, Lahmey, and their two children.

The officials were rude and short from the start, informing Baaba Kaarya that their community, which was made up of some 500 people, would have to move; the government needed their land for a cocoa plantation. Yes, that was how they put it. They did not speak at first of buying land, only of getting it. They said that, because the Aanke let some trees grow in their fields, it would be good land for cocoa, which needs some shade to grow well. But the main reason they needed the Aanke land was because it was next to land they already had, and this land was earmarked for a large plantation.

Baaba Kaarya did not understand what they were saying, so the officials repeated themselves. When realization dawned, he said: "My mother's basket is full of straw. I have no need to sell or buy."

Buying and selling land was an abstraction for the Aanke; they had never viewed their land in that way. They belonged to their land, not the other way around. Their ancestors had lived there and their spirits still resided among them. After every harvest, they held special ceremonies to honour these spirits. Without their blessings, they would not survive. Their children would continue to farm in Ferun. They would introduce new crops and farming techniques, and experiment, as each successive generation had done in the past.

The officials repeated their message, exasperation showing plainly on their faces, and Baaba Kaarya replied: "The land is like our skin. How can we move? If we did, we would surely perish."

"Things are changing, old man. You never bought your land; you just took it. No deeds, no papers, no nothing." The man who was in the lead waved a thick wad of paper at Baaba Kaarya. The government surveyors would be back in two weeks to survey the land and determine a price for it. It was for Baaba Kaarya to convey the news to the community and to prepare them. The government was in a hurry; they had no time to waste. They expected the Aanke off the land in a month and half.

Baaba Kaarya, incredulous, was reduced to silence. Fatimah, who had been observing from the sidelines, stepped up.

"That's impossible," she said.

The men ignored her. They placed the papers in Baaba Kaarya's hands and turned to go. Baaba Kaarya could not read; he passed the papers silently to Fatimah.

Amadu came home then, and the whole conversation, if one could call it that, started up all over again. He asked to see the papers, which Fatimah was trying to read. Not only was the content hard to grasp, she was in such a state of shock that she found it impossible to focus.

Amadu read for a long time and the men started fidgeting. One lit a cigarette; the other took a newspaper out of this bag and scanned it. When Amadu finished, he looked up, his face taut with rage, and flung the papers at the officials.

It had all gone badly, very badly, right from the start, Fatimah said. The papers amounted to an eviction notice, Amadu declared.

"We do not want to leave, you understand? We are not going anywhere," he said.

The officials turned to Baaba Kaarya and repeated what they had said before. Ignoring the papers scattered in the dust, they walked to their scooter, hopped on and took off.

Over the past five years, the Aanke had noticed changes, first in Gewe, the district capital and nearest city, and progressively in their immediate surroundings. Gewe had grown bigger and richer with the influx of money and people from outside. And city people had started buying land in their area to grow new crops, often for export—cocoa, tea, coffee, even cotton. They had heard of plans for exotic fruit orchards, and plants for making bottled fruit juice and canned fruit.

The Aanke continued their way of life. The land they lived on had always been fertile, and they hardly needed chemical fertilizers or pesticides. There were some years when new pests attacked their crops. Then they went to Gewe to buy those products. They practiced crop rotation, using complementary plants and allowing part of their land to lie fallow each season so it would rejuvenate.

A month before the officials appeared, they heard that 20 acres of land adjoining their farms was going to be developed by the government. They knew that a new Land Act had been passed the year before, but the provisions of the law were not clear to them. They had heard that all land was now looked upon as held in trust on behalf of the governor of each state, and when land was bought outright, there was no resettlement policy for the farmer.

The next day, Baaba Kaarya, Amadu and a few senior members of the community went to Gewe to talk to some shopkeepers they knew there. The verdict was the same: they would have to move. They had no choice.

"Your fields are in their way," one shopkeeper said.

"Remember that cotton plantation the German company started last year? They had to buy from some farmers, too."

"But we don't want to move!" Baaba Kaarya said with a sudden touch of anger.

Pat came the answer: "A chicken's prayer doesn't affect a hawk."

When they got back, they assembled in Baaba Kaarya's compound, all the men, except him, talking excitedly. Fatimah was frightened by what she saw in her father's face. It was as if he was haunted, haunted by a ghost, or an evil spirit.

Perhaps they should contact her husband's elder brother, Abubakar, who was the chief in Madafi, she suggested. Surely he would have some good advice.

"Let us speak of this all together, tomorrow," Baaba Kaarya said quietly.

The next day they held a meeting in a large clearing in the centre of the settlement. They invited the whole community, and everyone came. Amadu and some of the young men wanted to hire a lawyer and contest the authorities. The elders ruled this out. It would be a big expense with an unknown outcome. They would move, a few to Madafi and the rest to the Northwestern Highlands. They would contact their relatives at both these places; they were sure that they would be made welcome.

"There is still some land to be had in the Highlands," someone said.

"Take land in the old way and have it taken away?" Amadu said. "Is that what you want? The land tenure system is different now; we must understand it. Or they will strike us down again."

"You are both right, you Fasi and you Amadu," Baaba

Kaarya said. "We need to move and start our lives again, and this is possible in the Highlands, and for a few in Madafi, perhaps. In any case some people must go to Madafi, those with book learning, like you Amadu, so they can understand the new ways."

"There is a government scheme, is there not, that gives land to cooperatives?" Fatimah asked. "I think they said something about that on the radio. Perhaps we could form a cooperative and get land that way."

"These are all good ideas," Baaba Kaarya said. "For now we must contact Abubakar and also Fola and others, in the Highlands."

That night, Fatimah's mother, Masumi Kasi Ditta, had a dream that sealed their decision. Masumi was not only the chief's wife; she was also recognized as a Wise Woman and Seer. Shaikh Misfar Yasa Madafi, their greatest teacher and spiritual leader, whose tomb lay in Madafi, addressed Masumi in her dream: Most of the community must head for the Highlands to found a new village there called Alfajiri, and some people must go to Madafi.

In the morning, Masumi excitedly called all the adults to the clearing, and narrated her dream with customary flair. The vision appeased the community, particularly the elders, and it was decided that they would follow its dictates. They liked the name of the new settlement that they would found, Alfajiri, which meant dawn in Arabic, as well as Bisseau, their mother tongue. Amadu and some of his young friends were unhappy with the decision, but they had to go along.

When the surveyors came, accompanied by the two officials whom they had already met, Baaba Kaarya, Fatimah, Amadu and a few elders went to meet them. The surveyors were friendlier than the officials; one was even somewhat apologetic.

"You have fantastic farmland here and you will be well compensated. You will be rich men soon!" he said laughingly.

Then the thin, grim-faced man from the Agriculture Ministry spoke, explaining that they would survey not only the farmland, but any assets the land had, such as trees and other vegetal features, water sources, and so on. Soil quality, drainage and other factors would also be considered.

"What about the land our homes are on, and the materials we've used for them?" Fatimah asked.

"A smart lady we have here," the surveyor who liked to play the joker said. "Don't worry, everything will be looked into. Though your homes are mostly mud and straw, are they not?"

"The windows and doors, the pens for the animals and the fences are wood" Fatimah replied. "There are nails and metal clasps. There are poles supporting the roof, and wooden sticks in the roof itself. All these are valuable."

The joker frowned, and the official from the Agriculture Ministry kept himself immersed in a folder.

The Aanke had expected an immediate offer at the end of the survey, but that was not how it worked. They were told that the offer would come soon.

"But how can we move if we do not have the money?" Amadu asked. "We will have to pay bus fare and buy some donkeys, a few carts, for some who will come on foot. And there are other things for which we need money."

"Oh, you will get a moving allowance. Don't worry, we have thought of everything," the joker whose main interest now seemed to be to get away from Ferun said.

"Can't you give us an estimate?" Fatimah asked.

"No, that's not the proper way," the joker said primly.

In the days that followed, two distinct realities claimed Fatimah. Outwardly, she was engrossed in innumerable practical matters that the moves entailed, including taking care of wailing women, and men who sat immobile, staring into a distance. Even as she moved among them with seeming assurance, along with her mother, menacing shadows hovered at the edge of her consciousness, and she felt an ominous, oppressive weight bearing down on her. The beloved village where she had lived all her life, the compound, the trees, the woods, the fields, the pond, the wells, would suddenly glaze over before her eyes, becoming opaque, a mirage in reverse.

This scared her; she wondered if there were some evil spirits about. She was also acutely worried about her father. The turn of events had struck him with the force of a sledge-hammer, and though outwardly calm, she felt that he was losing strength day by day. She herself had mysterious aches and pains that came and went, she, who was never sick. Now her ankle hurt, now her head throbbed, now her hand felt numb. But there was no time to speak about this with someone, not even with her mother, who had a keen knowledge of herbs. She had to carry on, despite being anxious, furtive, fatigued in a way she had never been before.

At night she heard the elders recalling the old days, saying over and over that such a situation would have never come to pass during their time. She noticed how her father stayed silent, his head slightly bowed, and felt a pang. The elders were very disturbed not just by the sale of the land, but also because all the land would be used for a single crop. How could the government, who had so many employees with so much book learning, make such a grave mistake? And why cocoa, an alien crop that might harm the soil?

Meanwhile, the young men had been scouting around in the area, talking to people whose land had been bought by the government, or by private companies. They wanted to compute what would be a fair price for their own land.

The information they got was confusing. Some people had been offered a reasonable amount, but many had had to settle for a pittance. Much more worrisome was the fact that the government had not always paid, even after both parties had signed all the papers. Still, the men managed to put their heads together and come up with a price.

The week before their departure, they were called to the Gewe District Municipality and given a paltry sum of money as the moving allowance, which set them worrying anew. The land offer was still not ready, they were told. But it would come through soon. Finally, the day before they moved, the Joker came again, with one of the officials, and reams and reams of paper. The heads of families were asked to line up. The communal land was treated like many separate pieces of land and there were the individual plots, which did have specific owners. The Aanke already knew that this is how it would be.

It was a bizarre arrangement, but for the sake of the valuation, they had tried to divide up the communal land between the families as equally as they could. It had not been an easy task, and had led to many arguments. Two men had even come to blows, but better sense had finally prevailed. There was no compensation for the considerable land that their compounds covered, nor any building material. That was just how it was.

The rigidity of the system baffled them. They had their own customs and rules, which in many cases were strictly enforced by the Chief and a council of Wise Men and One Wise Woman. But in day-to-day matters there was always much negotiation. Compromise and common sense were prized, but both these values were absent from their dealings with the government.

The papers passed from official hands to heads of households to Amadu and his troop. These young men went under the shade of a tree and studied the contracts with care. The prices offered seemed reasonable. This came as such a surprise that the men kept going over the figures, anxious that they had perhaps made a mistake, while the Joker looked restless, and finally called out that he did not have all day.

Amadu's troop now approached the elders, showed them the contracts and explained them the best they could. The papers said that they would be compensated within two months.

Soon after, the heads of the households signed the contracts with their thumbs dipped in ink.

It was lunchtime when the officials left, and the sun was high up in the sky, but no one went to eat. Even the children did not ask for food. They all sat in small groups, in that open space between dwellings and fields, and talked.

An elder man suddenly cried out: "What have we done! Y'allah! We've sold our land! We have sold our land! We will be punished! I tell you, we will all be punished!"

Baaba Kaarya did not say anything, but Masumi went over to soothe the old man, and Fatimah followed her.

Soon came the many journeys. Baaba Kaarya, his elder sister, Bisa, Fatimah, Lahmey, their twins Hawa and Jelani, Amadu, and a few others, headed for Madafi. Only eight of the 43 families that lived in Ferun accompanied them. The rest followed Masumi to the Highlands. Lahmey had grown up sons, Eze and Kosey, his children from his first wife who had died giving birth. They chose to go to Gewe to find work, so they would have some ready cash to send their families. Their wives, Arza and Feeza, came to Madafi with their children. Amadu wanted to go with his brothers, but Fatimah insisted that they needed someone with advanced book learning to go with them to Madafi.

About a dozen young Aanke men went with Eze and Kosey. Many more would have gone, but Masumi cried out that they needed the strength of youth to found the new village. Lahmey's two grown-up daughters from his first marriage also went to the Highlands with their husbands and children, and so did Fatimah's two sisters, brothers-in-law and a brother. The farewells were heart breaking. The only person she didn't mind seeing go was her brother, a wastrel.

On the eve of their departure from Ferun, a slow burning anger claimed Fatimah. All this time, there had only been anguish over the multiple losses—land, home, family—lost, broken, scattered. In her pain, she had witnessed Amadu's rage, her father's sorrow and her mother's strength. That night, their last in Ferun, lying in the Women's House beside her mother, wide awake, she made a resolution that she would find a way to bring them all together again. They would unite, to till their own land, land they could legally claim as their own. Land they would be bound to through paperwork. Paperwork, she and Amadu had realized, was what mattered. That, and money, paper money. Amadu had told her that one day, soon, he would open a bank account, the first ever for their family.

Fatimah Lahmey Ditta, daughter of Kasi Umar Kaarya and Masumi Kasi Ditta, evoked her ancestors, the spirits of the land, the deity that presided over the Feruni River, and Shaikh Misfar Yasa Madafi, vowing that she would not rest till there was a fitting end to their story.

CHAPTER 3

Madafi

$\mathbf{M}$ADAFI WAS A pleasing assembly of compounds, large and small, lightly fenced, each containing circular huts of re-inforced mud with conical, thatched roofs. Between the com-pounds, there were little paths, and beyond them, fields. The paths did not form any sort of a pattern but flowed here and there with the sinuousness of running water. At this hour the goats were out grazing and the hens confined to their coops, with only the tall, hardy, charcoal dark Aanke and their slen-der, doe-eyed children in view.

Kibwe parked the car at a gap between compounds; there was no official entrance to Madafi. As Anjali and Elizabeth started making slow progress towards Fatimah's compound, a few barebacked children run up and greeted them in Morga, Kamorga's national language.

The Aanke greeting among adults required inquiring after a person's health, and that of the husband or wife, the children, the parents, other family members, the house, the fields, the livestock and work. If something particular was going on, like harvesting, that was included as well. The other person had to give an identical answer to each question: "There is no trouble." Among themselves the Aanke spoke Bisseau. With others they used Morga, if they knew that language.

It had been difficult for Anjali to learn Morga, supposedly an easy language. She had started with a private tutor who came to her house two evenings a week, but soon she was too busy at work to continue. Her progress was at best halting, though Elizabeth assured her that she was learning fast. Grace did not think so, Anjali was cerain, assuming a patronizing manner when Anjali spoke Morga in her presence.

Anjali trailed behind Elizabeth, letting her handle the greetings. Since she had started visiting Madafi, Anjali had come to appreciate the brevity of a hello, how are you, a handshake, or a Namaste. She confined herself to greeting the children, who merely had to be asked how they were: *kabari ani*? The response was a simple, *hoori*, good, or *hoori mana*, very good.

Anjali beamed her attention on the sights, sounds and smells—girls braiding hair, women pounding grain in wide, wooden mortars with tall, wooden pestles, the mouth watering smell of roasted yam (the odour of animal waste a low hum under all the other smells), calibrated human voices, a rebellious cock embarking on a series of crows, then abruptly falling silent. Having visited a few villages on different continents she knew that the idea of a cock crowing only at dawn was another urban fantasy about rural life.

After a few minutes they reached Fatimah's compound. Anjali took the lead, opening the gate with an air of familiarity. Hawa, Fatimah's pre-teen daughter, came up to greet them, smiling shyly. She relieved them of their purses. Anjali used to protest when rural children came forward routinely to carry her belongings. She had learnt that it was no use;

this was yet another custom that could not be tampered with. Their respectful attitude was flattering; she wished Rahul would display an iota of such courtesy.

Past a couple of huts, in an opening, stood three mud hearths in a semi-circle, a pot steaming on one of them. Nearby there was a ragtag, blue, plastic awning, held aloft by four wooden poles.

"Anjali, Elizabeth," Fatimah said in her low, rich voice as she advanced towards them.

Everyone in Kamorga had a different way of pronouncing Anjali's name. Anjali liked the way Fatimah said it. It was a jagged sort of a name, but she rounded it off, making it sweeter.

As they settled down under the awning, rigged especially for the guests, who were sensitive to the strong, tropical sun, Fatimah said: "Come, sit, eat." Having more or less used up her English vocabulary, she laughed out loud.

Nobody spoke for a few moments. With the Aanke there was a slow start to conversation.

"How is Rahul?" Fatimah asked, switching to Morga.

"There is no trouble," Anjali said, lying.

Rahul had made an impression when she had come here with him and Jeremy. Fatimah had slaughtered a chicken for the occasion. Anjali, a strict vegetarian, had felt embarrassed; Rahul had eaten the meat with great relish. Afterwards, he had shown Jelani, Fatimah's son, one of his favourite games —Space Aliens—on the Game Boy, with Fatimah looking on approvingly.

Rahul had better Morga than Anjali. He had surprised her by selecting Morga as an elective at school, though he had the choice of goofing off in the library during that class. He had even put in some work and got decent grades. Since that visit, Fatimah always asked after him, and usually sent him a treat. Once it had been mangoes, another time berries. Today she suspected that it was going to be corn. Half a dozen heads lay in a reed basket under the awning.

"How is Jeremy?" Fatimah asked.

"There is no trouble," Anjali said, more sincerely. She inquired after Lahmey and other family members. Now they could pass on to real conversation.

"I have submitted the application for the cooperative," Fatimah said proudly. "Two weeks it has been now."

"*Hoori, hoori mana*. Good, very good," Anjali said enthusiastically,

The paucity of her vocabulary in Morga, always frustrating, bothered her the most at such moments. *Hoori, hoori mana*, good, very good—feeble words to express her admiration for such an impressive action! But no other adjectives had come forth. She wondered if she should clasp Fatimah's hand, or hold out her hand for a handshake. She wanted somehow to add to her paltry utterance. But those gestures seemed wrong, and the moment had passed. She should have responded in English, letting Elizabeth translate.

Fatimah rewarded Anjali with a big smile.

The Cooperative Land Distribution Scheme, the first of its kind in sub-Saharan Africa, was a mighty feather in the cap of the Kamorgan government. It was the only progressive aspect of a new Land Act that the government had passed a year ago. Funded by HIVOS, the Dutch development organization, it had been lauded by multilateral agencies, the big aid organizations and media at a global level.

On Anjali's first visit to Madafi, Fatimah had asked for her help to write a proposal under the Land Distribution

Scheme. She wanted all the displaced farmers from Ferun to come together again, under a cooperative structure, to farm on a large tract of land near Madafi that they had already scoped out.

The earlier Aanke settlers in Madafi did not farm seriously; they only cultivated some grain and vegetables for their immediate needs. There were always one or two members in every large family who worked full-time in the informal sector in Makaenga. Others did some part-time work to help along. The Aanke from Ferun however were eager to farm.

Anjali, impressed by Fatimah's initiative and eager to help, had followed up with the Agriculture Ministry in Venimeli. She had brought Fatimah and Amadu all the information about how to apply, and had commented on successive drafts of the application.

Hawa had deposited their purses under the awning and disappeared. Now she came to them with glasses of goat milk, fragrant with herbs.

"It is good. I am happy," Fatimah said. "But the compensation, there is no good news about that."

Of the forty-two Aanke families that had left Ferun, only eight had received compensation so far. Fatimah followed up assiduously on the pending claims with monthly visits to the Ministry of Agriculture in Venimeli.

"If you can do something," she continued.

"Unfortunately, I cannot," Anjali replied. This dialogue is also a formula that they repeat every time. It was not for Anjali, Acting Executive Director of HELP's Africa Regional Office, to make such enquiries.

Hawa showed Anjali her English homework. In the Kamorgan public school system, they started teaching English at the secondary level and Hawa has recently begun secondary school. As Anjali admired her work, she thought of Rahul. He had to finish a science project that evening. To the best of her knowledge he had not yet done much work on it.

"Let's go," Fatimah said suddenly.

"Where?" Elizabeth asked.

"To the land."

"But we've seen it already," Anjali said.

"Let's see it again. It is always good to see the land!"

Anjali consulted her watch. This would add at least half an hour to their day. Fatimah was looking at her as expectant as a child. Anjali turned to Elizabeth.

"Okay," Elizabeth said. Anjali nodded. It was hard to deny Fatimah this small pleasure. The land meant so much to her. It was hard to deny Fatimah anything.

When they reached the car, the three young Aanke men sitting inside with Kibwe, chatting, hastily came out.

Fatimah told Kibwe where to go. Anjali expected him, puffed up from the admiration that he and the car had undoubtedly received, to go into a display of machismo, firing the engine and driving fast, as he tended to at times, much to Rahul's delight. But he quietly engaged the gear and drove carefully over the few bumpy miles. Thorny branches brushed against the closed car windows from time to time.

Dust everywhere, so much dust, Anjali thought. Dust on her clothes, hair, skin; dust in her eyes, sometimes. Dust bringing a hint of hoarseness to her voice. Fortunately, dust made her happy. For what is dust after all but earth turning dry and rising up to greet the air, which takes it in its embrace and fox trots it around? Here in Kamorga she encountered the same dust, unfettered and elemental, that she had wallowed in as a child growing up in India. Dust, like air, sky, sun, wind, water, was the same everywhere, no matter what corner of the planet one might find oneself in. Anjali took great comfort from this idea.

Soon the track grew wide, the bush thinned, and they were in open country again. As the land dipped a little, Kibwe brought the car to a halt and they all got out. Smiling expansively, Fatimah took a deep breath. Anjali looked from her to the spreading expanse of earth before them. The area, which they had visited a few months ago, made no particular impression on her, then or now. But she knew what it meant to Fatimah—hope, community, continuity, and the future.

This parcel of land had the power to unite all the Aanke from Ferun. Torn from their roots, dispersed, it could help them put their life in order again. They would have to work hard to become owners, by paying the full price of the land, in instalments. And this they wanted to do, more than anything else, Fatimah had assured her.

"So?" Fatimah looked keenly from Anjali to Elizabeth.

"Very nice," Elizabeth said.

Anjali decided against saying *hoori mana* again, instead she asked: "What's that bird?"

A little brown bird had alighted on a low bush a few yards away. She had never seen this bird in her garden.

Kibwe said something in Morga.

"He thinks it's a lark," Elizabeth said.

Maybe it will sing, Anjali thought. Her knowledge of birds was miniscule. But she knew the songs from *The Sound of Music* by heart. She found herself humming under her breath: "To laugh like a brook when it trips and falls over stones on its way; to sing through the night, like a lark who is learning to pray ..."

On their first visit, Fatimah had explained the lay of the land. The slight dip would provide some protection from the wind. And given the slope, the rainwater would drain downward and irrigate the fields. They would construct grooves to channel excess water. Having talked to the local people, they knew that the water table was good here, and the Land Certificate they had managed to get with great difficulty from the Makaenga Municipality had confirmed this.

They would also build a wind barrier with trees; they always practiced mixed farming. The word Anjali knew was agroforestry, and it was trendy. She had suggested that they use it in their application. An age-old concept, agroforestry had been revived in the 1970s by the aid industry, and subjected to worldwide research and promotion.

At first there was resistance. "But this is not forest at all, just trees that help the plants," Fatimah had said. Elizabeth had explained to Anjali that Fatimah understood something quite different by the word forest. Anjali in her turn had said that using phrases like prevention of soil erosion, increasing tree cover, practicing agroforestry, and linking these to concepts like enhancing local food security, sustainable agriculture, experimenting with local species to increase yields, protecting the water table, and preserving biodiversity, would have strategic advantage. This was how the Aanke farmed anyhow. Kamorga was losing its forests, and half-hearted reforestation programs introduced in the mid-1980s had not been particularly successful. Fatimah and Amadu had finally understood the importance of jargon, and agroforestry had been mentioned many times in the application.

Elizabeth glanced at her watch. "Time to go?"

As they got into the car, Anjali looked back at the bush; the lark had flown away.

"Thank you *mana*," Fatimah said, when they dropped her off in Madafi. She had not been as quick to smile or proffer thanks when Anjali had first met her, but she had quickly adopted new mannerisms.

Soon they were driving through Makaenga, a place with considerable vigour and variety. Small though it was, as the only town within a large radius, it had to serve many needs, be many things to many people, and this it accomplished with aplomb.

Almost at the other end of town stood the field office of the Health, Education & Livelihood Skills Partnership. The distinct compound housed a well-equipped health clinic, a primary school, a kindergarten, and a vocational training centre. All the services were free of charge. A similar set-up existed in Iberu, the oldest slum in Venimeli. HELP also operated in two other African countries, and in South Asia and South East Asia, with a head-office in Toronto.

Around the compound was a low, wire fence, more to mark territory than to provide security. Kibwe drove to the iron gate that stood wide open, and nodding at the guard, swept right through, bringing the car to a halt in front of the squat administrative office.

Nathan was looking through a report when Anjali stepped into his cluttered office. Dr. Nathan Kalish was in his late 20s, brown-haired, bespectacled, with an air of earnest, good health.

"Anjali, good to see you," he said heartily, getting up and extending his hand.

"Same here." Anjali shook his hand, smiling. With his ruddy wholesomeness, he brought a pleasing whiff of Canada into her life.

Elizabeth had already been whisked away by Nathan's

secretary; she was always in demand here. Anjali's main task at the field office was largely solitary. Carmen Melita, the communications chief in Toronto, was planning on an organizational history of HELP, with an accent on Best Practices and Lessons Learnt. She had talked Anjali into looking at all the old records at HELP Kamorga and extracting useful information from them. As Research and Organizational Development Coordinator at the Toronto office, a post she would return to when she finished her contract, she was undeniably the best person to do the job. Anjali made regular trips to the field office to review messy paperwork, most of which was in English (some of it in very bad English). Grace had grudgingly agreed, with pressure from Mathew, the Executive Director in Toronto.

Nathan and Anjali chatted for a few minutes, then parted, he to go to the clinic, she to the stuffy, little room around the corner where she had set up a work desk. Later they would meet as usual for a late lunch at the cafeteria. Julie, Nathan's wife, a volunteer-teacher at the primary school, would join them, along with Elizabeth.

CHAPTER 4

Tropical Garden

A PROFUSION OF mass and colour dazzled her as she pushed open the red-painted, metal gate. Directly ahead, bordering a paved path made of warm-toned, stone chips, was a swatch of Iris—purple and yellow. Their slim profiles contrasted against rotund, evergreen bushes, that marched towards the house, the house that Anjali lived in, but could not quite think of as her own. But the garden, that she claimed with relative ease.

Anjali's eyes moved to the neatly mowed lawn, bordered by ruby-red impatiens that grew close to the ground, nesting amid shapely, dark green leaves, going on to drink in the pretty little lily pond with stones set at different levels so that the water rose and fell, gently, ever so gently, with the lightest of murmurs, infinitely soothing. No less tranquilizing were the pristine white lilies that grew there. And oh, the delicate lily pads that displayed sometimes a blue-bodied dragonfly, a squirmy tadpole or a blackish water beetle. True the pond also bred mosquitoes, the malarial kind, but you couldn't escape those in Kamorga.

She had walked into an Eden, replete with fern and grass,

water and stone, flowers, trees, bushes,—all the elements artfully fitted together to make a harmonious whole. She made her way to the roses and magnolias. For a moment she stood still, letting their perfume pleasure her senses.

She caught sight of Fudu, wizened, with a crop of white, crinkly hair and twisted spectacles that were held together with wire and twine, and kept somehow in place over his one good eye, the other being milky and useless. She had given him money to buy proper glasses, but he had not done that. He seemed to have other priorities.

It was late. Why was he still here? Giving her a half-toothed smile Fudu shuffled past her, out of the gate and away. She was alone, splendidly alone.

Immediately, she was ashamed. He lived, she imagined, in an airless room, with children and grandchildren (she knew he was a widower), in one of Venimeli's poor suburbs. How could she deny him this beauty? She must accept the fact that he practically lived here. His gardening duties did not take up much time, but he pottered about, resting, in the hot afternoons, under the inadequate shade of the decorative lemon tree, refusing the comfort of the veranda. He brought his own meagre lunch, usually declining food from Mary, Anjali's maid, though he accepted tea.

Still, she was glad he was gone, and she had this splendour all to herself.

First there had been a cramped, second floor flat in Bombay, shared with her parents, sister and grandmother, moving on to a room in a student residence at the University of Toronto, shared with a Chinese roommate. A two-bedroom apartment, this time on the fifth floor of a condo at Young and St. Clair, followed. Here she lived with her husband Manish, and later with Manish and Rahul. She had kept it after their separation.

No earthly paradise in any of that.

This was the very first time that she could claim a piece of earth. This was what had brought her back to Venimeli, for the second time, and committed her to a year-long contract, this dream garden that would be hers, mostly hers. That was the story she told herself now, though she had come armed with more practical reasons for the move.

Two years ago, Anjali had attended a conference in Uganda, Kamorga's neighbour to the east. Mathew had suggested then that she take a couple of days in Venimeli. She had stayed at a nice hotel overlooking Lake Mathilda, and Anne had invited her home for dinner. She recalled being transported when she had stepped in through that gate, red even then. She continued to be enchanted, though many other first impressions had degraded and failed the test of time.

Her gaze went to the whitewashed, two-storied house. It was a graceful building, both house and garden British fancies, colonial conceptions of what life should be in the tropics.

Anjali walked in. The front door was shut but not locked. John, the night watchman, would arrive soon. Really, they all needed to be more security conscious; she heard about robberies every now and then. Why not a day watchman as well, she had asked Anne. "Well, Fudu is there during the day," was the reply.

Fudu as a guard, what a joke! But she had not hired a day guard; she wanted to change as little as possible. She had inherited Mary, maid and cook, as she had Kibwe, Fudu and John. She was like a plantation slave owner, with his privileges, and his duties and obligations. She had not realized back in Canada that privilege could be a trap, tying her down with responsibilities.

She paused on the veranda with its wicker chairs. She and Jeremy had often had an evening drink here. How short it had been, the time they had had together!

Walking through the living room with its potted plants and ethnic decor, she entered the kitchen. Mary was bent over a steaming pot, stirring. Anjali paused, a catch in her throat as she watched her. On the steps that led from the kitchen to the small back garden, where they grew vegetables, sat Gabriel, reading.

Hearing her, Mary turned around. She was short and slight, and wore a bold-printed dress. Ten-year-old Gabriel already came up to her shoulder. Her eyes exuded warmth. Her smile was large; it encompassed the world.

"*Kabari ani*?" Mary said. Dropping the spoon back into the pot, she came towards Anjali.

"*Hoori. Kabari ani*?"

Mary filled a glass of water from a pitcher she kept in the fridge and gave it to Anjali. There was a twist of lime in it.

Gabriel looked up from his book and smiled. He was a slim, silent boy with bright, observant eyes. When you spoke to him, he really listened. He had the same sort of luminosity as his mother, but in his case it was turned inwards.

She could see that he was reading some sort of an action adventure—one of Rahul's books. Gabriel usually had a couple of books on the go. The books he got from his school library were in English and Morga, and Anjali brought him books from the expat library in Jamesville that she thought he might enjoy—abridged versions of James Herriot, Roald Dahl, *Alice in Wonderland* and *The Jungle Book*. Old-fashioned, familiar, they comforted Anjali as she leafed through them. While these books didn't hold much attraction for Rahul, Gabriel seemed to enjoy them. She had also seen him glancing through Rahul's collection—books about mechanics, trains, inventions and nature.

Mary beckoned Anjali to come up to the counter. Together, they peered into the pot—sweet potato, green bean and spinach stew, which Mary would serve on *gali*, coarse boiled cornmeal that was a staple in Kamorga. And there was a tomato, cucumber, spring onion salad made with fresh produce from the garden. Mary would fry a couple of chicken legs for her Canadian son who needed meat at least a few times a week.

"I call Martha," Anjali said. She spoke to Mary sometimes in stripped down English, the sort Mary used herself, though mostly she spoke Morga. Mary did not seem to notice Anjali's grammatical confusion or her inadequate pronunciation in Morga.

Martha picked Rahul up from The International School along with her son Jerry when Anjali could not make it. Both the boys were in the same grade, Jerry's sister Dana two years younger.

"Darling, how are you?" Martha said when she got her on the phone.

"Good. Just back from Makaenga."

"Lucky! I am stuck with these brats. I hate to do this to you, but could you please, please drive over? I can't make it."

"Of course."

"Thanks, Hon. Richard's still not back, and there was a bit of a ruckus. Dana tumbled down a couple of steps. That was okay, but the boys laughed at her instead of helping."

"Oh no!"

"So she started crying. I did get them to apologize."

"Well done."

"They were not too sincere, but what the heck. They're all watching cartoons; they needed to simmer down. Of course, Salima is here, but ..."

"I'll come right away. It's no problem at all."

She drove leisurely to Martha's house. As usual, Kibwe had parked the car in the garage at the back. She enjoyed driving in Jamesville, the expat area where she lived, but did not venture out elsewhere on her own, though she vowed everyday that she would change that.

She feared the disorderly drivers in Venimeli, especially the Matata drivers. In the absence of public transport, private operators ferried people around in badly maintained mini-vans called Matatas, for a small price. In Jamesville everyone had a car, but elsewhere, Matatas dominated. They were like so many disagreeable, brown cockroaches, Anjali felt; they infested the city. The lack of public transport here, and in many growing African cities, was a disgrace.

Martha greeted her with a beer in hand, though Dixy, the grey and white fox terrier, got to her first. Anjali bent down to stroke him.

"Drink?" Martha asked.

"Not today. Thanks."

Martha Hines was a pert-looking woman in her early 40s, with auburn curls and crow's feet. Her husband, Richard, was a senior diplomat at the American Embassy. A lawyer who had practiced at one time, she had followed her husband abroad.

Anjali walked into the playroom to say hello to Jerry and Dana, even as Rahul was saying goodbye. He took up his school bag, large on his slight frame. After saying goodbye to Martha they were off.

"How was school?"

"Good."

"Tomorrow is Photography Club, no?"

"Yeah."

"Lots of work left on the science project?"

"Sort of."

"Hungry?"

"No."

"Did you eat something?"

"Banana."

Anjali focussed on the tarred road lined with houses with high walls. Here and there a tree provided shade. It was nice that their house had a thick hedge around it, not a wall. But perhaps they would be safer behind one of those formidable looking walls, some with jagged glass pieces wedged on top. Anjali wrinkled her nose in disgust.

She glanced at Rahul. He had his Game Boy in his hand but he did not use it. He was looking out of the window, his head turned away. He was usually silent in a car, had been that way since he was a little boy.

Tyla tithe nahi avadnar. He won't like it there.

When Anjali had called her mother, Indumati, in Bombay, from Toronto, with the news that she was planning to move to Kamorga for a year, Indumati had responded at once with: *Tyla tithe nahi avadnar.* He won't like it there. She was referring of course to Rahul, speaking in Marathi, their mother tongue.

"*Ithe aastha tar mech tyla thevla aastha.* If you were living here, I would have kept him," Indumati had said. "And

Vandana, she does not have any time, or he could have stayed with her. America is just like Canada, *nahi ka*, isn't it?"

Aai, mother, I would never leave Rahul behind and go anywhere, even if it was with you or my sister. Aloud Anjali had said: "*Tithe changli shaala aahe.* There's a good school there. And Mary has a son, Gabriel, who is also 10."

"Oh."

"He goes to a good Jesuit school, not a public one."

"Really? Must be expensive. How can she pay that much?"

"Mary used to be the cleaning woman at the Jesuit seminary. She used to take Gabriel there when he was a baby and one of the Fathers took a liking to him. Paid the fees. And I think Gabriel has a scholarship now."

"*Accha.* OK. Does she live in the servants' quarters with the boy?"

"Yes."

"I see. And her husband?"

"No idea."

"Left her no doubt. Better no husband than one who beats you."

"Gabriel knows English and Morga, their language. That will help. He will be able to translate for me. Gabriel will be company for Rahul, don't you think? And Mary is great, Anne's always telling me."

"Maybe. *Tyla tithe avadnar nahi.* I still feel that. Children are like that, Anju. *Bagh, mala je vatle, te me sangitle.* Look, I told you what I felt."

"*Tu kalji nako karoos.* Don't worry. It'll be okay. Rahul will be all right," Anjali had said, trying to reassure herself as much as she did her mother.

But he had not been all right.

Rahul went straight to his room after dinner. He would

sit down at his desk right away and concentrate fully on the assignment. When she took him a glass of milk at 10 o'clock, he was still at it. How like his father! Manish always put his best foot forward at the eleventh hour.

How could Rahul embody so strongly the habits of a father who had left when he was five?

When Anjali decided to go to bed half an hour later, the light was still visible under his door. She always checked to see if the mosquito net was properly tucked in around his mattress. She knocked on the door and opened it.

"Almost done, Ma. Just revising," he said, looking up.

"Good night *beta*, son." She wondered if she should go over and give him a goodnight kiss.

"Good night," he said.

She closed the door softly and went to her room. Turning out the light, she got into bed, but she could not sleep. "Oh Mary, Mary," she said, under her breath.

Mary had started feeling unwell a couple of months ago. The symptoms were vague, such as tiredness and bloating. On Anjali's insistence she had gone to a public clinic, then to a public hospital, but it was not clear what was wrong. Anjali had taken her to the International Clinic in Jamesville, where she and Rahul went. A couple of visits and some tests had revealed the problem—ovarian cancer. The disease was at an advanced stage; it would take Mary's life in a few months.

Anjali hadn't reconciled to the news; how could she? She continued to swing between shock and sadness. Sometimes the heart lags behind the mind. More often it races ahead and grasps the entirety in an instant, while the mind trails, seeking reasons, cause and effect, harping on the notion that life must make sense.

After debating with herself for some time, she had told

Rahul about the situation. Looking stricken, he had asked at once: "What'll happen to Gabriel?"

"I guess he'll live with his aunt Edith," she had said.

"Does he know, mom?"

"Don't think so, and we must wait for Mary to tell him."

Then she had added: "We'll leave them a good amount of money." Rahul's expression had not changed.

She had encouraged him to be kind to Mary and Gabriel and had noticed that he was more present with them now. He would linger in the kitchen, talking to Mary, and would stroll over to the back garden, Gabriel's favourite haunt, seeking him out.

Gabriel. She thought often about this silent, self-sufficient child, with few friends. Perhaps not surprising. A servant's boy living with an expat family, in a room behind the main house, going to a school where few people from his background would go. If he had lived like his aunt he would be surrounded by children his age.

Jeremy had also taken to Gabriel. He had talked, or rather he had lectured, and Gabriel had listened! It was not out of mere politeness, she felt; Gabriel had posed questions, had shown real interest in what Jeremy was saying. Mary's disease hadn't cast a pall on Jeremy's visit; this was before the diagnosis, though Anjali fervently wished that they had found out earlier, much earlier.

Despite her disquiet, Anjali managed to fall asleep, but she woke up a little past midnight with a burning sensation in her stomach. She used to have a touch of acidity when she lived in Toronto, but it had worsened in Kamorga, had blown up into a full-fledged medical condition. She got out of bed to take a pill.

Moonlight beckoned, and she went to the window. There was a beautiful, clear night sky with a half moon that was glowing and growing its way to fullness, even as time was drawing the final curtain, an impenetrable shroud, over Mary's young life.

Sakhu bai, their maid in Bombay, had lived with them when she and Vandana were young. While Indian maids usually slept on mattresses placed directly on the floor and never ate at the Master's table, Indumati had given Sakhu bai a proper bed, though she did sleep in their covered balcony, crammed with all sorts of belongings. Sakhu bai also sat and ate at their table, though only after she had served the family and they had finished their meal.

"*Vichitrach aahe tuzi aai*," Anjali's grandmother muttered from time to time. "She's strange, your mother." But Indumati's will prevailed in this as well as other matters.

Though Anjali liked Sakhu bai, she had taken her for granted. She knew nothing then about making a home, how much went into it, and how only some people had a real talent for it. Mary fed them wonderfully, kept the house spic and span and brought order and warmth into their lives. She had made them a home in this new country where they moved about with hesitation, on unsure ground. Anjali could never be able to repay her.

She got back in bed.

Mary would die at 30 and Gabriel would become an orphan. Anjali didn't know who Gabriel's father was. All she knew was that he wasn't in the picture, and not about to ride up and rescue him.

It was people like Mary that HELP needed to help. If she had had access to a proper health clinic, a doctor like Nathan, they would probably have found out about the cancer on time. At HELP, they always had to pick and choose who they could serve and who they would pass by—the "regulars" and the "irregulars"; the luck of the draw. Their work was just a drop in an ocean of need. A drop, yes, but a precious drop, Frank Maier, HELP's founder, had said many times in interviews. Before she moved to Kamorga, Anjali had believed this to be true, believed that what they were doing was good enough. But now she was not so sure.

She didn't believe in an afterlife either. If only there was the guarantee that Mary would reap the rewards that she so deserved, elsewhere. But Mary's life would abruptly end, just like that, with no light to shine upon it. There was no comfort in any of this, only anguish that scarred both body and spirit.

CHAPTER 5

Graceland

THE CHILDREN RECITED their multiplication tables in unison, standing stiffly behind their desks, their hands by their side. Having started at two, they were now at four; Grace wanted them to go till six. Dressed in white shirts, navy blue shorts or skirts, blue ties, white socks and black shoes, their hair tidy, they looked like little choir boys and girls, their faces shiny, their eyes alert.

Grace walked through the aisles, circling them. They weren't making a single mistake; she liked that, she liked that very much.

By the time they finished Grace was standing at the head of the class.

"Excellent, let's give ourselves a hand," she said.

Little hands come eagerly together.

"Let's write all the tables down in our notebooks. That way we'll always remember them."

Grace looked over the rows of bent heads, 30 in all. What a change from public schools in the city, which had at least twice as many students per class. In the villages that had primary schools at all, children from different grades were bunched together.

Grace was proud of the way they were working, undistracted by the many sounds that entered the first floor classroom—music, voices and mechanical sounds were among the ones she could identify. After all, the primary school was located in the heart of Iberu, the oldest slum in Venimeli.

Soon, Rose, the regular Class Three teacher, would come back and relieve her from her volunteer duties. A pity that. Grace could have taught for the rest of the day, the rest of the week, the rest of the year. Decades ago, she had taught primary school. A wealthy private school it had been, not that it made any difference. All you needed was a classroom and children, a blackboard and chalk for the teacher and slates and chalk for the students. Textbooks, notebooks, pens and pencils helped, but were not strictly necessary.

Oh, how her father had scoffed at the idea of his, Godfrey Dia's daughter, working as a mere schoolmarm.

"Why don't you sit for the civil service exams and work at the Ministry of Education?" he had asked.

"Because I want to teach," she had replied.

After graduating with Biology Honours, she had taken a two-month teacher training course in Kenya, the only one offered in the region at that time. What did her father think she had done that for?

Godfrey Dia, at that time the Departmental Secretary at the Ministry of External Affairs, was as stubborn as his first-born daughter. He had let her work, bringing home promising young civil servants, who would call her later and ask her out.

Grace had gone out with a few, finding them limited and boring. She had worked for two years, then decided to do a Masters in Education. She would do extra credits to make up for the lack of a B.Ed. She was researching programs in

Ghana and the UK when her father brought home Joshua Madaki, a promising lawyer. He was somewhat older than the others, good-looking, intelligent and impressive. Six months later they were married. Godfrey Dia had given his daughter away at a lavish wedding. As the couple took their wedding vows, there had been, perhaps, a triumphant glint in his eye. But Grace, the very picture of a happy, glowing bride, had not noticed.

The children wrote on, Grace continued sitting on the hard, wooden chair, and the sun shone brightly. All was well in this corner of the Lord's Kingdom.

Iberu (hope in Morga) tumbled down a hillside at the western edge of Venimeli, a sea of silvery grey rooftops. When they hit level ground, they spread out in the shape of a fan. The shacks higher up had their back against jagged, basalt rock. The hill was called Mary's Mount because of the small shrine to the Mother of God that nestled amidst a copse, on high, the only spot of greenery in an otherwise arid land-scape. Not for Iberu the broad streets lined with trees, the children's park edged with flowering shrubs, the homes surrounded with gardens that defined Jamesville and Masakeni, the neighbourhood where Grace lived.

In Iberu, the roofs knit a quilt that hid its abundant life from prying eyes. That's how the inhabitants liked it. They wanted, above all, to be left alone, unmolested by politicians, city officials, the police, social workers, proselytizers, drug dealers, people looking for prostitutes, and do-gooders of various ilk.

Housing about 20,000 people, Iberu was a maze of alley-ways that slipped and rose amongst 10 ft. by 10 ft. shacks, which sometimes climbed one on top of the other. These narrow paths wound their way among bars that brewed their own beer, eateries, bakeries, groceries, beauty salons, barber shops, video theatres, dance clubs, cassette sellers, gambling dens, massage parlours, prayer rooms, hatcheries, butcheries, tailoring shops, informal crèches, schools, stores that sold Western and herbal remedies, fortune tellers, tenement hotels, and a community radio station. Besides all that, there were four churches and two mosques.

Iberu started taking shape in the 1950s, when a massive miners strike in Northern Kamorga resulted in a spate of layoffs. Before that, there had been a few scattered huts, but not a community. Many of the unemployed miners came to Venimeli to find work and gravitated towards the then distant, western edge of the city, where they built lean-tos and lived by their own rules. The municipality ignored them for the first few years; by the time they decided to evict them, it was too late. The colony had attracted other homeless people and families. They dug their roots in deep, refusing to budge. They organized their own militia to stand guard against opportunistic thugs and corrupt policemen. Though crimes here ranged from domestic violence to robbery to a fight ending in a man being stabbed, or have his head bashed in, Iberu had a low crime rate.

Into this scene stepped Health, Education & Livelihood Skills Partnership, in 1981. Frank Meier, the son of German immigrants to Canada, had made his millions in the retail business and established the Basic Needs Foundation (BNF) in 1978 to fund international development work in Africa. He met Sister Juta Lallemand, a Belgian nun, at an international health conference in Kampala. She ran a small, charitable centre in Iberu that also held prayer service and Sunday school.

They hit it off at once, and Sister Juta invited him to come and see her work in Iberu. Maier liked Iberu's energy and entrepreneurial spirit, and set up an office in Venimeli that went on to become HELP's Africa Regional Office.

HELP leased land on a long-term basis from the Venimeli municipality and built, over time, a four-storey structure in Iberu. The organization stood apart from the battles that raged on about eviction or rehabilitation. Keeping its nose to the grind, it got work done. Nothing much had come from these urban development debates. Instead, the residents went ahead and helped themselves, installing water pumps and stringing electric cables from the nearest power sources. They organized garbage collection, sorting and burning, and tried to address problems of annual flooding during the rainy season in the lower parts of Iberu.

Other international, non-profits also worked in Iberu, but no one else had an office right in the midst of it. HELP, being one of the earliest, had secured the confidence of the residents. They liked the fact that HELP had never sided with the government, nor with any particular group or faction, and had the backing of the popular Sister Juta.

As Grace left the HELP building, the children's words, sung in unison, echoed in her ears: "Thank you, Mrs. Madaki." It was always the same routine: Rose returning to the classroom and asking the children to thank Grace. Grace felt it was she who needed to thank them.

They were still hiring teachers from outside. But in a few years, students who had finished primary school in the very same building, and had been supported by HELP to go on to secondary school, would get their B.Ed. and teach here. That idea buoyed Grace's spirit every time she volunteered in Iberu.

Her chariot, a light blue Nissan Sentra, was parked near Mother Mary's shrine, in the shade of a tree, where she felt it was better protected. She distrusted some of the younger Iberu residents. They might make off with a hubcap or windshield wipers or even a tire. Robert, her driver, was not the most vigilant soul.

He was waiting for her inside the car, the door open to let in some air. As soon as he saw her he sprang out of his seat and came around to hold open the rear door.

Margaret, the maid, greeted her in Kakwa, their mother tongue, as Grace walked into her house.

"Lunch?" she asked.

"Not yet."

The idea of eating alone in the cavernous dining room with its massive table depressed her. She wished the children were back from school. They were all so busy with their own activities now. Lunches had once been merry affairs with the kids and her mother-in-law. After her father-in-law's death, she had lived with them. Joshua's distant aunt, who had made their home a refuge, used to be at the table as well. Both the old women had passed away a few years ago.

Grace traversed the high-ceilinged living room displaying a somewhat ratty lion skin, spears, shields, rifles, and a well-stuffed rhino head, that she had never liked. Inheritances from her father; she didn't know why they had kept them.

She made for her first-floor study, which overlooked the back lawn, green and soothing. A vase of long-stemmed, yellow roses sat on her desk. Margaret had instructions to refresh them weekly. Sometimes they wilted in a couple of days, but they had to be kept a week. And the color was always yellow.

Grace's eyes rested momentarily on the framed certificate on the wall. It was her Bachelors of Education, done through a British, distance education program. She had managed to get the degree while she had had four healthy pregnancies in quick succession. When Nairi, the youngest, turned three, she had started working in an Irish-funded NGO that promoted adult literacy, rising to become the Executive Director in a few years.

Much later, when she had joined HELP's Board, she had worked her way to the Chair's seat in two years. She had left the literacy NGO a year and half ago. She had not got along with the new Director who issued unreasonable commands from Ireland.

There was only one letter on her desk—an invitation to inaugurate a women's employment project, sponsored by the Women's Wing of the People's Democratic Union (PDU). The centrist PDU was Kamorga's ruling party. Joshua was the General Secretary of the PDU and an elected MP. There was no avoiding this one, thought Grace, though it was a lacklustre project that provided sewing machines to poor women and taught them tailoring.

The phone rang abruptly. It was Joshua's secretary telling her that he would not be home for dinner. He had an important meeting that evening. Grace slammed down the receiver. Yes, he had a meeting all right, with the curvaceous Thema, and his children by her.

The HELP quarterly report that Anjali had sent her recently also lay on her desk, and it caught her eye now. She had already read it, and marked a couple of changes in red. She must return it so it could be printed and sent to the Board members in advance of the Board Meeting. She wanted to read it again and see if she could suggest other improvements. It was hard to admit that it was almost perfect. She wanted to seize the neatly stapled document that seemed to mock her, fling it to the floor and stamp on it! Getting hold of herself, she turned away and walked stiffly down the stairs. She entered the veranda through the side entrance, to avoid running into Margaret who would ask again if she wanted to eat.

It was now around 1 pm, and the heat was palpable, even on the well-shaded veranda. As Grace paced up and down, it pressed against her skin, while a red-hot anger scorched her stomach.

Joshua and her father—they were both cut from the same soiled cloth.

Godfrey Dia had had two wives, and one mistress, the two wives located in the same compound, the mistress not far away. Grace's mother, the timid Efie, half his age, always had to defer to the elder wife. Godfrey Dia had everything —ancestral land in a village near Venimeli, his work, first under British rule, then as an MP with the People's Democratic Union. He had his hunting trips with the British officers of high rank, and later, junkets abroad.

Grace touched the small, gold cross that hung on a slim chain around her neck, her mother's. May her soul rest in peace. As for her father ... then her heart softened. He had been jovial and generous, even while he was selfish and controlling. Perhaps he deserved a place in heaven as well.

As for Joshua, she hoped his soul would roast in hell for eternity.

"There you are!" a familiar voice said in Kakwa.

Grace turned to see her brother, Peter, advancing, arms extended.

"Oh Peter!" she exclaimed, moving swiftly into his strong embrace. "Have you eaten?"

"No."

"Come and eat."

They moved to the dinning room with its 20-seater, mahogany table from the time when she and Joshua had entertained on a grand scale, a time before Thema's ascendance.

"Why don't you get a smaller table?" Peter asked as they sat down.

"Wish I had time to get this place organized."

Margaret came around with another maid and set down pots of steaming beef stew, *gali*, fried fish, an okra and green banana curry and dumplings stuffed with shredded, sweetened coconut. Grace felt a sharp rise in her appetite; she had hardly eaten any breakfast.

She ladled a large helping of the stew on Peter's plate, before serving herself. "Where have you been? Haven't seen you for so long! If I knew you were coming, I'd have made one of mama's recipes."

Peter shovelled a spoonful of *gali* and stew into his mouth, chewing noisily. After a minute, he said: "Was here and there. Went to the Dakar car rally."

"Of course. Forgot about that. How's Tina? And the children?"

"All fine. Grace, tell me about this Anjali."

CHAPTER 6

Hassan

ANJALI WAS GLANCING through the in-tray, sitting at her desk in her office at HELP Venimeli, when the phone rang.

"Hello Anjali, I called ten minutes ago," Grace said.

The office worked from 9 to 5, at least as far as regular staff was concerned. Grace had a habit of calling before 9, even though Anjali rarely came in that early and Grace knew that.

"When are you sending me the financial report?" she asked.

The Board Meeting protocol demanded that they get a quarterly report to the members five days ahead. Grace reviewed everything first.

"I am waiting for it," Anjali said.

"But Leonard said he sent it."

"He didn't."

"But he told me he had."

Anjali looked at the in-tray again. There was nothing there.

"It's not here," she said.

"Send it to me soon. I don't want things to be delayed."

"Neither do I."

"Why don't you call Leonard?"

"I'll go and see him. I called him yesterday and left a message."

"Goodbye."

"Bye."

Slowly, Anjali replaced the receiver. There was a possibility that Leonard had sent the report the day before, and it had got misplaced between the first floor, where he sat, and her second floor office. He would only send the document through the internal, office delivery system, even though the report was overdue and this was not a large office. They were about a dozen people in all, not including the driver, the watchman and the cleaning maid.

The internal delivery system, which seemed simple enough, did not always work. Anjali had tried to investigate why when she had first got here. She would wait for certain documents to arrive, and when they did not, she called the relevant staff person. She was usually told that the document had been dispatched. So where was it? No one knew. She closely questioned the office assistant who carried things back and forth, the receptionist who contributed mail to the in-trays, and the staff who had sent the document, to find that their stories did not mesh.

Most of the documents would eventually get to her. She had come upon a couple of them herself, one on the back veranda, and another in the resource centre. She presumed people had forgotten them there. But when asked both colleagues swore that they had put the documents, properly labelled, in the in-tray.

Anjali took another report that she needed to send Mathew, and went into the passageway where the photocopier sat on a large table strewn with paper. She started the print job, but minutes later the photocopier stopped working. There was a thump and the purr of an engine. The electricity had gone off and the generator had kicked in. Power rationing in Venimeli followed an erratic schedule. Sometimes it was severe, with no electricity for 10–12 hours at a stretch. At home, Anjali shared a generator with two neighbours. She restarted the photocopier and glanced at her watch.

She had a call scheduled with Onuwa Chukwu, the Executive Director of HELP, Nigeria, in half an hour. She called him about once a month. She did the same with Alima Samake, the ED of HELP, Mali. It was her business to find out how things were going at their offices, and give them updates from Venimeli. She looked forward to these conversations. Over the months, Alima had become an ally. Alima was experienced, and had that rare skill—good listening. Anjali missed Rani Maharaj, her vivacious colleague and friend in Toronto. They had promised to stay in touch but it was difficult.

Mali had experienced student-led, anti-government riots earlier that year. Then Colonel Amadou Toumani Touré, head of the President's Personal Guard, had arrested Moussa Traore, Mali's President and military leader, and suspended the constitution. HELP management had feared unrest and instability, but Touré had initiated a transition from military to civilian rule. A draft constitution, a charter for political parties, and an electoral code had emerged, and the situation looked promising.

They were far more concerned about the fallouts of the Gulf War. Last month, the Arab League had passed a resolution calling for an Arab-led solution to the conflict, warning against further outside intervention in the region. Soon after, the UN Security Council Resolution 665 had come into effect, placing economic sanctions on Iraq. Kamorga's Northern neighbour, Sudan, had aligned itself with Saddam Hussein.

Kamorga supported Iraq's withdrawal from Kuwait, as did most nations in the Arab League. Meanwhile, Hussein had taken Western hostages and demanded that American troops in Saudi Arabia be replaced with an Arab force.

Putting the copy of the report in an envelope, Anjali took it back to her desk and wrote the Canadian office address on it. She was supposed to turn to Elizabeth for administrative support, but she found it absurd to give her silly, little tasks, when she was capable of so much more. She asked her to come to most of the meetings she attended. Anne would return to her post when Anjali's one-year contract ended. The more Elizabeth knew the easier that transfer would go.

"Why you bring Elizabeth everywhere like your shadow?" Grace had asked, more than once, in Elizabeth's presence.

When she was alone with Grace, Anjali patiently set out her reasons. This was not her decision alone. She had taken it jointly with Anne, and Grace knew that. Anjali had always apologized later to Elizabeth.

"Oh, I don't pay attention," Elizabeth had said.

"I don't pay attention." Anjali could not understand how people did that, how they didn't feel insulted and angry.

She went downstairs to see Leonard. The door to his office was wide open, as always. No one closed doors here. Anjali found that awkward at times, and closed her door when she was speaking to one of her colleagues from abroad. Leonard, she had noticed, was not much at his desk. And when he was, there would be other colleagues in the room. A jovial type, he had the girls laughing a lot of the time. Anjali missed the jokes, which were in Morga.

"I haven't sent the report. Later today," Leonard said as soon as he saw her. He was a lightly graying, portly man in his early 60s.

"For sure?"

"Definitely."

"I've sent the rest of the report to Grace. She's asking for the financial report. In fact she called me about it this morning."

There was no point asking him if he had told Grace that he had already sent her the report. She had learnt not to take things at face value, or expect what two people said would match.

Back at her office, Anjali took out a folder marked Internally Displaced Person—IDP.

The people who had an identity card for the Makaenga clinic were informally called "regulars". They were the ones that HELP Makaenga officially served. The ones for whom funds were raised and reports written. But people without cards, the "irregulars," came as well, in even greater numbers since the government had introduced a small consultation fee for public health services, as part of the Structural Adjustment Program. According to official HELP policy, these patients were supposed to be turned away, but this was impossible in reality. Regulars were given priority, and if the doctors had time, they examined the others, giving them a diagnosis and writing out a prescription. The irregulars did not get highly subsidized drugs or free supplements that the regulars received. On busy days the irregulars had to be turned away. But such was their need that they showed up the day after and the day after that, lining up on the veranda, spilling out into the sun-roasted compound, waiting patiently for hours and days on end.

The Aanke who had arrived from Ferun had requested identity cards from HELP; the Aanke in Madafi were regulars and had them. The request had sparked a heated discussion between the Makaenga, Venimeli and Toronto offices. The

Toronto office felt that the Aanke from Ferun were IDPs, though not officially recognized as such, and therefore entitled to identity cards. But in Venimeli, Grace headed a faction that vehemently opposed this view. The Aanke from Ferun were not IDPs at all, she said, as they would be paid for their land, which had been bought by the government. Nathan, the African doctors in Makaenga, and some of the nurses supported Toronto. The others in the field office just wanted a clear decision as soon as possible.

Anjali had argued that everything they knew pointed to the Aanke having been forced to sell their land, and though they were supposed to be compensated within two months of signing the papers, more than a year had passed, and the majority of the families had received no money. Therefore they should be treated like IDPs and issued identity cards on humanitarian grounds.

People moved and populations grew, that was normal. HELP always had to issue a certain number of new identity cards every year. But what if a much larger contingent suddenly arrived in an area they served, perhaps in dire need? Some of them might be fleeing ethnic strife or civil war, mentally scarred as well as physically spent. HELP had not planned or budgeted for such sudden swells, nor did it provide services like trauma counselling. Yet there were already a substantial number of IDPs in Africa and Asia, and the figures were growing. Lacking a clear policy on IDPs, or for that matter, refugees, they dealt with them on an ad-hoc basis.

A year ago, HELP had finalized a much-needed HIV AIDS policy, with Anjali coordinating that exercise from Toronto. More recently, the management had initiated an international committee comprising of HELP's international staff and outside experts to share research, discuss and formulate an IDP policy. Many questions needed answers, including whether they should go with accepted UN terminology regarding IDPs or come up with their own. Anjali was again the coordinator, operating this time from Venimeli instead of Toronto. They had all met once, at the beginning of the process, and she had orchestrated regular conference calls among the committee members during the last few months. Given the state of the phone lines in Kamorga, this hadn't been easy, but she had managed, and a first draft of the policy was now in circulation. Anjali had become immersed in the topic and started reading about it beyond the requirements of the task.

Engrossed in an article by a South East Asian expert, she did not hear the soft knock on her door.

"Good morning."

Looking up, she saw Hassan, debonair in an elegant white shirt with a black patterned collar.

"Hope I'm not disturbing you."

"Not yet," said Anjali, folding her hands across her chest, her expression quizzical.

Hassan laughed, showing a row of perfect teeth. He took a seat.

"How are you?" he asked.

"Good. And you?"

"Surviving. Look, I have a present for you." Opening his briefcase, he took out a thick wad of paper, stapled together. "The report. Draft only."

Hassan was a consultant who specialized in program evaluation. He also taught part-time in the History Department at the University of Venimeli. Two years ago, HELP had piloted a youth program in Iberu. Aimed at high school dropouts, it used a combination of sports, music, literacy and life skills to try and keep boys and girls off the street, motivating them to go back to school, or directing them towards vocational training. Now they wanted to expand this program. An American Foundation showed interest in providing funds, but their application required detailed facts and figures, which HELP did not have. Two months ago, Anjali had commissioned Hassan to find this data.

"Amazing. I wasn't expecting this before next week," Anjali said.

She ruffled through the pages, before looking up at Hassan who was saying: "Had to rush it. I have DANIDA breathing down my neck. Last minute approval of that project I was telling you about. The usual."

"I'll look over it this weekend."

"Working on the weekend?"

"Usually. Don't you?"

"Not me! I'm a lazy, African man, remember?"

"Oh yeah, how could I forget?"

They smiled in complicity.

"There's an interesting event Tuesday afternoon. It's a launch for a new biography of Thomas Sankara, written by Dr. Aimé Nikiema. Know him?"

"Afraid not."

"Eminent sociologist. From Burkina Faso, like Sankara. He's going to be there. My department got the book translated into English from French."

"I'll try for sure. Could you please grab a copy if I don't make it?"

"Sure."

"Fascinating personality, Sankara. I wrote a paper on

West African politics when I was doing my Masters in Toronto. Finally Sankara didn't figure that much in it, but I really enjoyed reading about him."

"They took some of our best as slaves and killed off our brightest, directly or indirectly. Not just Sankara, but Amilcar Cabral, Lumumba, Machel, Biko."

"And people hardly know about them abroad."

"The Western press won't talk about Nyerere or Nkrumah. They only feature the worst African despots and dictators."

"They cover Nelson Mandela, but that's about it."

"Are we supposed to be thankful for that?"

"Certainly not. You have every reason to be angry. The Western press is terrible when it comes to India too. It only shows the negative side."

"Frantz Fanon got it right when he said that sometimes people hold a core belief that is very strong. When they're presented with evidence that works against it, the new evidence is rejected. They will rationalize, ignore and even deny anything that doesn't fit in. By the way, have you read Fanon?"

"Not really. But I do know that he said: 'Oh my body, make of me always a man who questions.'"

"I'm impressed. That's from *Black Skin, White Masks*. Read *The Wretched of the Earth*."

"I will," she said.

After he left, she dwelt on their conversation, savouring it. It was nice when they had a stimulating exchange, without arguing. She recalled how he had reacted when she had called herself Indo-Canadian.

"You can't be both," he had said.

"Why not? It's a cosmopolitan identity. Multiculturalism —that's Canadian policy."

"That's the worst kind of compromise. Either you're on the side of the oppressor or the oppressed. You can't do both."

"And an Indian living in Canada under a Canadian passport? India won't even let me have dual citizenship!"

"You can call yourself an Indian immigrant."

"It's possible for me to be Indian and Canadian at the same time and still stand for my values. All of them."

"Really?"

"Yes, the world's a complex place."

"All the more reason to take a stance."

She liked it better when he teased her; then she could tease him back. Teasing was a legacy from her childhood. Everyone had teased everyone else, mothers, fathers, sisters, brothers, cousins, aunts and uncles, schoolmates, friends. Even their servants had got into the act, though more cautiously.

After immigration, a part of her had internalized the unspoken rules of Canadian political correctness. Teasing was at odds with a culture that strived to give no offense, at least outwardly. Now she was unpredictable. A phrase or a word could push her buttons, could leave her feeling that the teaser had gone too far. Yet she yearned for the easy intimacy that teasing brought, with its clever repartee and friendly combat.

She was rusty, yes, that was it. Teasing was like playing a musical instrument; you needed practice to carry it off. There were not many people she could tease. Not Rahul, certainly not, and she teased Jeremy only occasionally. Hassan though was fair game; she would continue honing her skills on him.

CHAPTER 7

Discord

SOMETIMES A CROW would perch on a branch of the mangosteen tree outside Anjali's office window. She had moved her desk right next to it. Staring at her, head slightly tilted, he would caw loudly. She considered him a messenger, if only she could decipher what he had to say! She was sure it was always the same one, a raucous male. He had a tendency to visit first thing in the morning. She was glad to see him. Today, he wasn't there. At home, crows sometimes descended on her veranda in a squabbling, unpleasant group. It was Gabriel's duty to shoo them off.

What am I doing here, staring out of the window, Anjali thought. I better go down. The board meeting will start soon.

Elizabeth had ordered a sumptuous meal catered by a women's cooperative for the HELP Board Meeting. The dinner was winding down and Anjali had come up to get her papers.

When she entered the conference room, Elizabeth was already there, placing copies of the quarterly report in twelve places, for the nine board members and the three staff people—Anjali, Leonard and herself.

Anjali sat down and started fussing with her notes. She

had done innumerable presentations and would be presenting the quarterly report in English, but she was never at ease presenting here, in Venimeli, under Grace's fastidious gaze. Grace usually dispensed with the niceties so beloved of her Canadian colleagues—do you think you could, could you please, thank you, that's great, would it work for you if, what do you think, shall we do it that way then. She rarely received smiles or inclinations of the head, handshakes or a quick touch on the shoulder from her.

The board members trooped in slowly, speaking animatedly in Morga, and settled down in the bulky, blue chairs. Three of them were male, the rest female. Anjali had been somewhat surprised to find that more women than men populated the international development sector here as well.

Grace, charmingly dressed in a delicately embroidered light blue silk kaftan and a head wrap fashioned out of the same material, took a seat at the other end of the table. All the women were well dressed, Kamorgan style. A board meeting was a more dressy occasion here than in Canada. Anjali wore a semi-formal beige suit with small, pearl earrings. Her straight, shoulder length hair was held back with clips.

The women Anjali saw on the road wore long brightly coloured skirts with bold prints and elaborately draped head wraps. The skirt, blouse and head wrap were an unhindered exuberance of hue, pattern and cut, which she would never dare assemble herself. In contrast, the observant Muslims wore white, or other chaste colours. The men could be seen in long, lightly embroidered tunics and *kufis*—short, round, brimless caps, while the women wore head scarves and a long, loose over garment. The Aanke, who practiced a form of Sufism, did not dress like the Sunni Muslims.

People continued talking loudly after they had sat down. She would have to call the meeting to order soon, speaking over everyone's voices. Only Grace was silent, erect and un-smiling—an imposing presence. The door opened and Hassan, who was Board Treasurer, came in. He had told them that he would be late. He took the only chair that was still empty, on Grace's right.

"Let's start," Grace said in a commanding voice. A hush fell almost instantly over the room and all eyes turned to Anjali. Elizabeth flipped open her pad; she was the note taker.

After Anjali read through the agenda, Grace raised her hand and said that there was an item she wanted to take up at the end. Noting this, Anjali went on to present her report and the formal part of the meeting proceeded smoothly to the end.

The members turned to each other and started talking and one of them left the room. Anjali wondered if they should call for an official washroom break. Then Grace rose and looked around the room. A hush fell over the crowd again. A born leader of the old-fashioned kind, thought Anjali. She wondered why Grace was standing up like that, then recalled she had another matter to discuss. She hoped that it was something minor; she wanted to see Rahul before he went to bed.

"I am glad things have gone well today," Grace said. "I am happy to see that the full Board here. I had said I would bring up an important matter at the end—something that has been disturbing me for some time. I have not spoken about it so far, though perhaps I should have mentioned it earlier."

She paused; she had everyone's attention.

"I want to start by thanking Anjali Bhave Bhagat for taking on the position of Acting Director of the HELP Africa Regional Office. It's a difficult task and she had to step into large shoes. Though Anjali has tried to do her best, I am afraid she has been stepping off the path for some time."

There was a stir. Some people inclined forward in their chairs, while others sat back. Anjali clutched the sides of her chair.

"We permitted her to make regular visits to Makaenga to do some important research there. You know about it. We expected that this work would not affect the work in this office. Unfortunately, this has been the case."

Anjali gasped.

"Anjali has been using staff time and the staff car to interact with an Aanke woman of questionable repute. She has been visiting Madafi, the Aanke settlement in Makaenga, and acting as advisor to this woman, though that is not her task. In fact, she has been inciting some of the Aanke to take wrong steps. That's why I bring this matter before the Board."

There were exclamations and people turning to each other, speaking in Morga. Anjali looked at Elizabeth; she looked utterly surprised.

Grace held up her hand.

"Silence please," she said. Then she turned to Anjali. "Well, Anjali, we are waiting to hear from you."

Anjali stood up, feeling like a child who is hauled up by the teacher. "I don't understand the charge at all," she said firmly, looking directly at Grace. "The Aanke woman you refer to is called Fatimah. I met her at the HELP office some months ago; she is among the people that HELP serves. She is a remarkable person, a leader in her community. Her people were displaced from their agricultural land in Ferun, land that the government is not compensating them for."

Now Anjali had everyone's attention.

"A chilli pepper on its plant, why should that make you hot?" Grace said in Morga. Then in English: "Some families have got compensation and the others will."

"Very few have been compensated. The process has been very slow; it's not good enough. And it is our business to help the people we serve, any way we can. The second time I saw Fatimah, she asked me if I knew about the Cooperative Land Distribution Scheme and if it was a good idea to apply for it. I said yes. You may not know this, but the Aanke community in Ferun is now split up between those who found shelter with their relatives in Madafi and those who went to the North-western Highlands. They're all having a tough time. I got Fatimah information about the scheme and she developed a good proposal. I gave her some feedback, that's all. If it comes through, the Aanke will be together again on new land that they legally own. What I did is within my right. And in any case, I had a small role in the whole thing."

"It was not your job to turn advisor, and without consulting us about it. That is definitely outside the scope of HELP's work and your work as Acting Executive Director," Grace said.

"Can you please explain to me how?" Anjali had raised her voice a little. "Helping people resettle is not our official mandate, but helping them gain livelihood skills or improve their livelihood is our work. And this has in no way adversely affected my work in Venimeli. I take grave objection to that charge."

"You know the job description in your contract. Or at

least you should. We provide people with training. That is very different. First you stepped outside our mandate and your mandate. Second you did this on company time, and used the HELP vehicle to visit Fatimah. And this had an adverse effect on your work here, no doubt about that."

Anjali looked around. Most people looked distinctly uncomfortable. Some lowered their gaze to avoid meeting hers, others looked away. Elizabeth was the only one who met her gaze, her eyes full of concern.

"That's not true!" Anjali said, her voice shaking. Swallowing hard, she continued more steadily: "I have been fulfilling all my responsibilities. Some things have been delayed, I admit, usually through no fault of mine. I have been working overtime and I have kept my own record, as I am supposed to. I can show it to anyone who wants to see it. I was not trying to hide anything. A process was discussed and finalized for my visits to do research in Makaenga, in which you were also involved."

"I never approved any visits to Madafi," Grace said.

"The Makaenga visit takes a day, so going to see Fatimah did not take up extra time. It is not as if I can come back to Venimeli and work, when I go to Makaenga. You know I often take work home. I have a log about it. I repeat that helping the Aanke is within our mandate. It's true that Fatimah has become a friend. Nothing wrong there."

She had decided not to address the issue of going to see Fatimah in the office car. It was too petty. But if Grace challenged her further she would bring up the matter of Grace using the office van for her personal work.

"You favoured this woman; you diverted valuable resources towards her," Grace said.

"I have nothing more to say. I think we're just repeating ourselves."

Fancy Gaoli, the Vice Chair of the Board, raised her hand. Grace nodded.

"I think we've heard both sides. This dialogue is also on record. Do any of the members have anything to say?"

There was silence. No one looked up at Anjali or Grace, though a few members exchanged glances. Anjali looked at Hassan, who was doodling. The slime ball!

"Let's move on then, it's getting late," Fancy said. "If the Board Chair wants she can take this matter to the international board or the head office as something that is coming from her, unless she wants to propose a formal motion and have us vote on it."

"That won't be necessary," Grace said.

"Please inform us about whatever action you decide to take," Fancy said.

Grace nodded again.

As soon as Anjali formally closed the meeting, people gathered their papers and made for the door. Usually they dispersed gradually, lingering to chat. Arthur Saleh, their oldest board member, shuffled over and shook Anjali's hand. He had forgotten his cane by the table.

"Thank you for everything, Anjali," he said simply. He had a tendency to nod off during meetings, though this one had kept his awake. Saleh walked away a little stiffly; he had arthritis. She felt sorry for him. She noted that Hassan had already left. The coward! Grace was talking to Elizabeth. Anjali gathered her papers and went upstairs.

Sitting down at her desk, she stared into the darkness. How pitch black it was! She shuddered involuntarily. The streetlight near them had not been working for a while. Anjali had suggested calling the municipality but Elizabeth had assured her that it would be a waste of time.

She opened her purse and took a pill for her headache.

"So, you work at Grace's NGO?" someone had remarked at a seminar she was attending when she had first got here.

Grace's NGO, that described it well. All her staff, except for Elizabeth, kowtowed to Grace. Perhaps Elizabeth had options they lacked. Perhaps she just happened to have a backbone. Grace was de facto the Executive Director of HELP Kamorga, but without the responsibility that the position entailed. And she, Anjali, was the ED, with all the responsibility but not enough power to take final decisions and make things happen.

No one on the Board had dared to open their mouth in front of that all-powerful person, not one of them. Hassan, the independent thinker who liked debating with her, had been a sheep as well! Three of their Board Members had considerable status. One ran one of the largest NGOs in Kamorga. Another was the second in command at Oxfam Kamorga. And Fancy was the ED of a well-regarded and well-funded women's NGO. But who would dare oppose Grace?

Anjali rested her head on the desk. How could she carry on with so little support?

Everything was a struggle, even little things, though she tried so hard. She could not make anything stick, because Grace ruled in parallel, at times undoing something already accomplished.

Anjali had tried out Jeremy's gym in Toronto once or twice. She had hated it. The treadmill particularly, where you huffed and puffed in one place, going nowhere. That's how much of her work here felt.

She pitied her colleagues. They had two bosses. She thought of them as spineless, but their behaviour was understandable, really. They threw in their lot with Grace. She was here to stay. This was only her first term on the Board. No doubt she would stay on for the next, while Anjali would be gone in a few months.

She wondered again how Anne managed to get along with Grace. All she had said was that Grace had a personality. Grace didn't merely have a personality; she had an agenda to undermine the Acting ED of the Africa Regional Office.

"*Allahu Akhbar!*" the Muslim call to prayer from the nearby mosque roused her from her slump. She sat up. With eyes closed, she let the sonorous chant travel through her. *Allahu Akbar. Ash-hadu an-la ilaha illa allah …*

A knock on the door. Elizabeth entered, closing the door behind her.

"That was horrible," she said.

"I'm glad someone's on my side."

"The members didn't oppose Grace, but no one supported her either."

That's not good enough, Anjali thought. But maybe it was something. She had not thought about it that way.

"Do you think Grace is right in any way?" Anjali asked.

"I think she has a narrow interpretation. Our work is people to people, we can't be rigid."

"I really believe that I am being true to Frank's vision when he set up the Basic Needs Foundation. I wanted to say that, but I didn't get a chance. How can farmers farm if they have no land?"

"You're right. I am sure the Board members saw it that way."

Why didn't they speak up then, Anjali wanted to ask. *Even you didn't say anything, Elizabeth.* But she knew why. They were all Kamorgans and there was an unspoken code; support your own people against a foreigner. Besides, Grace was a powerful person, why antagonize her?

They heard the sound of a scooter driving up outside.

"It's Kamau, I think," Anjali said.

Elizabeth's husband came to pick her up when she worked late.

Elizabeth laid her hand on Anjali's shoulder. "Try and get some rest," she said.

"Thank you, dear."

CHAPTER 8

Past Tense

SHE LAY BACK against the seat as Kibwe drove her home. Having a driver was a boon sometimes. She sensed the city as it passed by. How dark the nights were in Kamorga! Such utter, absolute blackness! She had never known it before. And she hadn't got used to it after all these months. Was it only because there had been more lighting everywhere else she had lived? Or was there more to it? Some nights she felt as if she was on a slow train that travelled back in time, back to the beginning of time, to the beginning of the world, the beginning of the human race.

She dreamt of trains that had many coaches, all of them empty. They moved and heaved from side to side as the train lurched along the tracks, light from the windows cleaving through, cutting swatches, momentarily, through the shadows, the rattling loud in her ears. Was she inside the train or hovering above it? She could not be sure. Then a high-pitched whistle would shake her out of the depths of sleep. Momentarily. To be plunged back into that infernal journey.

Empty vistas also haunted her dreams. She walked through arid landscapes, alone, always alone. Sometimes the scene was faintly, eerily lit, a bit like a sepia photograph, but often it was night, pitch black—the darkness dense and smothering. The endless stretch of land robbed of light was sheer terror, and she would wake up shivering and sweaty.

Such fears!

She had talked to Jeremy about them. Why did she have these nightmares? How could she rid herself of them? "You feel what you feel, Anju. Emotions aren't rational. You're under a lot of stress, and you're away from home," he had said, taking her hand. She had snuggled close. They had discussed stress-relief strategies, but Anjali had not found the time to implement any.

She opened her eyes for a moment, and then closed them again. The CN Tower loomed before her eyes—that overhyped Toronto landmark. She found the image reassuring. Technology, perhaps, had culled the West of its worst monsters. She doubted that there were any ghosts in Toronto, though ghost stories had populated her Indian childhood.

The day when Mathew had offered her the African contract seemed long ago, though only about nine months had passed since. He had called her into his office and said: "You learn languages fast, don't you?"

"Pardon?"

"You learn languages fast, right?"

"I don't know. Why?"

"You learnt French here, and how many Indian languages do you speak?"

"I had French as an option in secondary school. But I really learnt to speak at the Alliance, here. And I speak Marathi, Hindi, and a bit of Gujarati."

"That's five languages."

"Four-and-half."

She wondered what he was getting at. Then he told her that Anne had to head back to Canada and they needed a reliable replacement. They knew this was coming. Anne was an only child and her mother was alone. She was in the advanced stages of Parkinson's disease, living in her own house, refusing an assisted living facility.

Frank Maier had made it a policy that Canadian Executive Directors of HELP who worked in the field learn the local language. They had to have the basics, working to improve their fluency over time.

He had made an attractive offer. Anjali wanted to buy a house; the African contract would help her save and make a big down payment, cutting down her mortgage. It would look good on her resume. Not only was it an Executive Director position, it was in Africa, a part of the world that was always in the development spotlight.

The job was not that demanding, everything was in place, Anne had told her on the phone. Mary and Gabriel were gems. The American International School was superb. Venimeli was a liveable city. And to top it all, Kamorga was a peaceful, stable democracy!

After the divorce, when Manish had returned to India, Anjali had opted for a post that was more of a desk job. She knew that she was a lucky, rare immigrant who had found work easily in Canada, and that too in international development. Not many immigrants, especially people of colour, were to be found in this milieu, even though they were the people who had grown up in developing countries and many of them were well educated and qualified.

She had managed to negotiate a deal to travel only once

a year. She would drop Rahul off in India during his summer vacation, and then travel for work. Rahul spent most of his time with his father in Delhi and some time with Anjali's parents in Bombay.

But she missed the more frequent field visits that her earlier job had allowed, and she wanted Rahul to have more exposure. Living in Canada, how could he understand the issues that mattered to her—poverty, inequity, and the solutions that non-profits diligently sought for these seemingly intractable problems? In Kamorga, he would directly experience other ways of life. And Jeremy had been encouraging and supportive, promising a visit half way through the year.

She had envisioned more time at home with Rahul, a life rooted in community, the opportunity to meet people and make new friends—a sane, balanced life in a warm, tropical country; a shared adventure. But the dream had soured, except for one thing: Gabriel had become a companion for Rahul. She had failed to provide Rahul with a brother or sister, though she had always expected that she would have two children. But in Gabriel he had at least found a playmate who was close at hand.

Suddenly, the past washed over Anjali, a huge wave that swept her up and deposited her in the city by the sea, where she had been born.

It was 5 pm as usual when Anjali and Vandana got home from school that day. As they entered their flat, their maid Sakhu *bai* said, "*Todun takla sagla, thithe, Vishwas Bhau Colonit.* They destroyed everything in Vishwas Bhau Colony."

"What?" said Vandana.

"*Municipality che lok aale hote.* People from the municipality had come."

Anjali dropped her heavy school bag on the floor.

"*Chaal*, let's go, Vandu," she said, taking her sister's hand.

"Where you going? Don't go like this!" Sakhu *bai* called after them as they ran down the stairs, out of the apartment building and onto the street. They hailed a rickshaw and jumped in.

Ten minutes later they were face to face with the horrifying devastation: a cyclone had blown through Vishwas Bhau Colony. There was debris everywhere—pieces of wood and tin. Smashed pots and pans. Clothes lying in heaps in the dust. Sheets of plastic that had insulated the roofs lay bunched up here and there, snagged by a stone or a clump of dry grass. They rushed forward, Vandana nearly falling over an overturned kerosene stove, leaking dangerously into the soil.

They had been here last weekend at the adult literacy class as volunteer teachers. Eight months ago, Indumati's friend had got them involved in a program to teach the women to read and write Marathi. The class took place on Wednesday nights and Sunday afternoons, in a storage space that was partially cleared so that they could have a classroom with waist-high brick walls and a tin roof.

Gangu *bai*, one of their older and brighter students made her way towards them. The big, red *bindi* on her forehead was smeared; her eyes were wide with distress.

"*Bagha kasa kele*; look what they did," she said. Suddenly her face collapsed and she started crying. Vandana held her in her arms, her eyes moistening.

Anjali's heart felt hard, hard as stone and black as coal. She strode forward, looking at the women who squatted here and there in the dust, their littlest ones huddled against them, a pitiful cloth bundle or two lying by their side. The men sat together on the ground in groups of four or five, smoking. Some sat alone, vacant-eyed.

Someone will pay for this, she thought. Oh yes, someone is going to pay for this all right.

Vishnu sat with his back against a collapsed wall, glassy-eyed, flecks of white in his wild hair, his shirt half undone. He gave her pause. She knew him as eccentric and wily. What had happened to him? She squatted beside him, wondering if he was in a drunken stupor. That would be like him. She smelled no alcohol on his breath. His expression did not change; he seemed not to see her.

"Vishnu," she said. "Vishnu, *ooth*, get up." She shook him lightly by his shoulder. Still no response. She grabbed his wrist; there was a sluggish pulse.

"*Kai zala yala*; what's happened to him?" she yelled out, looking around. No one heard her. She noticed then that some of the older children were walking around aimlessly. A little boy she knew as Nandu came and stood beside her. He often came to class with his youthful mother and sat staring at the blackboard, a thumb in his mouth. He was about six, and somewhat slow.

He looked at her, his mouth open.

She felt anger rising, building into a rage as big as a bonfire. The government had done this, their own municipality! "How can they? How can they do this? Bastards, motherfuckers!" she screamed in Marathi.

She had never used those words before. She had heard them often in Vishwas Bhau Colony, and had recoiled from them, found them offensive.

Nandu's eyes widened. He put his thumb in his mouth and stumbled away. She reached out for him but he was gone.

Out of the corner of her eye she felt Vishnu stirring, and turned towards him. Awareness was returning, slowly, to his eyes. He groaned, then coughed, sitting up a bit straighter.

"*Kai Bhave bai, kasah kai*; Bhave madam, how are you?" he said hoarsely. He always addressed her by her last name, with mocking formality, while he addressed Vandana by her first name.

Catching his rough, dirt encrusted hand, she squeezed it, hard. Suddenly alert, he smiled at her. It was his usual smile, confident, cocky. It was as if there had been no demolition, as if they had met casually in one of the by lanes of Vishwas Bhau Colony. She felt the prickle of tears, and bit her lip. She would not let them come through, not then. She let go of his hand and looked away.

Someone is going to pay for this, she thought. They aren't just going to get away with it. No, definitely not.

CHAPTER 9

Mary's Dilemma

MARY AND GABRIEL sat on the middle seat of a Matata, waiting for it to fill up; it would leave only after all the seats were taken. A cloth bag with some clothes and food lay at Mary's feet, and there was a school bag on Gabriel's lap. As usual he had homework to do that weekend, a weekend they were going to spend with Edith, Aissa and John.

The Matata driver was not yet behind the wheel. The conductor, a boy who seemed to be a couple of years older than Gabriel, stood just outside, shouting, "Warringa, Warring, Warringa. *Tua ya, tua ya, tua ya* (step up, step up, step up)." This particular Matata was headed for the Warringa Central Bus Station.

Gabriel watched a passenger climb in, smoking. Mary had no eyes for him, or anyone else.

Lucky Gabriel had the window seat; he could see Matatas taking off and arriving, often double-parking, squeezing skilfully into any empty space they could find on that busy street. Around them, the swirling bodies of customers, embarking and disembarking.

Intriguing words—embarking and disembarking, Gabriel

thought. Barking was a word he commonly associated with dogs. Though he had also come across Lieutenants barking orders, in books.

Women with baskets on their heads bearing eggs, fish, fruit, vegetables and loaves of bread joined the melee. Occasionally one of them carried a thatched, closed basket with live chickens inside. The slits provided a glimpse of an eye, a beak, a feather or a foot. Men appeared with bales of cloth, rolls of matting, spools of wire, wooden stools or plastic buckets tied together with rough rope, all of which were loaded on the tops of the Matatas. They paid extra for this service.

Street kids in soiled clothes, full of impish energy, half begged half teased the people, who shooed them off. Adult beggars also solicited the passengers. Every now and then there was one who limped badly, had a stump for an arm, or a sightless eye. Women with babies on their hips, hands extended, palms turned upwards, eyes beseeching, begged wordlessly, trailing a second child behind them.

Street vendors sold cola, water, snacks, peanuts and bananas. Small kiosks on the pavement displayed more hearty food, toiletries, newspapers, cheap plastic and rubber toys.

It was impossible to take it all in, but Gabriel wanted to, desperately. His eyes darted here, there and everywhere: from a pretty young girl squatting on the sidewalk, selling slices of water melon to a large woman, wearing a lot of make-up, balancing a tray loaded with lipstick, nail polish, face powder, eye pencils, combs, hair clips, hand mirrors on her shoulder, to a young man making Michael Jackson moves on the pavement, 'Just Beat It' blaring from a ghetto blaster placed nearby, to a lurching drunk, who, in trying to cross the road, had caused a car, a Matata and a scooter to come to a standstill around him. Horns blared and curses rang out in the sultry, mid-morning air.

Gabriel stole a look at his mother. She sat slightly hunched, hands limp in her lap, lost in thought. She had been absent-minded since they left home that morning. Every time they crossed the road, she reached for Gabriel's hand, a gesture that embarrassed him. It didn't make sense; he'd been going out by himself on errands for a long time. He wanted to protest. Dissenting words rose to his lips, then fell away.

Mary's mind was focussed on a single idea: she must speak to Edith today. She must. I don't know how I could have left it for so long, she thought.

There was a reason why Mary had not spoken to her cousin Edith, a very good reason. Right then, her brain was fighting hard to keep that reason out of sight, submerged, allowing her to think: I must speak to Edith tonight. I must. I really must. So great was the effort to pull off this deception that all other thoughts, even perceptions, were cast out. Only that single, preposterous idea remained: she must, she must speak to Edith that day, she really had to.

"Warringa, Warringa, Warringa. *Tua ya, tua ya tua ya,*" said the conductor urgently. The Matata was almost full; one more customer would do it. Soon a middle-aged man arrived with a little girl; they took the front seat beside the driver. Kids below five rode for free; Gabriel was riding at half price.

Dropping the cigarette he was smoking, the driver leapt in, and noisily fired the engine. The conductor was still out. As the van started moving he ran alongside and leapt in. Wish I could do that, Gabriel thought. The conductor thrust half his body out of the open window and stayed that way through most of the ride. Gabriel eyed him enviously.

Twenty minutes later they were at the Central Bus Station with its slew of Matatas, an army of them, as well as private buses that ran between Venimeli and other cities, near and far.

Gabriel's eyed a row of buses run by a new company called Supersonic. They were mammoth, with shiny, steel-grey exteriors painted with a batman like figure in horizontal flight—firm jawline, crew cut, a purple cape billowing out from behind his head, eyes masked. How impressive they looked! Unlike the rundown buses of other companies. He had heard that they were made in Korea.

One day, when he was older, he would ride a Supersonic. He would get tickets for his mother, Aissa, John and Aunt Edith. Where would they go? Up north, to Mapaanji. On board, they would all eat oranges, which he would buy with his own money. He imagined sitting comfortably at a large window, looking out on a bare, brown landscape, suffused with the scent and taste of oranges, orange peels in his lap, seeds scattered at his feet. Heaven!

Oranges were rare and expensive in Kamorga, imported in small quantities from elsewhere. Anne bought them sometimes and so did Anjali, but fruit was not accessible to Gabriel in the big house in the same way as other food. Ama, Mary, bought a bunch of bananas for them when she went shopping. Sometimes their employers let the last of the oranges languish. Then, with a nod from Mary, Gabriel took one, overripe, or a bit shrivelled and dry, but still enjoyable. Mary always bought fresh, delectable oranges on his birthday, which all five of them enjoyed, and he got to eat one or two all by himself at home.

As they made their way through the crowd to catch a

Matata to Melunge, the suburb where Aunt Edith lived, Gabriel thought, as always, of his mother and aunt setting foot in Venimeli at the Central Bus Station, for the first time, coming all the way from Mapaanji, the bone-dry town up-north where they were born. Coming to work in the Big City was so daring of them! Gabriel knows that they took two buses; he had overheard them talking about the exhausting, two-day journey. He had been on the journey too, curled up inside Ama's stomach! She had been so afraid that the rocking bus, as it bounced and bumped along the road, would hurt her little baby.

His mother and aunt spoke often about life in Mapaanji. Many a story has he heard about his grandfather, silent and strong, who worked in the mines. His grandmother was an angel, he's been told. She ran a tiny, wayside eatery, stretching a tarp over four poles and cooking under it in a large pot, blackened with age, the only one she owned. She cooked and sold meat stew made out of animal guts. They lived in a brick and tin shack next to the motor road that led out of town, her husband gone for three months at a time.

His grandmother died giving birth when Mary was still a child. The baby died as well. Even now Mary's voice grew tremulous when she spoke of her. After her mother's death, Mary kept house the best she could for her elder brother, Otieno, and their father. Then a stepmother entered the scene. There were stories of the stepmother's cruelty towards Mary. It was always Aunt Edith who told these stories while Mary listened, her head bowed.

One day, Aunt Edith's mother, who was his grandmother's elder sister, took Mary to live with them. Mary holds her aunt, a cheerful, kindly woman who worked as a housemaid, in high regard. Uncle Otieno continued to live with the stepmother and Gabriel's grandfather. Being a boy, he was treated better, Mary said.

Now Uncle Otieno worked in Juba, in Southern Sudan. It was a river port on the Nile and Uncle Otieno did something with boats, repairs perhaps? Gabriel has never met his uncle, but he knows he will, one day. His uncle does not write often, but when he does, Gabriel reads the cryptic messages to Mary and Edith. Ama can't read or write; Aunt Edith can, but she gave him the letter reading-writing task because he got so good at school. For four months there had been no letter from Uncle Otieno. He knows Ama is waiting anxiously for one.

Ama and Aunt Edith loved talking about the past. They could go on for hours. Yet, despite their large supply of stories, there was one person always missing, an important person. This person, never ever mentioned, was Gabriel's father.

A great desire coiled like a snake in the pit of his stomach; he wanted to know who his father was. But not a word from Ama or Aunt Edith, never a whisper, a passing mention, a casual reference.

Nigiyo, no, nothing.

Some nights Gabriel willed himself to stay awake, pretending to be asleep, eavesdropping, but his father was still not mentioned.

I must have a father, Gabriel thought. Maybe his father was dead. Maybe he had been a soldier. Deep in his gut he knew that his father was alive, but how would he find out about him? By asking his mother. Yet this he can't do. Every so often, the question formed and reformed in his being, never reaching his lips. He must have asked his mother about his father when he was younger, after he saw his friends with their fathers. But he knows he never did, because if he had, he would have the answer, the answer that he desired the most.

His father would be mentioned someday. He just has to wait, be patient, and Gabriel is good at being patient. Meanwhile, the snake sat tightly coiled at the base of his belly. One day, if he doesn't get the answer, it will rise up and strike.

They climbed into the Matata bound for Melunge. Luckily, this one was nearly full, so they took the front seat beside the driver.

Sitting between his mother and the driver, he had an unimpeded view of the road, unrolling before him, the sharp smell of diesel in his nose and the heat and shudder of the engine under his feet. This was the most exciting seat of all and he had it!

I must speak to Edith today, Mary thought, frowning in concentration. There was no time to lose. Today it would be, after the children sleep.

Aunt Edith lived on a little, twisting lane. The road turned to sludge when it rained. The building had 20 rooms, built in a row. A couple of families had two rooms side by side, but most had just one. There were two squat toilets, two bathrooms and a communal tap, an improvement over the last place that had one toilet and bathroom between as many rooms.

An open, foul-smelling drain ran on one side of the building. Edith's room, closer to the other side, avoided the full effect of the stink. Everyone, however, had equal access to the plentiful flies and mosquitoes.

Aissa came running up to meet them. She was thin, her large eyes taking up most of her small, oval face. She threw herself at Mary, while John, a year younger than 6-year-old Aissa, claimed Gabriel. Edith stood in the background, in a faded, house gown, smiling enormously—a tall, slim woman with braided hair. When the children released them she hugged them close. Then everyone started talking at once:

John wanted Gabriel to go out and play ball with him, Aissa wanted him to be a horse, Edith wanted Mary's opinion on how to treat a painful boil on her hand.

An hour later, sitting on a mat on the floor, they shared a meal of plantain stew with *gali*, and discussed the weekend. It was decided that Gabriel would mind the children while Mary and Edith visited a grand-aunt, twice removed, who had arrived in Venimeli from Mapaanji, and was staying nearby with her son and his family. Aissa, John and Gabriel had already met her. The old lady was not well, and the children tried her patience. The next day, Sunday, Edith and Mary would take the children to the parade ground to see a travelling fair, giving Gabriel time to finish his homework in peace.

"Why can't Gabriel go with us? I want him to come!" Aissa said.

"Darling, we will bring a balloon for Gabriel. Would you like that?" Mary said. Taking a sweet dumpling from a box that she had brought with her, she gave it to Aissa.

"You can make me a drawing of the fair when you get back," Gabriel told Aissa.

"Me too! I'll make a drawing too!" John jumped up and down, waving his pudgy arms.

Edith insisted that Mary take it easy as she brought the utensils out in the courtyard to wash. John followed his mother, while Gabriel gamely crawled around making neighing sounds, with Aissa riding him, hooting with joy. Suddenly, he started braying.

"What animal am I now?" he asked.

"Donkey!" Aissa yelled.

Mary sat with her back to the wall. She was tired; she tired so easily these days. The strain of maintaining the illusion that she was going to talk to Edith and ask her to take on Gabriel's responsibility had added to her fatigue. Now that idea had gone flat, like a collapsed balloon. It was obvious that she could not do this; Edith was already responsible for John and Aissa, and barely made ends meet. Mary knew that night would fall, the children go to sleep, and she would not say anything to Edith. The thought sat heavy, a physical weight, making her stoop.

Edith had wept noisily and berated fate when Mary had told her about the cancer, but she had not asked what would happen to Gabriel after Mary died. Edith was like that; she lived from day to day. But Mary did not have that luxury. She must plan. She must find a guardian angel for Gabriel.

Her thoughts, held at bay since morning, ran helter-skelter. She cannot send him back to Mapaanji to live with her ailing father and heartless stepmother. Sending him to live with one of Edith's sisters, one of whom also took care of Edith's mother, was also not an option. Both had large families and burdens of their own, and Gabriel had never met them.

As for Otieno, it was his duty to look after Gabriel, and he had a bit of money. One day he would return to Kamorga and assume the responsibility. Of that she was sure. But why didn't he write? Was he still in Juba? She had tried to get people in Mapaanji with some contacts in Sudan to investigate, but there was no news yet.

There was another problem, a big one. She must ensure that Gabriel stayed in Venimeli and went from St. Anthony's Primary School to St. Anthony's Secondary School for Boys. Gabriel would be a Big Man one day, but only if he continued in a good school like St. Anthony's.

Night arrived and everyone went to sleep, one by one.

First Aissa and John who played themselves into an exhaust-ed, cranky state and slept, after an outburst of tears. Then Gabriel, who hung out with the boys in the courtyard, came in and fell asleep as soon as his head touched the pillow. Soon Edith, who has been darning one of John's shirts as they chatted, catchy Congolese music playing on the radio, de-clared that she was done for the day.

Mary lay down too, but sleep eluded her. The air was still —warm and stifling. She tossed and she turned, afraid that Aissa, who had flung an arm against her, would awaken. Mary's thoughts tossed too, like seaweed on restless waves that peaks on a strong up thrust and just as suddenly, disappears, pulled down by a powerful undertow.

Mary's disease had disturbed her equanimity, not shat-tered it. But Gabriel's unresolved future was tearing her apart. What was the secret behind her habitual calm, her quiet contentment? Mary followed the two precepts for hap-piness that come hard to most of us. She lived in the present and gave herself fully to the task at hand. And she remained focussed on other people, the world beyond herself. She did not have any grand desires. All she wanted was to be in the world and interact amicably with it.

When the disease came, she was not terribly troubled, death being no stranger. First it had taken her mother, then other relatives, friends and neighbours, suddenly, inexplic-ably. She had not dwelt on the injustice of these deaths. Life and death were natural, ever present, beyond questioning. "When you live next to the cemetery, you cannot weep for everyone." People did not plan babies; babies happened, and once conceived were welcomed into the world. Some of them died. That was sad, of course, very sad, and their mothers mourned them with all their heart. But the sadness passed and they lived on, not looking backwards, nor dwelling too much on the future. The present was quite enough.

She was born, and now she must die. That's how Mary thought about her own death. When you got right down to it, it was as simple as that. Except that it was not, because there was Gabriel, whom she loved above and beyond everything.

Gabriel had a strange life, she mused, living between worlds. She didn't know what kind of strength he had to handle her death. They were close, she and Gabriel, interdependent. They tried to shield each other from the shocks of life. Under Gabriel's intelligence and seeming maturity she sensed vulnerability. She feared for him, feared her death would break him. Unless, unless he was supported by someone strong and dependable. That could help soften the blow.

There was always the good Father, Father Emmanuel, whom baby Gabriel had charmed in such a big way. She had worked with Gabriel strapped to her back, sweeping the floors of the residence for Jesuit Fathers. Some of them taught at St. Anthony's, others were priests, others theologians, teachers of religion, and social workers.

Sometimes Gabriel would crawl around as she worked. That was how, one day, he had collided with Father Emmanuel's feet. The good Father had picked him up, and Gabriel had looked at him, gurgling and cooing, making big, soft, sweet baby eyes, waving his little fists in the air, worming his way, in that instant, into Father Emmanuel's heart. Of course it had helped that Gabriel was an early talker, quick to learn, interested in his lessons. But it was that first instant of falling in love with baby Gabriel that made everything that followed possible.

She could approach Father Emmanuel to whom she owed a debt beyond measure. He was a Man of God, and it was his duty to look after God's children. This was what he had told her when he had enrolled Gabriel in St. Anthony's. If she asked him, he would not say no. He was simply too good, and loved Gabriel too well to refuse.

Gabriel would remember her everyday, and grieve deeply for years. That's how she had mourned her mother. But perhaps he would find some comfort in books and learned words. He loved so much to read; he read aloud to her sometimes. She was so proud of him then that she forgot to listen to the words. She just looked at him; watching his lips move in wonderment.

Father Emmanuel was the best choice for Gabriel. He too was a man of learning. Mary had dusted the books in his office and his room. And besides, he was the only one. She must approach him soon. If he took Gabriel in he might need to move out of the Jesuit residence and find a place nearby, but that would not be too difficult. Savings never go bad, and she had a little pot she had managed to fill, which she would gladly give the dear Father. She made more working for Anne, and now Anjali, than she would have working in a local household, with many expenses taken care of as well. Of course she had to spend on Gabriel's school uniform, pay for proper shoes and supplies; the scholarship only covered fees and books.

Before she could approach Father Emmanuel, there was another task before her, not a task but a mountain: she must tell Gabriel that she was going to die. All he knew was that she had some stomach trouble that drained her energy. This prospect sapped Mary's remaining strength, and she fell into a troubled sleep.

CHAPTER 10

Morning Prayer

Fatimah rose at daybreak. Normally she was instantly awake, but today her head felt heavy. Shaking off the shadowy visions that were still trying to stake their claim on her, she sat up on the thick reed mat that lay directly on the mud floor, covered with a rough cotton sheet.

Letting the patchwork quilt made by her mother fall away from her, she surveyed the interior of the circular mud and wattle dwelling. First light was seeping in already through the easterly window, gently outlining the form of her daughter, Hawa, sleeping a little way off. The light didn't quite reach her daughters-in-law and their children, sleeping in a row to her left.

She draped a scarf loosely around her head, and moved stealthily towards the exit. The wooden door always creaked, but the slight sound was unlikely to rouse anyone, all young, all good sleepers. Aunt Bisa, the widowed, childless, elder sister of Baaba Kaarya, had her own hut.

Outside, the compound stretched out before her. The cool air was pleasing. She washed her face and patted it dry with one end of her scarf.

Facing Mecca, she raised her arms, and with eyes closed, prayed silently. It was right that she welcomed the day on behalf of her family and community. This was how Baaba Kaarya used to conduct himself in Ferun, and now she followed in her father's footsteps. He had not lived long in Madafi; the mighty Baaba Kaarya had succumbed to a sudden, high fever, two months after their arrival.

Arza, Feeza and Hawa would soon be up. Feeza, the designated Water Woman, would go to the community water pump, carrying a large plastic bucket on her head, and smaller buckets in her hands. Hawa would accompany her. On return, it would be time to milk the goats. Arza, the eldest daughter-in-law, and therefore the designated Cooking Woman, would light a fire and make a thin, sorghum gruel for breakfast.

Fatimah touched her *Tawiz*, then she put on her rubber slippers from among the neat row lined up outside the Women's House, and headed out of the compound, onto the track that led through open ground and vegetation, to Shaikh Misfar Yasa Madafi's shrine. It was Friday, a holy day.

She had sensed Yasa Madafi's presence as soon as they had reached the settlement, after an arduous, three-day journey from Ferun, on foot and by bus. They were made welcome in Abubakar's spacious compound, and served water, followed swiftly by a meal.

The very air in this settlement, so similar and yet so different from their home in Ferun, was imbued with Yasa Madafi's auspicious presence. Fatimah did not have words to describe this feeling, but it was as palpable as her own breath. The air in Madafi was super charged; turgid like a cloud before a shower. Embraced by Yasa Madafi's spirit, Fatimah had felt deeply comforted, as she tucked into the meal, graciously served by Ebun. Perhaps things would turn out all right after all, she had thought.

She had also noticed how struck Amadu was by his cousin, Ebun. The normally garrulous young man had gone silent, staring at her and then staring some more. It made Fatimah smile. She had heard so much about Ebun's beauty, but this was the first time she was seeing her. She had met Abubakar and Sabra, Abubakar's elder wife, only once, at her own, long-ago wedding in Ferun. But she had never met their daughter.

What a luminous presence Ebun was: tall, long limbed, graceful; an oval face with liquid, almond shaped eyes, a high forehead and cheekbones, a flaring nose, and a perfectly shaped, generous mouth. Her neck was long, as were her fingers, her head covered in tiny, tightly wrought braids that fell almost to her waist.

Fatimah willed her mind back to the present. En route to the shrine, she did not want her consciousness to be prisoner to memories from the past or fantasies about the future. She needed to walk in silence and spaciousness, emptying her mind of Things of This World.

As she walked on, she came abreast of a large-scale Thing of This World—the many-chambered granary. The Things of This World had a way of bearing down on human beings.

The granary was a living symbol of their link with their Mande ancestors. The walls were made of bamboo strips, with straw, mat liners. Some sections were held together with wood and rope. In Ferun, they used to make their own rope, but here in Makaenga they bought it quite cheaply from a nearby shop. The floor was covered with straw mats, with a mud coating on top. Rocks under the base elevated the structure 30 centimetres above ground; the Aanke always followed precise measurements set down by tradition. Each section had a conical, thatched roof. The area around was swept clean every day.

The granary held the harvest from their communal fields. Grain from the women's fields was kept in the Women's Houses. Sabra kept it on a raised platform under the roof. Fatimah had stored the grain Sabra had given them in jute sacks stacked against the back wall. They had been planning to build a platform, which would protect the grain better from mice, insects and rainwater, but they had not done so yet. So much time, labour and resources had gone into building a basic compound for themselves, on the land near Abubakar's compound. She was thankful that they had at least that.

The sight of the granary always lifted her spirits. It took her back to Ferun, where they had several such granaries, not just one. The granary stood for everything she held dear—the bountiful land, the hard work they all put in together to make crops grow, the laborious but joyous effort of harvesting. The granary was precious, sacred; it stored the grain that held the community together and provided security in case of a bad crop.

Beyond the granary were musambya trees—small, upright, slender, with crooked branches and a soft, green crown. How lovely they looked! They reminded her of Hawa, who was going to step into womanhood, any day now. She must remember to scrape off some tree bark on her way back; it helped with menstrual cramps.

Now she was far enough along the path that she spied the tip of the pointed white dome of Yasa Madafi's shrine. She closed her eyes and bowed her head.

The shrine was a tall, conical, brick structure that they

whitewashed every few years. It was 150 years old and not marked in any way; Yasa Madafi's followers knew it at once for what it was. Here, their ancestors had planted some nsambya trees that shone with yellow blossoms every spring. They were green now, dignified guardians of this hallowed ground.

The worshippers kneeled before a door that was etched on the shrine in charcoal. Not a real door, but a representation. After each whitewash, the Aanke redrew it again, carefully, with solemn ceremony. The shrine contained relics, the bones not only of Yasa Madafi, but also of his learned father, making it the holiest place for the Aanke in all of Kamorga.

Pulling her headscarf a little lower over her head, Fatimah kneeled down and bowed her head. Reverence came unbidden here. She recited the root prayer written by Yasa Madafi, who taught that all things exist as light, beginning with the Absolute Light, the Light of Lights, God. Then the light spread to angels and to other heavenly beings, including Muhammad and other prophets, radiating out to all the Sufi sheikhs, and finally to their followers. Each being reflected the light from above to creatures below. The world shone as the divine light spread through innumerable beings, radiating outwards, downwards, onwards, penetrating further and further till nobody and nothing was left in the dark. Yasa Madafi had emphasized the duty of each Aanke to pay frequent homage to this beautiful, radiant latticework, which he likened to an illuminated spider's web. More formal prayers would be offered later that day at the banco mosque in Madafi.

After she was done, Fatimah continued kneeling for some time, letting the words work their inevitable magic, spread slowly, surely through her entire being, nourishing her very soul. Then she raised her head to the clear blue sky that doomed the space and started praying for the health and well being of her family and community.

Peace be with her dear father, whom they had lost so unexpectedly. It was not the fever that had killed him, such a strong man as he. It was heartbreak—pure and simple. In leaving Ferun, he had been forced to walk away from the only earthly abode where he wished to be. Losing the will to continue, he had sickened and died bit by bit, day by day.

When the fever had risen so high so fast that night, he had remained lucid, forbidding Amadu to go and get a doctor. He had asked instead that all his family, and Abubakar's, gather around his bed. Then, fixing his reddened eyes on Fatimah, he had proclaimed her, his eldest, his successor.

Fatimah, who had restrained herself till then, burst into tears, placing her head on her father's flaming chest. Baaba Kaarya, stroking her hair, had addressed Amadu, saying that he was now a man, and must take all his responsibilities seriously. Then, turning to Abubakar, whose eyes were moist, he had thanked him again for his hospitality and said that he was glad to leave his family in the care of one so honourable. He had sought out Lahmey's eyes and merely smiled at him, calling out feebly, "Elder Sister," as his strength failed him and his eyes closed.

Bisa had firmly grasped his feverish, shaky hands. She had stood like that, all through the night, dry-eyed, strong as a baobab, eyes fixed on her brother, lips moving now and then in prayer. He had not opened his eyes after that, and had passed away at dawn. Fatimah too had sat by his bedside, but had dozed off at some point. It was Bisa who had shaken her gently awake and conveyed through a look that her father was no more. Then she had started reciting the verses that were customary when a person passed way, her old voice thin but firm.

Now Fatimah mourned her father, tears flowing without reserve. Grief overtook her every Friday, when she kneeled before the shrine. At home she had to put on a brave face. Here she opened her heart, keeping no secrets from Yasa Madafi.

After a few minutes, she dabbed her cheeks with the end of her scarf, and continued her prayers. After praying for everyone, she asked that the forthcoming union of Amadu and Ebun be blessed. A heart deep in love has no patience. So Lahmey had approached Abubakar a couple of months ago, and the engagement had taken place. Fatimah prayed for new land and compensation.

"Our young will drift, lose their way, Allah, I beseech you, beg you, we must have land, and we need the money. With your blessings, it will be done."

It hadn't been easy to ask so directly, but once she found the words, this prayer had become the most fervent of them all.

After this, there was still one prayer left. She hesitated every time before starting on this one.

It was 12 years ago that she had borne Hawa and Jelani to full term, with great difficulty. Before that there had been two stillbirths, and a miscarriage had followed the birth of the twins. Lahmey had insisted then that she start using contraceptive herbs; she had nearly died when she had miscarried. She had done his bidding ever so reluctantly.

Before taking that step, she had tried special herbs to become pregnant, and charms, chants and fasts, but nothing had worked.

Worst of all, Masumi had been discouraging. She had read the portents and sighed deeply—no children would come forth from Fatimah's womb. Clasping her eldest-born to her breast, she had lamented loudly. When her mother had approached the spirits for counsel, Fatimah had sat dry-eyed through the ritual. She had not spilt tears on receiving the terrible news, but many were the nights when she wept silently in her bed. She could not contain her tears even on the nights when Lahmey came and slept with her at the Women's House. She would never forget how he had comforted her then, as a mother does her baby. Over the years that acute ache of longing had dulled but not disappeared.

And now, here they were in Madafi, not by design, but through a play of fate, with the HELP clinic and doctors like Nathan close at hand. She wondered if she might be able to conceive once again and deliver safely. The thought kept stinging her consciousness like a persistent bee. She was 35, not so young anymore, but ...

It shamed her to ask for so many things at a time when she is not even capable of giving *zakat*, alms, but she would make up for that later, when they had their own fields and became prosperous again. Allah, all-seeing, all-forgiving, would surely be sympathetic to her plight.

She bowed low and prayed for more children. She asked not only for the seed to take safe root, but also for the courage to talk to Nathan. Allah, Mohammed, Yasa Madafi—she appealed to them all.

CHAPTER 11

Gathering Force

WHEN SHE RETURNED home from Yasa Madafi's shrine, Fatimah went to the open hearth and sat down on one of the low, wooden stools. Arza had finished cooking breakfast and was squatting near the fire, looking absentmindedly at the glowing embers. Seeing Fatimah, she rose and went to the Men's House to call Amadu and Jelani.

Lahmey was already up, and would return soon, having gone, as always, for a casual inspection of his brother's fields. Sometimes, Lahmey went straight to his brother's compound and ate his first meal of the day there.

Amadu and Jelani emerged shortly. Being just past the harvest season, they slept later than usual. Fatimah considered this to be one of the many bad habits that the boys had picked up in Madafi. "Lying down when your elders are already up, it's shameful," she would say every so often.

It didn't help that Lahmey said nothing. He had suggested quietly to Fatimah that she should let little things be. If they rested a little more when there was no work, what was the harm in that? At times her husband's mild ways irked Fatimah, but there was nothing she could do.

Sometimes Abubakar ate breakfast with them; an honour. He appeared without warning, smiling mischievously, throwing the women into a tizzy.

Fatimah would send Hawa to the women's garden plot to pick berries and tell Arza to heat a cup of goat milk, and mix in some herbs. Then she would engage her brother-in-law in the traditional greeting and Abubakar would respond. Sometimes he answered irreverently in Morga instead of Bisseau.

When Fatimah presented the berries and the milk to him, with a bow, he would laugh, "Revered sister-in-law, don't fuss so. Leave off your Feruni ways here and give the milk to Feeza's little one. It'll do him good." The berries, which he loved, he ate eagerly.

Fatimah would retreat silently, walking backwards, always facing Abubakar, as was customary. She could not show her back to her elder brother-in-law. Outside, when dealing with communal matters, they may be on par. But here, in their compound, she would ignore his city ways and show him the respect that was his due.

Living on the outskirts of Makaenga, listening to the radio and having townspeople for friends had made Abubakar modern. But he was a honourable soul, and a High Chief, without whose hospitality they too would have had to go and eke out a difficult living in Alfajiri. Giving them land for a compound and helping them build their new home was his duty, but he had given without reserve and deserved admiration.

Following breakfast, Amadu started heading out to the fields, but Fatimah called him back. "Have you forgotten we are going to Venimeli?"

"I have not. But I promised Masa I'd help mend his fence. It won't take long."

"Anyone can do that job. The early bus is the most reliable. We must catch that one without fail."

Amadu sighed theatrically and went to the Men's House to get into his city clothes.

Amadu had changed. He had always been somewhat high-spirited, given to quick speech and action. Even so, he had become less respectful. He was in a difficult situation; a young man without fields, without a wife or children, who helped everyone a little here and a little there. But no one was in an easy situation—not Lahmey, not Fatimah, nor anyone else who had to leave Ferun.

She lamented again that Lahmey's exemplary sons—Eze and Kosey—were not around to guide Amadu as they used to. They had found hard, labouring jobs in Gewe, and sent money home every month. She missed these wonderful, vigorous men who had always showed her so much respect. Amadu missed them too, and said that he should have gone with them.

Some evenings Amadu went to a nearby place they call a bar, with his cousins and some other young men from the settlement. She was told that they sold alcohol there, and there was card playing and gambling sometimes.

Amadu told her that he did not drink anything but soda pop, and that was true. But there was no need to go to such a disreputable place, no need at all. When confronted he had laughed in her face and told her that the place was harmless, normal for Makaenga, and there was a television set there. It was very interesting to watch TV and he was learning some useful things that way.

She was not convinced. He could spend time with friends at one end of their compound, as he used to do in Ferun. Their compound here was much smaller, but he could use his uncle's that was more spacious. As for TV, Abubakar's youngest son, the one who had a small grocery store and lived at the other end of the settlement, had a set. It was strange that he did not live in this father's compound, but many things were strange here. He was the only one with electricity in his house, and Amadu could easily watch TV there. But Amadu said that the electricity was more off than on there. The bar, on the other hand, had a generator.

Amadu always had a ready answer, and this bothered her as well. Fatimah hoped that marriage and children will improve Amadu's conduct, and if he had his own fields to cultivate, he would be too busy and tired to visit the bar. She had prodded Lahmey to talk to Amadu, but he seemed to find his brother-in-law's behaviour unremarkable, not worthy of reprimand.

Amadu must set a good example for Jelani; she was afraid of the corrupting influence of city ways on her son. Jelani was obedient and doing okay in his new school, but he needed to be in the fields with his father and uncle. He needed to learn to work the land. What good was just book learning? Fatimah had tried to interest him in the women's garden but he paid no heed to that. There were so many reasons why they must have land as soon as possible.

Fatimah took up the cloth bag that held their lunch, and issued last minute instructions to Arza. Then brother and sister set out on the half a kilometre path to the bus stop. En route they met and greeted many people; Fatimah kept the exchange brief.

Today they would visit the office of the Agriculture Ministry in Venimeli. Fatimah has initiated a monthly ritual—

a follow-up visit for their application under the Cooperative Land Distribution Scheme.

She calls the person in charge, a sympathetic woman officer, from the Public Call Centre and gets an appointment. She always brought a gift for the woman. Today it is a small bag of amarula berries. She also follows up on the land compensation claim, but she does not see the two officers on the same day, even though they are in the same building. The officer concerned with the compensation is a rather distracted, older man.

"What's the point of pestering these people?" Amadu had asked.

"To aim an arrow is not to strike the target. If we are not there following up, it is easy for them to ignore us. That's what Anjali said. It is much harder to say no to a person who is sitting right in front of you, is it not?"

Amadu had to agree. "But why not take both appointments on the same day? The bus fare is not cheap."

"No need to tell me that, Amadu. Look, the officers may know each other and may be meeting and talking among themselves. I don't think its good to go from one to the other on the same day. The government owes us money and does not like to be reminded. The Cooperative scheme is something they are proud of. They boast about it to foreigners, Anjali told me. When we ask for the money they see us as a nuisance. But it is our due and we must keep asking. And we must also keep following up on the Cooperative application. But we must not muddle the two."

This had silenced Amadu for the moment. Couldn't he see that she needed him to go with her?

Having studied till Class 4, Fatimah could speak Morga

well, and read it slowly, but official documents confused her. There was no paper work involved at this stage, but she did not want to take chances. There was always the possibility of paper work. They might suddenly ask her to fill out yet one more form.

Amadu had completed secondary school. They had not paid his school fees for nothing. Besides, it was good to go with a man, a young, strong and good looking one at that. There was an emphasis, Anjali had told her, on the development of youth and women.

After coming to Madafi, Amadu had completed a small business development course offered at the HELP Training Centre. It was the only thing that had excited him since leaving Ferun. Fatimah had made it a point to mention Amadu's schooling, and the course, to the two officers. She hoped that it was not lost on the distracted bureaucrat in charge of the compensation that when they got their money Amadu would be able to do something useful with it.

Of the 42 families that had sold their land, only 8 had been compensated so far. Eight—such a shameful number!

"Our men like to talk big," her mother had said to her once. "But they are not good at following through. But following through is what matters. That is women's work. We know how to keep the fire going in the hearth. We may not have big, big dreams, but we know how to put *gali* in the bowl."

Fatimah never forgot those words.

CHAPTER 12

Wine & Cheese

$\mathbf{A}$NJALI WAS DRIVING to an after-work engagement: another evening away from home, and she was late. Damn!

The bad taste left by the Board Meeting lingered, despite the decision she had taken that night. Basic Needs was a concept that had emerged in the mid-1970s, partly through the work of the International Labour Organization. Frank Maier's first step into philanthropy was to set up the Basic Needs Foundation; HELP, funded through that Foundation, was the bearer of those ideas. In helping Fatimah get land, she was being true to Frank's laudable vision. Did she need anything more to justify her actions? It didn't matter what Grace thought. But the other Board members—why hadn't they said anything? Their lack of visible support continued to rankle her, especially the fact that Hassan hadn't spoken up.

The Nordic Aid Agencies had organized an event to commemorate World Food Day at the Alliance Française, an impressive art nouveau building that was a coveted venue. This is where she was headed.

After independence the Kamorgan government had renounced colonial structures to build their own buildings, most of which were unimaginative, even ugly. The Europeans had been all too happy to take over the old British and German constructions, housing their embassies, consulates, aid agencies and other institutions, while their senior staff moved into the empty residences of departed British bureaucrats. No need to exit Jamesville and go somewhere less familiar, and by extension, less safe.

The road she was on ran the length of the waterfront in Jamesville. Separating Lake Mathilda from the road was a ribbon of walking path and grass, and a string of streetlights, some of which were working. Very few neighbourhoods in Kamorga were blessed with streetlights. On her left were waterfront houses, shops and restaurants.

Jazz music came at her, momentarily, from one of the restaurants. A dull ache claimed her. They had gone to the jazz club in Jamesville, she and Jeremy. They had few dates alone; this had been one of them.

Tyla tithe nahi avadnar. He won't like it there. Rahul's face loomed before her eyes. Oh stop it, mother! Go away, leave me alone, leave me in peace, Anjali muttered.

And yet, would she be here in Kamorga if it hadn't been for Indumati? At home, she and Vandana had witnessed long evenings of political discussions. Indumati's friends were social activists, labour leaders, academics, researchers and journalists. No one shied away from heated debate or raised voices; rather, they seemed to revel in them. As a child Anjali hadn't grasped much of what was being said, but slowly, she had developed a way of looking at the world through her mother's eyes.

Anjali switched on the tape player. Rahul had his Game Boy; she needed her fix. The Kishori Amonkar tape that Vandana had mixed for her, from her mother's extensive collection of Amonkar's music, was already in it. She had been listening to it the day before.

Amonkar's distinctive voice filled the car and Anjali felt a wave of relief. Instant gratification was rare in Indian classical music; there was usually a long lead-up to the singer engaging the full melody. Her sister had thoughtfully given her this short-cut when Anjali had left India to study in Toronto.

By now she had missed all the speeches at the World Food Day event—a happy thought. She had also likely missed the servers bearing trays of duck pâté canapés and caviar spread on crackers. Good riddance! Luckily the wine would still be flowing, and they were lavish with cheese.

She easily found a spot in the large parking lot of the Alliance compound. Some people must have put in an appearance and left by now. She paused at the baobab, majestic in the mellow beams that bathed it from lights set at ground level. It wasn't as large or as old as others Anjali had seen, but it was still impressive.

As she entered the huge reception hall she spied Goodluck Ironsu. Dressed in a Western suit, he was speaking to a woman in striking African garb, probably a West African. Ironsu was quite high up in the government, a Secretary to a Deputy Minister. She had met him recently at another party. Overhearing him holding forth on the origins of Morga, she had sidled up to his group. Introductions had followed and the conversation had turned to HELP, and the Makaenga field office, which Ironsu had visited once. He was all praise for their kindergarten program, a first in Kamorga.

Anjali had mentioned that she had visited the Aanke in Madafi. She was curious how Bissau fitted into the linguistic map of Kamorga. Ironsu did not know.

"It's a West African language, not really from here," he said.

"I hope the government will pay the Aanke for their land soon," Anjali found herself saying.

"What's that?" Ironsu asked.

Surprised that he did not know, she explained the situation.

"You must not believe everything they say!" he responded.

"It's in our records too."

"You know they tend to exaggerate. How much land they had for example."

"I doubt that," she said stiffly.

"It's important to look to the future. Unfortunately, people like that live in the past. You have to make some sacrifices in order to have a better life. But they just don't understand."

"What better life? They have been practically robbed of their land and left nearly destitute!" Anjali burst out.

Ironsu frowned. "They farm the old-fashioned way. That does not work any more. They don't want to change, and they want the government to always give them something. They should also think about what they can do for the country."

"They're small farmers, but what's wrong with that?"

"Now-a-days it is all about rights," Ironsu said, continuing on his own track. "Everybody wants rights. And the NGOs encourage them, whether they deserve them or not. God gives every bird his worm, but he does not throw it into the nest. Nobody is thinking of their duty. Of what they can do. As for sacrificing for the common good, that idea has been thrown away."

Anjali had wanted to ask whether he was willing to sacrifice, willing to give up his house, cars, stocks, bribes, girlfriends and foreign junkets for the common good, give up even a fraction of all that.

Heading in the opposite direction from Ironsu, Anjali made her way to the drinks table. Accepting a glass of red wine, she picked up a paper plate and piled some crackers on it. Then she cut herself some cheese: brie, a couple of harder cheeses, a crumbly, blue cheese. She was starving.

Next to the food table was a table spread with material generated for World Food Day. She picked up a one-pager that profiled hunger in the region. Forty-four per cent of people in the Central African Republic were undernourished, in Congo it was 42, in Sudan 39, in Uganda 19. For Kamorga that figure stood at 40 per cent. The total number for the world stood at 848 million people, or 16 per cent of the global population. That was bad, she reasoned, but ten years ago that percentage had been 21.

These statistics had been recently quoted in *The Venimeli Herald*, the English paper owned by the People's Democratic Union. The *Herald* could have also done something more relevant, she thought, like featuring news from the drought-hit North, or talked to the people who lived in Iberu or other slums in Venimeli. She dropped the paper back on the table.

As she turned she was face to face with Alfonso Salo, who worked at the Swedish Consulate.

"Anjali, welcome," he said warmly. She smiled at him. He was young and enthusiastic, not common characteristics in this crowd. "If you want a bit of real music, there's a cellist from Sweden giving an informal recital in the little room at the back."

She noticed then the canned music that was playing at a very low volume. New Age, Fusion? She wasn't sure how to describe it.

"Sounds nice. I'm surprised he's at the back. Why doesn't he play for everyone?"

Salo made a face. "We couldn't agree on the music. But he'll play here on Sunday, with two accompanists from Sweden. I hope you'll come."

"I'll try. Thanks."

"Namaste," he said, bringing his hands together, as he departed. Anjali brought her hands together as well.

She regarded the crowd again, wishing Martha was here. She had met her at the very first parent-teacher's meeting she had attended at the American International School. Sometimes Martha came for these events, and entertained Anjali with tidbits about the people present—their petty squabbles, their foibles, and their misdemeanours, some of them sexual: an affair with a maid, or someone else's partner.

She did not see Katherine Grey, who worked at the Canadian High Commission. Also absent were Shirley Osei and Hamida Musa, two Kamorgan women who worked at other non-profit organizations. Anjali had tried to meet both outside official events, but she had failed. Her African counterparts were enmeshed in large extended families that always kept them occupied. She had never succeeded in meeting Elizabeth outside work hours either.

Grace never attended these events, even though someone had once pointed out her husband, Joshua. Anjali had not gone over and introduced herself.

"Anjali, ça va?" said a breathy, female voice. She turned to find Désirée Boutin standing beside her.

"Très bien. Et vous?"

At first she had warmed to Désirée, a French anthropologist of indeterminate age who ran a small, non-profit organization fighting for the rights of the Bambuti, pygmy hunter-gatherers who lived in the Congo region. There was a small community of Bambuti in the forests bordering Western Kamorga.

Désirée's in-depth knowledge of this tribe and her fervour to do the right thing had impressed her. A forest people, Bambuti territory was not protected, and their claim to the forest and ability to hunt were compromised by deforestation, mining, plantation agriculture and forest conservation that worked against rather than with them. Désirée was obsessed with her mission. Once she got talking she carried on without a pause, tiring her audience. Anjali had also realized that Désirée had no interest in the Bambuti who had left their traditional way of living and migrated to urban or semi-urban areas, and were struggling to make a living there.

"You know, they won't let me enter Senegal," Désirée said.

"Oh?"

"I sent a paper to The Congress of Indigenous Peoples. Very important conference. Very good paper. When I apply for the visa, they refuse. Imagine! They refuse!"

So, even white people get denied a visa sometimes, Anjali thought. Vandana had tried to come and see her when she was studying in Toronto. She had presented proof of her status as a medical student, bank statements from her own bank and those of their father and mother, their parent's will which stipulated that Vandana would inherit half of all their assets, and a letter from the Dean of the medical college who had stated that he was confident she would come back to India to finish her studies. Canada had flatly denied Vandana a tourist visa.

"Désirée," someone called out.

"They have another person presenting on the Bambuti," Désirée said. "A Belgian professor who is ... oh, how you say ... a fake? I am the expert in the field. Okay, I will talk to you later."

Anjali contemplated her next move. Perhaps, listen to the cellist? She wondered why Désirée had been denied a visa.

"You seem a little lost," a familiar voice said.

Anjali turned to face Hassan, dressed in a blue suit.

"Not lost, just tired," she said coldly.

"You should take the weekend off," he said laughing. "Nice dress."

"Thanks," she said.

She was wearing a white *salwar kameez* with small, gold dots and a golden trim. Her chunni was black and gold. She was happy to air her Indian clothes here.

"Something wrong?" he asked.

"Yes. I loved the way you defended me at the Board Meeting."

Hassan looked surprised. "Oh that."

"Oh that. How casual you are! It was so awful to be confronted like that."

"I had to rush to another appointment. Didn't realize you were so upset." He looked contrite.

Anjali said nothing.

"It is not just the Aanke that got ousted from their land," he said. "There are other groups who got the same treatment, and they didn't even get to sign papers that could bring them compensation. Then there are the miners; no one has had it as bad."

"So the Aanke don't deserve to have someone defend their rights and look out for them?"

"One injustice doesn't cancel another. But a scheme where the government holds the power to decide who'll get land and who won't isn't the answer."

"What's the answer then?"

"People coming together—farmers, the landless, miners, the urban poor, labourers, workers of all kinds who are being exploited, and fighting together for more fundamental, structural change."

"A socialist revolution?"

Hassan merely smiled.

"Followed by a socialist state?" Anjali continued.

"Something along those lines could be one option."

"What a utopian vision! Look what happened in the Soviet Union."

"Socialism, real socialism, doesn't always have to fail."

"And what are people supposed to do till the revolution comes?"

"Educate themselves. Organize."

"I see."

She looked at him, expecting him to continue, wanting him to say more.

"We should talk about this sometime, but my friends are waiting. Why not join us?"

He indicated towards two men who were standing near a large window halfway across the room. One of them was Kamau Falana, Elizabeth's husband, a journalist with the *Kamorga Times*. The other man was white.

"Derek Foley, an Irish journalist. Visiting his girlfriend who works for Irish Aid. He's filing a few stories on the side," Hassan said.

Anjali hesitated for a moment, then agreed.

The other commitment he had had on the day of the Board Meeting was probably just a drinking date with a buddy, she thought. An ideologue who would always hold a Marxist view; nothing else would make an impression. Her mother was like that too, looking at everything through one lens—Nehruvian socialism in her case. Anjali had learnt the hard way that people like that were not given to empathy.

Kamau and Derek were discussing political scandals. Kamorga was a kaleidoscope of scams; they arrived like flocks of locusts landing on fields full of ripening grain, picking them clean within minutes. Yet, as a democratic and stable country that boasted a relatively free press, Kamorga remained the darling of Western Aid.

"We are lucky in one respect. At least we don't have oil," Kamau was saying. "Otherwise we would have even bigger corruption, perhaps even a civil war. Look at what's happening in Nigeria, and Sudan."

"You have some nice swindles," Derek said. "Let's see now, what's the latest? A European electric company allegedly got its contract after paying bribes that went as high up as the VP. The information was leaked by a European competitor. Supposedly."

"I actually think it was someone from the Socialist Workers Party," Kamau said.

"Yeah, that's the opposition for you," Derek said. "I also heard that the government signed a contract with an American firm to train jet fighters, even though a reputed German company had proposed that it could do the work for much less. We don't know who got paid how much."

"Not yet anyway," Kamau said.

"My favourite, fake exports of iron ore that cost the country nearly four per cent of its GDP last year," Hassan said. "That was impressive."

"Enforce laws! Bring back the death penalty, I say," Derek said.

Anjali had the impression that he was somewhat drunk.

"Oh that would not do. Trust me, they would just hang the wrong guy," Kamau said.

"There aren't any scandals involving land. At least we don't hear of them," Anjali said.

"Oh there are, definitely," Kamau said promptly.

"Really? Like what?" she asked.

"Hoarding land, in both urban and rural areas, is becoming more common," Hassan said.

"My colleague Milton has unearthed some strong stuff. But I am not allowed to say anything about it," Kamau said, with an air of self-importance.

"I heard someone say that the Aanke in Ferun were unusual in that they hardly had any absentee landlords and this has kept them strong," Anjali said.

"Somewhat true," Hassan said. "When land is abundant, as it has been in Kamorga in the past, communal rights can exist more easily. But as it becomes more scarce, individual rights advance, even with groups like the Aanke that are so communal at present. Absentee landlords are not necessarily a bad thing. If people who own land work in cities, they are able to make a bit of an investment in that land. They tend to lease it to relatives and send cash remittances."

"Has there been any land registration in this part of Africa? That would be a good move," Anjali said.

"It's expensive, and not exactly a hot election topic," Kamau said.

"There was some land registration done in Kenya," Hassan said. "It might happen if people demanded it, forcefully. We never had civil society here saying let's look at the land issue. Post independence, you had land distribution in some states in India, didn't you?"

He is knowledgeable, Anjali thought. He was probably referring to the communist-ruled, Indian states of West Bengal and Kerala.

"Yes we did, and we had the extraordinary *Bhoodan* or Land Gift Movement in Maharashtra, started by Vinoba Bhave. That's my state."

Hassan smiled.

"Have you heard of him?" she asked

"Yes, a little. Mr. Bhave, your namesake," he said.

Anjali was pleased but she did not want to smile at him. Not yet. Instead, she raised her glass to her lips, as Derek steered the conversation to the FIFA Women's World Cup that would be held in China the next month.

Her mind wandered and she was afloat, hovering above the heads of the group, before rising higher, above the heads of all the perfumed, chattering people, the voices in the room merging into a meaningless, muted cacophony. She closed her eyes momentarily, imagining grand, celestial music— Mozart, Beethoven, something like that.

Opening her eyes she looked up, taking in the elaborate, crystal chandelier that hung gloriously from the ceiling. She noticed for the first time that there was a moulding that edged the ceiling, painted a light blue, with a tasteful vine pattern on it. How hard they tried to recreate the world they left behind, the colonizers, both old and new! Instead of growing guavas and mangoes, or even mangosteen, they tried to nurture rose bushes and apple trees. Instead of wearing loose, light shirts; ample, cotton trousers, and flowing skirts, they wore close-fitting, black, Western clothes. She had spotted a couple of women in the little black cocktail dress with black stockings. Stockings would have looked out of place on the street, even in Jamesville, besides being too hot, but here, among vine patterns, chandeliers, a cellist, and brie melting onto the plate, despite the air conditioning, they could pass for normal.

Her eyes moved to the salmon pink walls. Ah, one had to come to the Alliance Française to be reminded that pastels were colours too! There were no geckos to be seen here. She wondered what they sprayed to keep pests at bay. She liked house lizards; had lived with them in Bombay. And she did again now, in Kamorga. They had managed to penetrate the exclusive neighbourhood of Jamesville, she was happy to note. She wondered how it would feel to slither down walls instead of walking on two feet. It was an interesting notion, though it made her feel somewhat dizzy.

When she brought her attention back to the group they were still on FIFA, now talking about the Men's Tournament. She glanced at her watch.

"I must get going."

"We should all meet at the Press Club for a drink," Kamau said.

"Sure, with Elizabeth," she said.

"Definitely. She's at a funeral just now. I slipped away."

"Oh, whose funeral?"

"An aunt—a venerable lady of 82."

Many people here don't even get past 50, Anjali thought as she made her way to the door. Death struck suddenly and more frequently, taking people of all ages. Her colleagues were often away attending funerals—elaborate affairs where extended family and friends gathered for days.

When she got to the exit, Anjali looked back. She had felt Hassan's gaze on her as she had walked away. He gave a little wave, smiling at her from across the room. This time she allowed him a slight smile.

Outside, she paused at the baobab and leaned against it—too much wine. What the hell, she deserved it!

Her mind drifted to Madagascar, Land of Baobabs. She had read that this was where those incredible upside-down trees had originated. Another theory had it that there were originally six species of baobabs in Madagascar and one on the African continent. She preferred the Madagascar origin story, which was at least partly true and much more romantic. The wind and sea had brought baobab seeds to the eastern shore of Africa, from where they had spread all over that continental immensity; the kind of colonization she loved.

She was the closest she would ever be to that beautiful, exotic island. Yet it was unlikely she would go there. A great pity. To be a baobab pod and travel backwards, from Kamorga to Uganda and Kenya, then bobbling over the waves of the Indian Ocean to Madagascar! That would be quite a journey.

Hinduism spoke of an unending chain of birth and rebirth, a cycle encompassing animal and plant life, and in there somewhere, after eons, the reward of a human existence. It was easier to believe that flora and fauna lived on through different lives, changed form and continued. Humans? Maybe. She could have well been a lizard or a baobab in a past life. Or a crow. The thought pleased her.

Perhaps... Mary would be reborn.

Anjali's mother was an atheist; her grandmother had been a believer, worshipping daily the many Hindu gods in her little altar. Both had transmitted their beliefs to Anjali, leaving her stranded in the middle of a fast moving stream of equally compelling faiths. Without a doctrine you can still have hope, can't you? Anjali thought. Be open to possibilities?

Yes, there was a chance that something good would come Mary's way after her death.

Anjali's head felt a bit clearer as she walked towards the car.

CHAPTER 13

Longing

DRIVING HOME, LISTENING to jazz on the car radio, Anjali enjoyed the warm-cool caress of the night breeze. This breeze, this tender freshness on her face and hair and hands told her that she was in the tropics. How wonderful! Beside her the inky expanse of the lake, light glinting off its surface here and there, reminding her of the beautiful, midnight blue, Kanjivaram silk *saree* that she had not brought to Venimeli.

Strange that I should live by a vast lake again, Anjali thought. Lake Mathilda, long and narrow, went North-South, from one end of Kamorga to the other, along its eastern border, covering 6432 sq. km. The Sun and Moon exerted their influence on this immensity, just as they did on seas and oceans. They conspired with the wind to cause little waves to form on its surface. Lake Mathilda too had its tides, lake tides.

If only Jeremy was sitting beside her now, his hand resting lightly on her thigh, life would be perfect. A sensuous thread extended from one to the other; they tended to touch when they were together.

She pictured him walking across the campus of University of Toronto, where he taught Economics. By now the trees would be dressed in yellow, russet, brown, orange and red. She missed fall—the stunning colours, the thick, crunchy foliage that coated the ground, the diffused, slanting light. A season the Group of Seven had loved as well.

She had met Jeremy at a HELP Annual General Meeting. A HELP Board Member had brought him along. Instantly attracted, neither had tried to get in touch afterwards. A few months later, Anjali joined a book club that discussed socio-political non-fiction. Here she had met Jeremy again and he had asked her out for coffee.

It was six months since Manish had gone back to India. Anjali had become a different sort of parent after he left, stricter, now that she was both father and mother. She tried to provide more structure during this difficult period in Rahul's life. There were problems at school and home: temper tantrums, sulking, withdrawal, but the storm caused by his father's departure had gradually subsided, if not passed altogether. She was struggling with parenting and her own pain, less sure of herself than she had ever been before. How had things gone so horribly, terribly wrong?

Jeremy had slowly filled in the crevices in their tenuous existence. Some of them ran deep and bled in the middle of the night, but that did not seem to deter him. He had older children—a son and daughter, from his first marriage. They lived with his ex, Suzanne, in Halifax. Jeremy loved his children, but he was not close to them; his divorce, nearly ten years ago, had been acrimonious. He had crevices of his own, which gradually came to light. Survivors of shipwrecks, they knew how to support each other because they had suffered the same calamity.

When Anjali got home she found Gabriel sitting on the veranda, reading.

"What are you reading?" she asked, though she could plainly see that it was *The Little Prince*, and she had got it from the Jamesville library herself. He held out the book to her.

"What do you think of it?"

He hesitated. "It's different," he said.

"A little strange, huh?"

He nodded.

"I read it as an adult and loved it. You don't have to read it, you know, if you're not enjoying it."

"It's fine, and I like the drawings."

"Yes, the drawings are the best," Anjali said, laughingly. "Don't stay up too late, though. I guess Mary's gone to bed?"

He nodded again.

In the living room Rahul had fallen asleep on the sofa; he had been watching a video. The movie was still running. She switched off the player and led him gently to his room.

The tap in the bathroom upstairs was leaking again. Anjali drew a deep breath. The house refused to be tamed. It enjoyed hitting back at the imperialists, old and new. There were sizeable cracks on the walls of her bedroom. The ceiling in Rahul's room leaked during the rains. The toilet in the downstairs washroom clogged constantly. The shower stall in the other one had a slope that allowed water to flow away from the drain rather than towards it! The dining room cupboard doors would suddenly spring open. And the light bulb in the passageway flickered on and off and off and on, a thing demented.

It was hard to get things fixed. Plumbers, electricians and carpenters played hooky. If they showed up, they did not have the right tools. If they managed to get the work done, they demanded a higher price than the one fixed at the beginning. But worse still, the repairs would not hold. A few weeks after their departure, the covered-up crack reappeared, grinning impishly, the tap gleefully resumed leaking, and the cupboard door defiantly swung open.

Mary had left food on the table in covered bowls: *dal*, a cauliflower vegetable and a tomato *raita*, all Maharashtrian style. Home food made by an African maid. Was this somehow the good side of globalization? Mary had mastered the dozen or so Maharashtrian recipes that Anjali had taught her.

Though there was no Indian presence in Kamorga, as compared to Uganda, Kenya and Tanzania, she had heard that a few Indian businessmen lived in Venimeli, and were exploring business options. Anjali had come with a bagful of spices from Toronto and got them replenished when Jeremy came to visit.

She sat down and tucked in. Right away, she was back in her parent's home. The kitchen had been tiny, and they had all clustered around the dinning table to eat. I must call Ma soon, she thought. She hadn't called for a long time. Indumati would be pleased to learn that Mary could cook Maharastrian meals.

When she went into the kitchen to put the food away, she found Mary sleeping there, curled up on the floor. Kneeling beside her, she softly called out her name. Mary came to, slowly. How tired she looks, Anjali thought. She had offered to hire a part-time maid to help out but Mary had refused.

Mary sat up, back to the wall, yawning.

"You should have gone to bed!"

Mary rose, smiling, and started putting things away.

"No, Mary, I can do that!"

She would not listen, as usual. Anjali stood by helplessly.

"Any news from Otieno?" she asked.

Mary shook her head.

"I wish HELP had contacts in Juba. I really should look into it," Anjali said.

Chances of finding Otieno though international development contacts were slim, but there was no reason not to try. Mary would be so relived if only she could locate Otieno again.

Mary nodded. Anjali grabbed her hand, impulsively. Mary looked at her, as if she was about to say something, then she seemed to change her mind.

"Goodnight," she said, softly.

"Goodnight, Mary."

Upstairs, in her bedroom, Anjali hesitated by the phone. She picked up the receiver; she had to call Jeremy, even though this is not their scheduled day to talk.

"Hello, you have reached Jeremy Shein. I am not here to take your call, but please leave a message, and I'll get back to you as soon as I can."

Anjali cradled the receiver for a moment before slowly replacing it. It was nice to hear his voice, and their official date was just two days away.

To think that they would be married next year! She pictured them together at their reception, she in a striking *saree*, he in a dark suit. But she could not stay very long with the wedding imagery. She liked best to think of them cuddled together in front of his fireplace.

Jeremy, Rahul and she had spent a week in Kirali, a pleasant resort town on Lake Mathilda. After Rahul went to bed, she and Jeremy sat under the gazebo in their hotel garden, holding hands, their fake engagement rings on their fingers, talking late into the night.

They had had time alone when they first started dating, followed by a period of activity, passing rapidly from court-ship to sharing everyday life, mostly on weekends. They had both been very busy; two years had swiftly passed. Kirali had been a gift, the pause when they could be together and take stock. After they had decided to get married they had spoken to Rahul, and he had responded well to the idea.

Anjali wanted to call Boston, but she knew Vandana would be at the hospital where she was doing her residency. Her husband Himanshu, a neurosurgeon, would not be at home either. Vandana was the first person she had called when she had learnt about Mary's illness, and she had com-forted her as usual. Her sweet, loving sister. Why had she left her behind and come all this way? Why had she imagined that being away from Jeremy for a whole year would be man-ageable?

The phone rang. Jeremy! But it was Hassan, calling from what sounded like a noisy bar; she could just about hear him.

"Hi," he said.

"Why, hello."

"I didn't realize what happened at the Board meeting, I mean... how it affected you," he said.

Anjali remained silent.

"I hope you believe me."

"I do, actually."

"Oh, I am relieved to hear that. Are you feeling better now?"

"Yeah, sure. I know I'm not doing anything wrong. In fact it's in line with HELP's mandate."

"You're right. You know what? You should come to one of our local bars. They're fun."

"They're certainly noisy!"

"And the singing hasn't even started yet!"

"Is there going to be an act?"

"No, the customers like to sing!"

"You too? I'd like to hear that!"

"I just listen."

"Pity. Anyhow, enjoy! I'm off to bed."

"Goodnight then."

When she hung up she was smiling. Even though Mr. Marxist hadn't exactly apologized, at least he was beginning to tilt towards humanism.

CHAPTER 14

Spark

Anjali and Rahul were having breakfast when Nathan called.

"Hello Anjali, how are you?"

"Fine. And you?"

"We're well, but there's some bad news. There's been trouble and Amadu's in prison."

"What!"

"Fatimah's at our house with Fehed and Linje, Amadu's friends. They were at this bar near Madafi last evening. They go there sometimes. Three men picked a fight with them. First they called them names. Then one guy took Fehed by his collar and hit him, and another went for Linje. Amadu intervened. Next thing there were cops there, and they arrested Amadu. The three guys just walked off. No one was hurt. We're planning to go to the main police station in Makaenga now, and see what we can do."

"That's awful!"

"Yes. Fatimah's in shock. She almost came over last night, but they decided to wait."

"What are the charges?"

"Not clear."

"Who were the men? Any idea?"

"Fehed and Linje didn't know them. Nor did the regulars at the bar."

"Nathan, I'm on the last day of a meeting with colleagues from the regional offices. Otherwise I'd have come down."

"Oh yeah, I remember. It's OK. We can manage."

"I'll call you at lunch."

"Sure thing. Try the clinic."

"Can you explain things to Fatimah and put her on for a sec.?"

"*Kabari ani*?" Fatimah asked when she came on.

Always the protocol that had to be followed. "*Hoori*," Anjali responded. "Don't worry. I'm sure we can sort this out."

"*Elewa,* I understand," Fatimah responded. She sounded quite calm.

When Anjali hung up, she found Rahul standing in the doorway. He looked worried when she told him what had happened.

"Don't worry, sweetie. I'm sure it's a misunderstanding. Nathan will take care of it."

The conference room at the HELP office was set up for the annual meeting of staff from the three African offices. Onuwa Chukwu from Nigeria and Alima Samake from Mali were there, along with their Communications and Finance Directors. The past two days had consisted of reporting on the country programs, and their plans for the coming year. Today they would consider overall HELP planning and strategy. One issue Anjali would present was HELP's possible expansion into Central and South America. The Toronto office had just dispatched a consultant to research and report on their options. Both Onuwa and Alima were totally against this idea.

"Why go there when there's so much more to do in Africa?"

Onuwa had asked at the welcome dinner Anjali had arranged at an Ethiopian restaurant in Jamesville. Senior staff at the Asian offices were also posing the same question, though with less fervour.

Anjali had explained the reasons, which the international staff already knew, but refused to accept. Central and South America mattered in Canada, and in North America as a whole. It was an area of growing geo-political importance. Last year, Canada had joined the Organization of American States (OAS). As a result, Canadian development assistance to this region would go up. Trade was expected to increase as well.

And Canada had a sizeable proportion of immigrants from that region, who expected Canadian non-profits to operate in their home countries. There were implications for fundraising and volunteer involvement, among other things. Rani Maharaj, Anjali's friend and colleague in Toronto, had been advocating for years that HELP set up a Central American office. She was originally from Trinidad. Anjali knew that she would be laying out these reasons, all over again, at the meeting that morning.

HELP's operations in Nigeria and Mali were large; they had more than double the budget of Kamorga, and if they worked at it, they could grow even more. HELP, initially funded through the Basic Needs Foundation, which was in effect a large trust fund, now did a lot of its own fundraising, through diverse strategies. The Toronto head office spearheaded fundraising, but the country offices had an important role to play. They needed to develop feasible plans for new projects, or project extensions, and send hard data that showed positive project results to Toronto.

The head office also needed human-interest stories and good photographs that they could feed the media, and use in publicity materials and donor updates. And the country offices had leeway to fundraise directly from European and American donors. The South Asian offices had done a good job of leveraging funds in this way. Anjali was sympathetic to the idea that the African operations needed to grow, but not at the expense of growth elsewhere. Onuwa and Alima and their staff needed to take more initiative to foster their own growth. Anjali felt that at times they displayed a sense of entitlement coupled with dependency, neither of which were justifiable.

The discussion about the expansion of HELP's African operations that morning was spirited, but not hostile. The meeting broke up on an optimistic note, with some good fundraising ideas being tabled.

Anjali had already instructed Elizabeth to lead their guests to lunch, where Grace would be playing hostess. She closed her office door and called Nathan's clinic. He came on the line five minutes later.

"Sorry, lots of patients. So we went to the police station. A hostile bunch, those cops. The Police Chief says Amadu was at fault. They've booked him for battery. Fehed tried to talk about how the other men had started the fight, but he shut him up real fast. Said they had witnesses who they could produce in court. Very strange. The guy was even rude to me. Asked why a foreigner was getting mixed up in local stuff. I said that whatever it was, this wasn't a grave offense. The three men were not hurt. They had not pressed charges. Asked him how long he planned to detain Amadu. Said I could pay bail. But he just wouldn't play ball. So I said we might just go to a lawyer. He said not to be hasty. Of course they wouldn't let us see Amadu."

"That's bad."

"Fatimah says let's wait till tomorrow. She's been saying something about people out there who want to get the Aanke. I asked her who did she mean, and she said the Kakwa."

"Wait a minute. Isn't that Grace's tribe?"

"Oh yeah? No idea."

"So why are the Kakwa out to get the Aanke?"

"She wouldn't say."

"She's not there, is she?"

"No, she isn't. But she has a message for you. If you can contact some higher ups in Venimeli, that may help."

"I'll try for sure."

"I'll go to Madafi this evening. Had to rush back to the clinic from the police station. Could call you after that."

"Thanks, Nathan. You've been great as usual."

Anjali went downstairs for lunch. Good thing Onuwa and Alima were flying out the next morning. She had enjoyed their company, but the timing was bad. Three other colleagues were staying back to visit HELP operations in Iberu and Makaenga; Elizabeth would take them around.

"There you are," Onuwa said as she entered the small lunchroom, which looked rather crowded. She noticed that some of her colleagues were out on the back veranda. Grace was talking to Alima at the other end of the table. "Elizabeth is taking us shopping this evening. Got to get something for the wife and kids. Any ideas?" Onuwa continued.

"There's lots of ethnic stuff—masks and bowls and table linen. But that may not be so different for you. I wonder what you could get that's unique."

"There are a couple of new boutiques that have really nice things. I'll take them there," Elizabeth, who was standing nearby, said.

Anjali glanced uncomfortably towards Grace, who seemed

to be totally engrossed in conversation. She wondered if she should go over and speak to her about Amadu.

No! What was she thinking? That would be dumb. Grace was sure to be unsympathetic. A pity; she definitely had contacts.

Taking some food on her plate, she drew Elizabeth aside and told her what had happened. She was as puzzled as Anjali, and very concerned.

"Do you think Kamau could help?" Anjali asked.

"He's not in town. Visiting his parents. Back tomorrow. I'll see if I can get hold of him."

A wrap-up meeting followed lunch. It finished promptly at 4 pm, as planned, much to Anjali's surprise. At the end, Anjali thanked everyone warmly. Their time together had been fruitful; the atmosphere had been positive and energetic. She was happy that everything had gone well.

There was a round of effusive goodbyes with the Malians and Nigerians inviting each other and the Kamorgans to come to their countries.

"It's sad you won't be able to make it this time," Alima said to Anjali.

"I know. Never thought it would be so busy. Anyway, we'll meet in Bangladesh."

The biannual meeting when select staff from all the country offices got together was going to be held in Bangladesh next year.

"I'm thinking of going to India for a holiday after the meeting," Alima said. "Last time we were there, I saw a bit of Delhi. That was it."

"You should do that. We'll talk about it."

After they left, Anjali went up to her office. Who could

she call? The Canadian High Commission wasn't going to be particularly useful, nor the Americans. She could talk informally to Martha's husband, Richard Hines. Then she remembered that he was away. Damn!

How about someone in the government? No one came to mind right away. Hassan? She dialled his number. When he was not at university he worked from home. There was no answer. At least he does not seem to have a mistress living right under his roof, she thought.

She sat still for a few minutes. It was quiet, except for the whirling of the ceiling fan. She looked up, affectionately. Old faithful, another reminder of India.

She picked up the phone and dialled Martha. They fixed up to meet at Café Lafayette, near the American International School. They had to pick up the kids soon, anyhow.

Café Lafayette was built on a strip of land bordering Lake Mathilda. She got there earlier than anticipated; traffic had been light. The terrace was already full, so she took an inside table by the wall that allowed a lake view.

The day had become cloudy; there was a band of mist on the horizon, crossing the vast stretch of the lake. A fountain had been built a few yards from the shoreline, on a concrete pier. Sometimes it worked, sometimes not, depending on the availability of electricity perhaps, and god knows what other factors. Today it was still. It was magical in the dark, when it did work, shooting jets of blue, yellow, red and green water high up in the sky.

Anjali ordered a glass of white wine. They had good, dry whites from South Africa here.

Turning around she took in the old black and white photographs that lined the opposite wall. They allowed her to imagine the life of the early white settlers, who had been mostly British and German. Martha had told her that the British settlers had developed orchards, while the Germans owned farms. Of course the main draw was Kamorga's mineral wealth.

It was pleasant on the lakeshore, the vast body of water somewhat moderating the heat. The villas here had been built not only by British administrators, army commanders, police chiefs and mine owners, but also by geologists, engineers, surveyors, managers and mining sector specialists.

The colonizers led hunting expeditions into what was then the thick forest of south-western Kamorga. They built boating clubs and held regattas. They fished recreationally. They tea-partied, picnicked, held balls, played cricket. They gardened. They ordered their servants about. They built some Anglican churches and did good works. They also built a couple of resort towns in the hills bordering the south-eastern shore of Lake Mathilda. One of them was Kirali, where Anjali, Rahul and Jeremy had gone during Jeremy's visit.

Must have been nice to feel that Kamorga owed them all this, thought Anjali. But could all of them have followed the ideas and norms of their society? Considered the blacks beneath them, believed unequivocally in a Christian god? There must have been people, even if only a few, who had felt uneasy about their lifestyle, perhaps gone so far as to question their role and purpose here; people who hadn't fitted in.

Martha walked in just then, in slacks and a t-shirt, looking a little harried. Her face relaxed into a big smile when she saw Anjali.

"Nice to see you ma chère," she said, planting a kiss on Anjali's cheek.

"Thanks for coming at short notice."

Martha sat down and ordered a beer.

"I never thought of this before, but is there a historical Lafayette?" Anjali said.

"Charles-Henri Lafayette," said Martha, pronouncing the name correctly. "He lurked around these parts in the mid 19th century, classifying flora. Something like that."

"And the James in Jamesville?"

"That's easy. He's the last British Governor General they had: James Adam Campbell. Like your Lord Mountbatten."

"We still have them in Canada."

"Oh yeah, dear Canada!"

"You're so well-informed! I had read about James Adam Campbell but completely forgot."

"Darling, I've nothing better to do than have tea with li'l old ladies who were born here and know this stuff."

"You're busy with the kids and the book," Anjali said. "How's it going?"

"Don't say a word about it. Everything else is fair game."

Martha had written a detective novel set in a made-up African country, just for fun, a few years ago. Otherwise she would have died of boredom, she had told Anjali. The book was published in the USA and had done rather well, to her surprise. Now she had a contract for a second book with the same publisher.

"I'm sure it's going to turn out well," Anjali said.

"Lafayette's an interesting guy. He wasn't the usual oblivious to his own privilege kind of coloniser."

"Oh yeah?"

"He protested against some of the policies of the time, like how the British ran the mines. Wrote about it for French newspapers. Didn't do much good. They just got rid of him."

"How?"

"When he went to France to see his ailing mother, they wouldn't let him enter the country again. Forgot the excuse they used. Was pretty flimsy."

"Sick."

Martha shrugged.

"Hey, I have a real-life mystery for you," Anjali said.

"Do tell."

Anjali told her everything.

"Huh, kind of thing young men get into," Martha said.

"Oh no, it really wasn't Amadu's fault."

"You're sure of that?'

"Yes. Fatimah told me once that he goes sometimes to this bar. She doesn't like it, in fact. He doesn't drink; I mean alcohol. The Aanke are still Muslim, even if it's a less ortho-dox form of Islam. There are times when they drink, at har-vest, marriages. But they don't drink casually."

Martha looked sceptical.

"I know Amadu quite well," Anjali said. "It isn't like him to get into a fight. Besides he has witnesses, right?"

Martha said nothing.

"When's Richard back? I'd have liked his advice," Anjali said.

"Not for a couple of days. I doubt he'd be able to do any-thing."

"So what's your advice?"

"You won't like it. But I think it's best you keep out of it."

Anjali sighed. "You sound like Grace."

"I'm sorry. Strange things happen here, we know that. People bend the law and get away with it quite nicely, thank you. The authorities do the same. I think you and Nathan be-ing seen as interested parties may make it worse. It could be intimidation tactics. Perhaps those friends of Amadu have enemies, and this is an act of revenge of some sort. Who knows? And my feeling is that it's going to blow over."

An American suggesting non-interference, that was mildly amusing. Aloud she said: "It's hard to do nothing."

"I know. It's the hardest thing. Look, Richard's going to call tomorrow. I'll ask him what he thinks."

"All right."

"Hey, tonight's movie night. *The Russia House.* Nine pm at Marilyn's house. Why don't you come?"

"Let's see. Nathan's supposed to call tonight."

They chatted for a while before going to pick up the boys.

That evening, Anjali stayed home, but Nathan didn't call. When she picked up the phone around 10 pm she found that the line was dead. Shit! This happened from time to time.

She didn't want to disturb her neighbours at this late hour.

If she had the car she could have driven to Marilyn's and called from there, or gone to the public call centre in Jamesville. It was a common service in Venimeli given that most people did not have a telephone and even fewer had one with long-distance capacity. Walking around at this time was out and Venimeli had an unreliable taxi service. Anjali decided reluctantly to go to bed.

An immense expanse of land filled her dream. She was walking, walking, through a hot, dry plain, barefoot. She knew that she had but a short distance to go, and then she would reach what she sought. It wasn't clear what it was she sought, but it was out there somewhere, waiting for her. She walked slowly but purposefully, her eyes on the faint track in the dust. The sun on her back was pleasant, not punishing.

Suddenly, she was in the middle of a desert storm, sand whipping around her, blotting out her vision, the wind swishing in her ears, almost toppling her over. She stopped short; her heart thudding against her ribs. She could not stand up to the sand and wind that hammered her. To her knees she dropped and stayed that way, the sand swirling round and round, the wind moaning, demonic, in her ears, her eyes shut tight, her arms wrapped around herself.

She woke up with a start, fully awake, alert; she would be unable to sleep for some time. She got up and drank some water. Taking a report out of her bag, she switched on the light and sat down on the sofa to read. These days she always carried one report or another with her. This one was a recent international survey of Internally Displaced Persons, IDPs, issued by the United Nations High Commission for Refugees.

In some ways the fate of IDPs was worse than that of refugees, the report said. While the latter were at least recognized by international law and human rights policies, there was no legal definition for an IDP, whose presence was denied or ignored by many national governments. Displaced within their own country by famine, flood, and other natural disasters, as well as ethnic strife, civil wars, at times genocidal campaigns, IDPs were also victims of development schemes undertaken by their own governments—hydroelectric dams, mining, plantation agriculture, deforestation, urban sprawl, displaced by some of the very same projects that were supposedly designed to improve the lives of people at the margins. IDPs also sometimes moved repeatedly within their country —victims of a series of evictions. Many ended up in slums in the hope of finding work in cities.

Anjali stopped reading and contemplated the window.

Internally displaced people, refugees, migrants, immigrants, people who were trafficked, locked into domestic labour, sold into slavery and prostitution, forced to do back-breaking, dangerous work. Human exploitation and misery took infinite forms, and academics and civil society organizations defined, classified, researched and documented them all.

Never before in human history had there been so much movement of so many people, over such large distances. Only a small percentage of these moves were entirely voluntary, as had been her move to Canada. Most of the moves were forced, like Rahul's move to Venimeli.

No, she wasn't going to go on that track. She needed to read something else, something more uplifting. Ah! The biography of Thomas Sankara that she had got from Hassan. She was only at the beginning of the book, and Sankara was still the undisputed, glorious hero. Worse would follow, but not for a while.

CHAPTER 15

Smoke

GRACE WAS AT the HELP reception, waiting for Anjali to come in.

Too much, it really is too much, she was thinking. Anjali had gone against her wishes and over her head far too many times. How docile and sweet she had seemed at first, all smiles and questions and thank you so much for the information. Grace had been so welcoming; she had explained everything to Anjali and had said that she could call her anytime she wanted, including on evenings and weekends. They were in this together. In Anne's absence; they both had equal responsibility for the organization.

Anjali had agreed, but not really! Two-faced and scheming—that was her real nature. At first she had put on a fine face and consulted Grace, though she had not necessarily followed her advice. As the weeks passed, her phone calls had dwindled, and she had started taking decisions entirely on her own, without a word to Grace.

Grace had become very concerned, and had started dropping in, every so often. What else could she do? After all, she had to find out what was going on. Anjali was new; she might well take the wrong decision. Anjali would look surprised when she saw Grace, and make one excuse or another —she had this and that meeting set up, and this and that report to write.

"Let's book an appointment," she would say. "Why an appointment?" Grace would answer, outraged. "I am here now, let's talk!" Then Anjali would get all upset, go tight-lipped, and disregard what Grace was saying. Once in a while, if she did sit down and talk, she would start presenting decisions and so-called solutions. She didn't want to hear what Grace had to say, oh no, she didn't.

And she would bring out her precious agenda book, which Grace noticed was full of little scribbles. She would flip through it and suggest a time to meet, which would be at least a week away. *Ridiculous! Who did she think she was?*

Lost deep in her thoughts, Grace was startled when she heard Anjali saying "hello."

Grace stood up and then looked pointedly at her wristwatch. Anjali looked at the clock on the wall. It was 9:15. She thought of telling Grace that Rahul had been a little sick that morning, that's why she was late. But she held back. Grace had four children, you'd expect her to understand. But no doubt she ran her household like an army barrack.

"I hear you've been chasing after Fatimah again?" Grace said. No greeting, thought Anjali. How did Grace know? Did she have spies?

Anjali said nothing, looking stonily at her adversary.

"I hear Fatimah's no good brother's in jail. And Nathan and you have been trying to get him out?"

Their receptionist, Esther, or the receptionist in Makaenga could have told her everything.

"Amadu's arrest was wrong, so Nathan tried to help. And he called to see if I could be of any use. That's all."

"What makes your heart bleed so much for the Aanke, eh?"

"And what makes you hate them? That you're Kakwa?"

Had she hit a tender spot? It was hard to say. Grace did not have an expressive face.

"Nathan had no business going to the police with Fatimah. I really will have to call Mathew about all this. It's too much."

"You do that. I have a lot of work to do," Anjali said.

Turning sharply, Grace walked out, her slim-heeled shoes tap tapping on the floor in explosive bursts.

Anjali waited till she heard Grace's car drive off. Then she told Esther, who had pretended to sort the mail all through the exchange, that she was stepping out for a moment. She wasn't going to call Nathan from the office.

Up the little lane that led to the main road was a restaurant called Mama Penda's. It had a phone centre on the side.

Anjali dialled Nathan's home. Perhaps Julie would be there and give her the news without all this spying.

"We've been trying to get hold of you!" said Julie as she came on the line. "We called you at home and then at work this morning."

"My home phone's dead."

"No wonder! Amadu was released early this morning. Just like that; no explanation."

"Thank god! Did you talk to him?"

"We haven't spoken to him, just to Fatimah when she called. She said he was treated like the other prisoners; no intimidation or anything. We thought he might be pushed around, but nothing of the kind."

"And the men who attacked them? Do we have a clue about who they were?"

"No, nothing. They have not been seen since. We feel they were not locals. Nor do we know who called the police. The fact that they arrived so fast, when the fight had just begun, it has to be a set-up."

"Oh, that I'm sure of."

"We asked Fatimah about the Kakwa. She said they were traditional enemies of the Aanke, way back when. But seems there's not been any confrontation or violence, hate crimes. It's all so weird."

"It sure is. Listen, I have to go soon. I'm going to ask the phone company to fix my phone, fast. Let's try and use our home phones as much as we can. It seems that anything we say on the office phones reaches Grace."

"Really?"

"Yeah. She just paid me a nasty little visit asking why we were interfering."

"Oh no, I'm sorry to hear that! By the way, Fatimah says a big thank you."

"I didn't do anything."

"She said we've been very supportive."

"Good to have some appreciation. It's rare. I'll let you know when the phone get's fixed."

Anjali walked back to the office. As she reached the HELP gate, Hassan drove up and parked nearby. She waited for him at the gate.

"I completely forgot that I had to have those papers ready for you! I'm so sorry," she said as he came abreast.

"No problem. I can come later," he said.

"Do you have a bit of time?"

"Sure."

"Do you think you could you drive me to the Kamorga Telephones office? My phone's dead. And I want to talk to you about something. We could do that on way."

"Okay."

"You won't be late for anything?"

"Not at all, Madam. I'm entirely at your service."

He made a sweeping bow that brought a smile to her lips.

As they drove away, she said: "Hassan, are you close to Grace?"

"What do you mean?"

"I don't know who to trust any more. Grace is more or less spying on me. I have never asked you what you think of her. I think we've shied away from the topic, actually."

Hassan said nothing for a few moments.

"She's complex," he said. "I admire her for some of the things she's done. She's smart. And I think she has a genuine interest in education. But I know she's authoritarian."

"She's not easy to work with."

"I can imagine."

"She's influential, right?"

"She comes from a political family and her husband's in politics too. Yes, they're influential. Though I don't think she gets along with her husband."

"Oh? Anyhow. You wouldn't want to antagonize her, I'd think."

"I wouldn't want to antagonize anyone! But I understand what you're saying. I try not to cross her in public. But it's not like I'm afraid of her. I have my connections too."

"No doubt. I'd like to tell you something and ask you something. But it's all strictly confidential."

"You can trust me, Anju!"

They were going down Lekeme, the main street from which the business district took its name. Banks, shops, government buildings and corporate offices lined the busy thoroughfare. Car horns tooted, Matatas tried rakishly to overtake the private cars and each other; in the absence of pedestrian crossings, people and stray dogs crossed the road any which way they could. A traffic cop dressed in khaki stood on an upturned drum in the middle of an intersection, trying ineffectually to direct the chaos. Hope he has a good life insurance policy, Anjali thought. She was glad she wasn't at the wheel.

"Sorry to drag you through this mess," she said.

"What mess? This is life in all its splendid glory!" Hassan said, grinning.

Anjali smiled; and so it was!

It took Hassan some time to turn into the side lane where the Telephone Office was located and find a parking spot.

"Let me come in with you," he said.

She agreed. Having a Kamorgan man who spoke fluent Morga with her wouldn't do her case any harm.

They registered the complaint and as they walked out of the building Anjali noticed a large group of men standing together at a street corner. These were casual labourers hired by the day or the week for all kinds of odd jobs. Sometimes they were driven off to a factory or a farm by the truckloads. If no one picked them up, they would often go from door to door, soliciting work.

Anjali told Hassan about Amadu's arrest and release. Somehow she had needed time to come to this moment of trust.

"I think it's a set-up, too," Hassan said.

"Is there a tribal rivalry between the Aanke and the Kakwa?"

They got into the car but Hassan didn't start it right away. Instead he turned towards her and said: "You know, foreigners always like to think of Africa in terms of clan and tribal relations. But there are many reasons why things happen here. It's not always ancient ties and enmities. Class matters a lot too."

He fired the ignition. Anjali waited for a moment before she spoke.

"I understand, but do you know anything about the relations between these two groups?"

"Not particularly, no. Tribal connections and animosities are complex."

"It was Fatimah who brought it up."

"Local people use that kind of analysis too, almost without thinking. We're conditioned to think like that. But in reality Kamorga is a rapidly modernizing state."

Against the backdrop of deep-seated traditions, like India. Aloud she said:

"Any guesses what could be going on?"

"Maybe it's an issue of land. Land is always contentious."

"You mean it's about the land Fatimah's trying to get hold of?"

"Perhaps."

"That's interesting. I never thought of that! And Martha mentioned intimidation tactics. But they say land is available here. It's not a big problem."

"There's land and there's fertile, arable land. There's the factor of proximity to a water source or a good water table. I don't think there's enough fertile land available in this country anymore. And some of the best land, which is around Lake Mathilda, belongs to the white settlers who stayed behind after independence."

Anjali thoughts were racing, but there was no illumination.

"Martha advised against me and Nathan getting involved," she said. "She felt it would be seen as interference."

"She's right."

Hassan parked in front of the office gate.

"Thanks a lot. I'll get those papers organized and give you a call," Anjali said.

She was about to open the door when he said: "May be this isn't a good time to propose what I was going to, but maybe it is."

Anjali paused.

"You've heard of The Odeon?" he asked.

"Not sure I have."

"It's a night club. Has great bands. Next week they have an act from Congo. Thought you might be interested."

"Oh."

"Thought you might enjoy getting out of the white ghetto for once." He was grinning.

"And if I feel at home there?" she shot back at once.

"Going somewhere else could be fun too."

"Let's see. I'll give you a call."

CHAPTER 16

Play

RAHUL WAS GUIDING the lemmings through a taxing level on his Game Boy. They came fast and furious, and though he blocked the way to the trap, there was no way for them to get out of the room with its steel walls and water on one side. Ah, maybe I could dig under the wall, he thought. But this would only get them to the next room, with more steel walls and water. *Yikes! Not good enough. But that room has a chimney. I could zigzag the stairs through the chimney.* That was a bit like building a Meccano scaffold. He almost got it done when time ran out. *Oh no! Well, try again.*

A little way down in the garden, Gabriel rode Rahul's bike, a splendid chariot drawn by four fine horses. It was sleek and black, with fiery red strokes on both sides, brakes that worked beautifully and levers that adjusted the speed to several levels. Rahul had shown him how they worked and indicated that Gabriel could ride the bike when he wasn't using it.

Maybe a shorter tunnel between the rooms would work, Rahul thought. This time he forgot to block the trap, and too many lemmings died. He decided to destroy the remaining lemmings to restart the level. He was determined to get it right. It would be a short tunnel, then a zigzag stair, and another trap near the top ... Level Complete! He looked up, triumphant.

Gabriel pretended that Rahul's bike was a motorcycle. He made motorcycle sounds as he pedalled around. He imagined gunning down the main road that cut through Jamesville, wind in hair, envious looks following his heroic rush all the way through.

Gabriel too had a bike, a simple one that helped him run errands for Mary.

Rahul looked back at the screen. He was a bit bored with Lemmings. He had been playing this game for a while now. He didn't care for the music either. But ... he pressed a button.

Finding himself at the half-open garden gate, Gabriel hesitated. Rahul was not allowed to leave the compound on his bike. This made no sense to Gabriel as the bike was designed for getting around efficiently. Yet the only time Rahul took it out was when Anjali drove him sometimes to an open ground at the edge of Jamesville.

Not lava! Oh please! Rahul thought. Oh well, I'll make a stair that will bounce on that column, then bash through this one. Frowning, he mechanically blocked the first lemming from falling into the lava pit.

As Gabriel stood at the gate, indecisive, Fudu emerged and gently closed the gate, latching it firmly. Gabriel swung the bike back towards the house, making a swift, dangerous arc at a near 90-degree angle for a thrilling moment. Then he went up the garden path.

Rahul's possessions were casually scattered around; Gabriel observed them and took mental notes. He had sneaked into Rahul's room a few times when he was at school, or at Jerry's house. Rahul's clothes, toys and books are too many to count. He had a Meccano set with shiny, metallic girders, plates, nuts and bolts, wheels, clutches, ball bearings, and a book with illustrated models. With it they could build cars, jeeps, even a helicopter.

Rahul had all the superhero action figures, and two loud guns that flashed when fired. He had all kinds of books too. Amazingly, a new toy or book arrived every few weeks to join this treasure-trove. Gabriel looked after Rahul's toys, bringing the Meccano set in from the veranda and picking up a superhero lying facedown on the lawn.

Most impressive of all, Rahul had his own camera. Not a kiddie camera, but an adult one—small, silvery and light. This, Rahul was possessive of, and he took good care of it.

Rahul went to a school with a swimming pool, and his friend Jerry had a swimming pool in his backyard. Gabriel cannot quite imagine Rahul's school. He would like to visit it sometime, just to take a look.

Gabriel does not covet Rahul's things, not really. Anyhow, he has ready access to most of them.

He has been observing foreigners, their customs and behaviour, since he came with Mary, five years ago, to live in Anne's compound. Even at that naive age, Gabriel had his eyes wide open.

Above all he wants to understand. And understanding requires patience. That's what Father Abraham had told them at school. Patience, reading, exploring, observing, taking notes, analysing, cultivating an inquiring mind—Father Abraham strongly recommended all these virtues. And humility; he particularly stressed that one. Gabriel believes that as he grows and studies, the world will unfold for him, revealing slowly its connections, its mysteries laid bare.

Of course, there were things worth having, like a motorcycle. But Gabriel was not in a hurry. The process of looking, reading and listening offered its own potent pleasures. And would eventually lead to possessions, a few choice, prized possessions.

As he neared the veranda, Gabriel got off the bike and picked up the cricket bat lying there. Taking the position of a batsman, he swung it at an imaginary ball. Once, then a few more times.

From the corner of his eye, Rahul caught sight of the bat, swinging. He had just finished a really difficult level and needed a break. Putting his Game Boy down, he picked up the ball.

They walked wordlessly to the lawn and started playing, without bothering with stumps. The bowler was also the fielder, most of the time, but if the batsman sent the ball flying away from the bowler, in the opposite direction, he dropped his bat and ran to catch it. Neither Rahul nor Gabriel were caught out, and they changed from one role to the other, in silent communion. Rahul, who had played cricket with his cousins in Delhi during his Indian summers, was happy to take it up again.

As Rahul and Gabriel played in the shadowy part of the garden, the late afternoon sun slowly lost its gaudy heat. Suddenly, they flung bat and ball on the ground and started rolling on the grass, giggling. This was something Anjali disapproved, but she was not around.

They collided with each other as they rolled. More giggling and a bit of scuffling, before they rolled away from each other, and lay enjoying the sky with its fluffy clouds. Gabriel saw a camel who went from having a single hump to two, then turned into a goat with an exaggerated beard.

In the tropics one lived with many creatures. Light brown house lizards slithered silently down the walls, cockroaches roamed despite poisons sprayed at them. A little mouse crept out of its hiding place. Frogs found their way into squat toilets. Flying creatures whirled around and crawly ones, like beetles, walked sedately along the edges of floors. Mosquitos and flies made a nuisance of themselves. Moths made a beeline for illuminated electric bulbs. There were at least two kinds of ants that formed queues and moved in an orderly fashion towards a singular destination. One kind was big and black and you could clearly see its body shape and feelers and legs. The other was tiny, oh so small, black or red, and deadly; it bit really hard.

Outside the house, crickets chirped. Some nights, a fleet of fireflies dropped by for a visit; butterflies and bees alighted on flowers. Little sparrows hopped about; crows sat on trees, observant; birds built nests and dropped shit on your head. A chipmunk or two ran among the trees, and yes, a ssssssssnake glided by sometimes, dainty as a swan.

Rahul's father lived in a house with a garden, but in Delhi he didn't get to hang around much. His schedule there was always full, with activities and visits. Here he could enjoy the life that teemed in the garden at leisure. He felt proprietorial towards all these little creatures, as if he was in charge of their welfare.

Rolling onto his stomach, he spied a furry, red ladybug. Gabriel noticed it too. Springing up he walked away. Rahul looked at his receding figure, wondering what he was up to, but did not call after him.

Gabriel reappeared with a matchbox, a torn piece of newspaper and a pin. He used the pin to bore a few holes in the matchbox cover. Pulling up two blades of grass, he squeezed them in. Then he placed the paper in the ladybug's path. She avoided it at first and tried to go in another direction. Gabriel placed the paper in her path again and again and finally she climbed on. Pop she went into the box!

Closing it, Gabriel presented it solemnly to Rahul, who received it respectfully, recalling that his cousin in India had conducted a similar operation once.

He would show the ladybug to his mother before he went to bed. Anjali would admire it, and ask him to put it back in the garden. Rahul was fine with that; he didn't want to hold the ladybug prisoner for too long. But he relished the idea of killing an insect, taking it apart, and putting a part of it in the box.

"Let's play checkers," Gabriel said.

"How about Titan?" Rahul responded.

Gabriel nodded. They have played this thrilling, combative board game before.

They didn't notice when Anjali came home from work and found them sprawled on the living room carpet, an empty bag of potato chips beside them. She paused. Here for a change was fantasy chumming up with reality: her adult fantasy that Rahul would find a playmate in Gabriel, and everything would turn out well.

CHAPTER 17

Nocturne

HASSAN'S CAR HAD surprised Anjali—a red Fiat. Not a colour she associated with him, he who dressed so tastefully, on the conservative side. She had expected blue, white or beige, perhaps black.

Now he was at her door in his flashy car, dressed in a bold, printed shirt, ready to drive her to the nightclub. She wore the only party top she had brought along to Kamorga: a slinky black and red number, over black pants. A light red stole covered her bare shoulders.

They got into the car and Hassan drove silently towards Masakeni. He seemed preoccupied.

"So, how's the red revolution coming along?" she said playfully.

He took her seriously, "Well, considering everything."

"Everything being?"

"The political culture of this country. The economic forces."

Anjali had heard from Elizabeth about the terrible working conditions in the mines in northern Kamorga, and the high accident rates. Such news did not always appear in the outwardly free Kamorgan press, but Kamau was aware of these issues, particularly because of the work of his colleague Milton Saneo.

"What's the role of the Socialist Workers Party in all this?" Anjali asked.

"They are supporting the unions and the Mine Workers Front. That's the organized miners movement. Let's say that the movement has confidence because this party exists, because it's active, and has not totally lost its ideals."

Martha had told her that the Americans were documenting incidents of bribery by foreign and local mining companies, as well as instances of political corruption. Both sectors were using militia and violence in an effort to keep the miners and their unions in check.

"What do you think will happen down the road?"

"You really want to know?"

"Of course!"

"I believe there will be a guerrilla war fought from the Northwestern Highlands. The Mine Workers Front won't be able to take over the mines or anything close, but they'll throw spanners in the works, big ones."

"But there'll be civilian casualties!"

"When elephants fight, the grass get's trampled. That's what we say. The Americans call it collateral damage. We've heard that term a lot in the Gulf War."

"Are the Aanke in the Northwestern Highlands involved? I mean the Aanke who've been there for ages, not the ones from Ferun."

"The Front is organizing among farmers and labourers there, so yeah, I expect some Aanke are involved."

"If there's a guerrilla war, it could go on for years!"

"Politics is a violent business."

Anjali felt deflated; she didn't want Kamorga to degenerate into some kind of a civil war. There were enough of those already. But she didn't believe in preserving an unjust status quo either. Things needed to change; the miners needed much better working conditions. And the wealth created through mining needed to serve the interests of Kamorgans, not leave the country, as it did now. If only ... if only the change could come about more peacefully.

Hassan, as if sensing her mood, leaned over and flicked on the cassette player. South African Township Music filled the car and Anjali took a deep breath. They were already at the edge of Masakeni. The traffic thinned out at night and one could get around much faster.

"You studied in Ghana, didn't you?" Anjali said.

"Yes, my Bachelors."

"How did you find it, doing your Bachelors abroad?"

"It was good, though not perhaps in the way it was intended."

She turned towards him.

"I was young," he said. "Those were the drinking, partying years. I think I would have been better off partying at home during my Bachelors and doing my Masters more seriously abroad." He laughed.

"Ah," she said. She was going to see his drinking, partying side today. She could hardly wait!

They had turned onto a lively street with restaurants and bars—lights, cars, voices, music and laughter. Anjali rolled her window further down. Suddenly she was glad she had come. She had been unsure about it, but now she knew that a night out was what she needed. That, and getting to know a

Kamorgan better. She had tried to socialize with Elizabeth and Shirley Osei and Hamida Musa, but it had gone nowhere.

Soon they were seated at a table in The Odeon's compound, Anjali taking in the outdoor setting, with tables and chairs set around a small stage. The trees in the compound were decorated with blue lights. The effect was very pretty. Canned Congolese Soukous music sounded in the background. A waiter soon appeared to take their order. Anjali asked for a cocktail called Snows of Kilimanjaro; Hassan ordered a local beer. They also decided on a couple of vegetarian appetizers.

"Let me tell you about the music," Hassan said. "It's Congolese rumba and the band's Marty Djembo and the Boys. Rumba became big in Cuba, and Central and Latin America later on, but it originated here in Congo."

"Really? Didn't know that. Always thought Rumba was Latin American."

"There's a Soukous influence in their music as well, but it's a different sound from standard Soukous. These guys have been around—Dakar, Paris, the U.S."

"I first heard Soukous at the Harbourfront Centre in Toronto. Local musicians actually, immigrants from the Congo."

"Yeah, it got around. I've not heard this band live, but I have a couple of their tapes."

Anjali was suddenly nostalgic for summer at the Harbourfront, when she had discovered Africa, through the incredible riches of African music. Manu Dibango, Oumuo Sangare, Papa Wemba, Cesaria Evora, Khaled, Youssou N'Dour, Salif Keita, Angelique Kidjo, Toumani Diabate, Miriam Makeba, Hugh Masekela, Baaba Maal, Souad Massi, Ali Farka Toure— the list of African greats went on and on. She had not brought her African music collection here; she missed it. The radio played either music from Congo or very local bands. Nor had she found her African favourites in the shops.

The drinks arrived, the Snows of Kilimanjaro a concoction of white rum, coconut milk, Angostura Bitters and a touch of citrus. She got Hassan to taste it and laughed when it left a line of foam on his moustache.

The place was filling up; the crowd was about 95 percent black, five per cent white. That was a change. She was the only South Asian there, as expected, but no one stared at her. The Kamorgans were discreet that way. The atmosphere was friendly; a few people caught her eye and smiled.

The first band was an international act from Senegal. It was a trio with a kora player who was also the singer, a drummer with a djembe and calabash drums, and a musician on a keyboard. As the gentle notes of the kora overlaid by the mellifluous voice of the singer swept over her, she was transported. How beautiful it was, smooth, flowing naturally like a rivulet, and just as life affirming. How different the world it evoked from the paper-pushing, issue-oriented one she lived in!

When she looked at Hassan, she found him looking ardently at her. She turned away. Suddenly the idea surfaced that Hassan found her attractive. *Oh my god!* It had been quite obvious all along, so how had she missed it? He was an interesting man, and good-looking, no doubt about it. It was quite unusual to be unmarried and childless in Kamorga, as he seemed to be. She expected girlfriends, perhaps even a mistress. He certainly knew women and their ways. Anyhow, there was no harm done, she told herself. The slight sexual tension was pleasing, even healthy, and wouldn't go anywhere.

"This music is just exquisite," she said.

"It's lovely. Glad you like it."

The act played for a blissful half an hour. Anjali was able to let go, become totally immersed. And then came Marty Djembe and the Boys—energetic, contemporary, eclectic—and people started taking to the dance floor.

"Should we?" he asked.

"Sure," she said, draping her stole over the back of the chair.

They danced to a few Soukous-inflected numbers, followed by a couple which were more Rumba influenced. She was not surprised to find that Hassan was a good dancer. The atmosphere was jovial. A couple of the dancers were fooling around, making comic moves, laughing. The last time she had danced, really danced, was at her farewell party, organized by Rani, in Toronto.

The band played a slower number, and some of the couples started dancing close. Hassan looked at Anjali again. After a moment's hesitation, she nodded. A warm hand lay lightly on her shoulder and the other rested on her waist. Her head came up to his shoulder. It was a little too perfect.

They moved slowly to the music, which wrapped itself around her like a snug winter coat. There was a tantalizing hint of Portuguese Fado in the rhythm. She felt she was floating, her body as light as her head. The parts of her body that touched Hassan, ever so slightly, were getting warmer, more lively. She was extremely aware of him, so close, so solid. She could smell his spicy aftershave. The hand on her bare shoulder felt intimate, too intimate. Why had she worn a top that exposed her shoulders?

Hassan shifted a little closer, his hands moving to mid shoulder. Now her shoulder was aflame and Anjali's head rested on his shoulder of its own volition. Their bodies touched, and his wide, generous mouth brushed against her hair. The base of her spine tingled. She held her pose, a little rigidly, even as her body was signalling her to melt into him.

She imagined her lips on his smooth, ebony-hued neck. It was a hair's-breadth away. She moved closer. Now they were welded together, even as each of her nerves stood distinct, like bristles on a stiff hairbrush. An external force seemed to have taken over: her nose was buried in his shoulder, as she inhaled his real scent; his lips brushed the top of her ear. Anjali shuddered. She felt him sigh, his lips moving back to her hair.

"Anju," he whispered. "Anju." Gasping, she pressed closer.

They stayed like that, united as one, for an eternity that flashed by, a resplendent comet illuminating the lush beauty of the night sky.

The music stopped. He released her slowly, reluctantly. Anjali moved back, breathless, purposefully avoiding his eyes. The lead singer was announcing that they were going to take a break.

Once seated, sanity returned by degrees, though the memory of her body pinned against his, and the desire to be back in his embrace, filled the evening.

They ordered a second round of drinks.

"What made you turn to international development work?" she asked. She wanted to try and re-establish their relationship as colleagues.

"It helps supplement my income. University lecturers don't make much here. And it's interesting work, in its own way."

"But you prefer teaching and research?"

"Absolutely, I love the university life."

"It's funny," she said, and stopped.

He looked inquiringly at her.

"I am not as happy with HELP's mandate as I used to be. Now that I am here, in Kamorga, I think ... I wish ... we were doing something that empowered people in a deeper way."

"That's another topic. It's not a bad organization, HELP."

They said no more, content to sit there, sipping their drinks, looking around. She felt as if she was 19, out on her first date in far away Bombay. But you are 36, a mother, and engaged to be married, she told herself.

When the band came on again she said: "Not sure I can stay too long. Would you mind if we left after 15-20 minutes?"

"That's fine." He seemed composed, and that stung her.

They went back to the floor and danced a few numbers. There were no more slow ones.

She bought a tape of Marty Djembe and the Boys on their way out. The kora music was not to be had.

"You must come to a local bar," he said as they drove home. "Sometimes they have live music. They're a good deal rowdier but fun."

"Was a great evening. Just what I needed."

"Anytime you feel like it."

"Richard and Martha may like to go too. You know them I think?"

"A bit. Nice folks. As long as I don't get into a deep conversation about politics with Richard!"

"That wouldn't do!"

When he parked at her gate she thanked him profusely.

"I'm the one who should thank you. What're you up to this weekend?"

"Barbeque at Martha's Friday night, children's day or something like that at the American Embassy on Saturday, plus Nathan and Julie will be down this weekend. We'll all go to the Waterpark with Rahul on Sunday."

"Busy lady."

"I'll call you next week. Maybe we could have lunch. I'd like to talk with you about the IDP policy."

"Sounds good."

He leaned forward and planted a soft kiss on her forehead, making her shiver. He stayed, his lips grazing her skin. Anjali had to stop herself from putting her arms around him. Then he drew back, his eyes full of longing. Anjali looked away. They were in plain view of the small wooden enclosure just outside the gate where John sat, dozing. The car hadn't even woken him up!

"Good night Anju," he whispered.

"Sleep well," she mumbled. Opening the car door, she stumbled out.

Kora music played in her head all through the following day. Hassan claimed her thoughts as well. She was restless. She daydreamed. She sighed. She sat in her office chair, arching her back, stretching like a cat.

A couple of days later he was in her dreams, dressed all in indigo—a Tuareg man on a camel, only his eyes showing through the voluminous drapes that covered him from head to toe.

Anjali reverberated with longing—a kora with its strings stretched too tight. The dream mingled places, had her sitting on a beach near Bombay, watching him ride up on his ungainly steed. He was some distance away and up close at the same time. Then, abruptly, she was on a ship, or a boat perhaps, standing aft, looking at the foamy wake stretching to the horizon. Cut to her sitting on a sand dune, Hassan still approaching, but this time on foot. He walked and walked; he had a long stretch to traverse. She rose, and now he stood before her. He opened his arms, and enveloped her in his robes, so that they were both wrapped tightly in each other's arms, swaddled in reams and reams of soft, indigo cloth, two mummies face to face, except that they were anything but dead. They stood together for a while and she heard the sound of the surf and felt the heat of the sun, pounding, pounding. Then she tilted her head up and his full lips were on hers, kissing greedily. Gasping, she pushed herself against him, her febrile flesh meeting his satin-smooth skin through flimsy cloth. When the dream dissolved she woke up, terribly aroused.

CHAPTER 18

Mary's Request

ANJALI WENT UPSTAIRS to Anne's study and settled down to write to her mother. She hadn't managed to call. She wanted to send her Rahul's photos of the house, his school and the swimming pool. Not exactly representative of Kamorga, but that's what she had.

This is such a nice room, she thought, looking around. I should use it more often. She wondered if Anne used it much. Usually Anjali worked on the sofa in the spacious bedroom.

Overlooking the back garden, the study had a cosy feel. On the walls were photographs of Anne with her parents, as a child and an adolescent. There was a watercolour of a cottage, at the edge of what she imagined was one of the ever-present Canadian lakes. Probably Anne's family retreat. The other wall decorations—posters featuring Nelson Mandela and Miriam Makeba—signalled Anne's journey from Canada to Africa.

Anjali started writing. Soon she had filled two pages describing everyday life in Kamorga and telling her mother about Amadu's mysterious arrest. Indumati already knew about Fatimah and the idea of applying for land under the Cooperative Land Distribution Scheme.

Hearing a sound, she looked up to see Mary at the door. She stood there awkwardly, looking down at her feet.

"What's up?" Anjali asked, getting up from her chair.

Mary looked up, her eyes full of tears. Then she hung her head again.

Anjali was by her side in an instant, holding her by the arm.

Mary started speaking in Morga and broken English, her voice suddenly loud and shrill, asking Anjali if she could please, please take Gabriel back to Canada with her.

"What? What are you saying?"

"Gabriel, he *angavu* (intelligent), he good! My brother, I don't know where he is ... Father Emmanuel yes, but no ... no." Mary paused, shaking her head sadly.

Anjali looked at her, unable to say anything.

"If only my mother was alive!" Mary cried out. "But she die. She die too soon!"

Anjali held Mary as she started weeping uncontrollably.

"And Otieno... Otieno ...,"

Anjali led her gently to the narrow antique bench, set against the wall, and made her sit down. She sat down next to her and fished out a handkerchief.

Mary dried her tears and wiped her nose. Then she looked at Anjali, silent. There was no pleading in her eyes now, just a deep sadness.

"Mary, do you mean I should adopt him?" Anjali asked gently.

"Dio. Yes."

"Oh god!"

The exclamation was out before she could censor it. Mary gave her a frightened look, then dropped her gaze. Anjali tried to compose herself.

"I mean ... have you ... asked him?"

"Yes, last week. At first he did not want to go. But when I explained and he understood, he said yes."

"But ..."

"It is very far, Canada, he knows. I talk Edith. She thinks it's a good idea."

"And Father Emmanuel?"

"He said he could help with the papers."

After a long moment Anjali said: "Mary, I understand why you are asking me. Gabriel is a wonderful boy. But I must think. It is all so sudden and it would be a huge decision ... And I must speak to Rahul, and Jeremy."

"Gabriel likes Rahul, and you, and Jeremiah. You are all so good to him."

Anjali looked silently at her.

"A man never stands as tall as when he kneels to help a child. A woman too," Mary said.

"I'm glad you came to me, Mary, I really am. I will think about it seriously. I am so sorry ..."

Mary laid a hand on hers. "Do not worry about me. I okay. I will be at peace if Gabriel is with you in Canada."

Anjali produced a wan smile. Mary smiled back radiantly, smudge cheeked and red-eyed.

She felt immensely relieved. When she had gone to see Father Emmanuel, waiting for him in his untidy office, she had looked around and realized that he was not a family man. He never could be.

He let his papers fall into disorder on his desk. And he tended to be absentminded, preoccupied. In a flash it had all become clear to her. The good Father could provide for Gabriel's mind and soul, but he could not ensure his physical well being, nor could he love him with the deep, abiding love of a mother for her child. No, she could not quite see him tending to Gabriel when he was sick, getting up several times a night to check on his fever, making him as comfortable as possible.

After she was gone, who would wash the two school uniforms that Gabriel had and make sure that one was always available, nicely pressed and smelling pleasantly of lemony detergent? Who would add extra onion to the okra knowing that curry made this way was his favourite dish? Who would put away the book that fell on his chest because he dozed off while reading, and switch off the light? Only a woman could to do all that, a motherly woman. A woman unlike her own stepmother. A woman like ... Anjali.

Yes of course. Anjali! Why had she not thought of Anjali? Anjali was such a good mother. And she had confided in her once that she regretted Rahul being an only child. Rahul and Gabriel played well together, he and Anjali liked Gabriel and Gabriel liked them too. And Jeremiah? He had been nice to Gabriel. Gabriel would get a great education in Canada. Anjali had the heart and the means to take Gabriel on.

When Father Emmanuel had finally entered the room she had told him about her idea, and he had agreed that this was the best way to go.

Mary took Anjali's hand and gave it a gentle squeeze. "*Mandi mana*. Thank you very much. Good night," she said, getting up and leaving the room, a smile lingering on her face.

Anjali was as stunned by Mary's departure as she had been by her arrival.

"Don't go yet," she almost called out after her.

Now that she was beginning to adjust to Mary's request, she had expected that they would discuss the situation some more. But no; Mary was gone, leaving the weight of a huge decision behind.

She continued sitting, staring at the dark square of the window, welcoming the discomfort of the hard bench. It helped her deal with her tumultuous emotions, to stay grounded. Otherwise she might have wondered if all this was a dream. From time to time her gaze shifted to the door. She could still picture Mary, standing there awkwardly, looking down at her feet.

Finally she got up and went back to the letter. She described Mary's request and asked her mother's counsel. Signing the letter, she put it in an envelope. Then she walked downstairs and stepped out into the garden. She needed air and trees and earth and sky, her true friends, particularly here in Kamorga. She let out a long, slow breath.

The adoption, if she went for it, would involve her and Gabriel and Mary and Rahul and Jeremy and Edith and Father Emmanuel and an ever-widening circle of relatives and friends. She would certainly have to talk to Mathew and Anne. Her mother and sister would be supportive, she felt. As for her father, he would go along, as he did with most things. She wondered what the Kamorgans would say, Hassan and Elizabeth, for instance. It could become a divisive issue that would make people take sides.

Very few African countries allowed international adoption. She knew that Kamorga was among a handful that did. She had met a Belgian woman at an event at the Alliance Française who had adopted a baby here. She also knew Canadian couples who had gone for international adoption. One had adopted a Chinese boy, the other an Indian girl. The two children were now a little younger than Rahul. They seemed to be doing fine, but perhaps they would have problems later, in their adolescence, when they began exploring their identity. Or perhaps they would fare no worse than Rahul.

You can help Mary.

It was always about her helping people here, but not in this case. Gabriel would bring responsibilities and worries, but also riches, riches she could barely fathom. Gabriel could be the second child she had always wanted, the brother for Rahul. She wondered if Mary had also wanted a second child, a brother or sister for Gabriel. She must have wished for that. Many children were the norm in Kamorga.

Anjali's decision would depend on what Rahul and Jeremy said. Rahul seemed to really like Gabriel. But having him for a brother, that was something else. He might feel jealous, insecure. She felt sometimes that Rahul had some bruises, deep down, somewhere.

But she didn't need to think for others. They would tell her what they thought about having Gabriel as a family member. She needed, first of all, to know if she wanted to become Gabriel's mother.

How happy they had been, she and Manish, in that second year of their marriage, when the pregnancy test result had come out positive. Anjali's mother-in-law had come down for the delivery and stayed with them for three months. Anjali had had a healthy pregnancy, followed by a comparatively easy delivery. The first few weeks after the birth were overwhelming, and Anjali had been thankful for her mother-in-law's help.

They had held a small naming ceremony at home with a few friends. Rahul—the name meant capable, conqueror of miseries. Her mother-in-law returned to India, and when her parental leave ran out, Anjali went back to her job.

Then her relationship with Manish started changing. At first slowly. She wanted Rahul to have minimal parental control so that he could discover who he really was. This was in keeping with Canadian ideas of child rearing and reflected in the school system. Manish, the outwardly relaxed one, believed in a more traditional approach. He also believed that this style was in keeping with Rahul's personality.

In hindsight, perhaps he had been right.

Manish dealt with life in Canada by turning inwards, towards the Indian community in Toronto, away from novelty. Anjali's response was almost exactly the opposite. Her friends were international development professionals and social activists, attracted to new trends, people who wanted to bring about change. Manish, an engineer, was not comfortable with this crowd. Anjali wanted to see an artsy film, attend a public lecture or take Rahul to a children's activity at the Harbourfront Centre. Manish wanted to stay home and watch Indian TV via satellite, or rent a popular movie. She wanted to try out the various ethnic restaurants that dotted the city. He preferred an Indian restaurant, or home food, which she had to cook. The deal breaker had been his turning away from liberal values and becoming politically more conservative.

Manish did his fair share of housework, if not the cooking, and he was a conscientious father. But real conversation between them was dying. Some evenings Anjali would come home late from a work-related event to find a sullen husband in front of the TV set, and Rahul playing by himself with his train or his Meccano set, or watching cartoons on the television in their bedroom, the second set that Manish had insisted on getting. As soon as Rahul saw her he would run to her and cling, crying.

Soon they were disagreeing about practically everything, and arguing. Afraid of the effect on Rahul, they curtailed their loud voices. Open dissent turned to simmering, festering re-sentment; their relationship had turned brittle.

We gave Rahul that one good year, thought Anjali, and then we really fucked up.

There had been another problem, a big one. Her mother had not taken to Manish. Indumati's approval never came easy, but she coveted it all the same. She was deeply hurt by her mother's response. Among other things Indumati was put off that Manish and Anjali spoke in Hindi with Rahul, not Marathi, their mother tongue. Hindi was his father's mother tongue. Anjali and Manish had decided that it was more practical for Rahul to learn Hindi, the national language, and too complicated to expose him to two languages at home.

And Anjali was angry with her father for always being neutral and disengaged. When she was growing up she had liked his easygoing ways, a foil to her mother's domineering personality. She had been rather proud of her "cool" parents then. They allowed Anjali and her sister much more freedom than most middle-class, Indian parents. But after immigra-tion, she had longed for a mother who would grind and mix special *masalas* for her to take back to Canada, and a father who posed anxious questions about the Canadian winter. Indian parents spent months on end with their children who lived abroad. Hers visited for a month, moving on to Van-dana for another two-three weeks, before flying back home.

Mary did not know that Anjali was not a good mother. She had judged her by appearance alone, and was beguiled, no doubt, by the image of Canada she had in her mind. How it dazzled people, the West. No, it blinded them. They didn't realize just how complicated immigration was, how it could diminish and break people. Immigration could gore into the heart of a family, deform something that had been sane and whole before. What was that word they used all the time? Dysfunctional. They were so good at coming up with a clinical sounding word for everything, robbing life of emotional content, rendering it "safe." It wasn't pretty—seeing a person or a family fall apart. She wondered if Mary had any idea about racism in the West. Probably not. She was already at the bottom of the ladder in Kamorga, though maybe that was not how she framed it in her mind. She must have so many hopes for Gabriel, so many dreams.

It worried her that Mary already seemed to think that she was going to adopt Gabriel. The way she had smiled at the end, it was a smile of relief and certainty. But what about what Rahul felt? And Jeremy? Mary had laid the burden of the decision on her and her alone.

And yet, and yet she did understand. Would she not have behaved similarly if she had been in Mary's shoes?

Anjali had been walking around the lawn, without really seeing it, but now she looked at the border of impatiens, the lily pond, and beyond it the hedge that separated their house from the road. There was a bit of light coming in from the street. Being in the garden usually brought her peace, but not today. She paused in her pacing, and went and sat down on the veranda steps. How still the night was, how beautiful! Everything in the garden was in perfect harmony, not a single element out of place. How out of balance her life was, by comparison!

If she took on Gabriel's responsibility, he would need not only a lot of love and support, but also guidance and discipline. She had brought Rahul to Kamorga, and that had been such a challenge. Taking Gabriel to Canada would be a far greater one. Or was it more fair to call it a gamble? Perhaps, perhaps she was too burnt out to take it on.

And what about Rahul's feelings? He liked Gabriel, and the two got along well, but Gabriel as a brother after being an only child for 10 years? Another challenge thrown at poor Rahul! Hadn't he already faced enough adversity by dealing with his father's departure to India and coping with the move to Kamorga?

She wished she was more like her sister. Or Mary. They were both so kind, so accepting and spontaneously loving. She was afraid that buried somewhere within her was an Indumati—quick to judge, hard headed, difficult to please and undependable. Yes, undependable, because her mother's love and approval were conditional, and that was not how it was supposed to be.

She had tried to love Rahul unconditionally, without reserve. Her battle as a mother was about suppressing Indumati and bringing out her nurturing self, her true self. But could there ever be a true self, separate and pure, untainted by Indumati?

Anjali looked up at the starry sky. Out there were constellations, galaxies and celestial formations she could not see; entire worlds spinning away, weaving their own dreams and realities. That unlimited space also contained the future —the uncertain outcome of taking Gabriel to Canada.

She wanted to adopt him; yes, she wanted to look after him after Mary's death. She wanted to call him her son; she wanted to take him to Toronto.

And yet, could she really be his mother? She was afraid that she would not, could not be a good, loving mother to Gabriel.

How perverse life was; how mixed-up her emotions! She would call her sister tomorrow, and soon after, she would talk to Jeremy. She would talk to her mother as well.

She wished there was an elder around to give counsel, someone like her grandmother who had lived with them. If her grandmother had lived to see her married to Manish, she would have accepted him as family. She would not have treated him with disdain, as Indumati had. Her mother had already put a stamp of approval on Jeremy, whom she had met on her last visit to Toronto. That was something.

Anjali made her way, slowly, back into the house and up the stairs, picturing the baobab at the 'Alliance Française. Marvelling at its wide, wise girth, she imagined leaning against it and drawing in its genuine strength.

CHAPTER 19

Conversations

ᴘARKED OUTSIDE THE American International School, Anjali was waiting for Rahul to come out. She had called Martha and asked if she should pick up Jerry, to learn that he was at home with a sore throat.

When she saw Rahul come through the school gate, hesitate for a moment before seeing the car and heading for it, she was struck by how small-built her son was, compared to many of the other boys. How vulnerable he seemed, the school bag far too big on his slight frame! Was it fair to subject him to another upheaval by taking up the subject of adopting Gabriel? She planned to talk to him after dinner.

The night before, Anjali had spoken to Vandana and Jeremy about Mary's request. Anjali had expressed again her fears of not being a good mother. Vandana was the only person to whom she had ever expressed these sentiments.

Vandana had embraced the idea of the possible adoption without reserve. Anjali would be a good mother, she had said; she was a good mother, of course she was. Why did she doubt her ability so much? There was no need for her to do so at all. Vandana was also confident that their mother Indumati would support an adoption. As for their father, he would go along. He never had a strong opinion about anything. All he wanted was to be left alone to play Bridge.

While her sister's position hadn't surprised her, Anjali was taken aback by Jeremy's response. He was keen to father Gabriel! He had really enjoyed talking to him, he said. Gabriel's desire to learn had impressed him. Such an interest in learning wasn't common; in fact it was quite rare, and well worth nurturing. Yes, there would be many challenges, he agreed; yes, it wasn't going to be easy for any of them, particularly Gabriel, but the effort would be well worth it.

"You don't want to think it over?" she had asked.

"I don't need to, not really. But the final decision, the final choice, must be yours, Anju. I would understand if you decided against it." Even as he said that she could feel his desire to have Gabriel in their life coming straight at her through the crackling telephone wire.

Perhaps Jeremy was disappointed that his nearly grown-up children were not interested in the intellectual life, that he so loved, Anjali thought as she hung up. Jeremy's son wanted to be a woodworker, and his daughter had won a scholarship to study dance in New York. Rahul didn't show any particular potential for an academic future. How ironic that Gabriel with his scholarly bent resembled Jeremy the most!

Both Vandana and Jeremy had agreed with Anjali that Rahul's response would the crucial, deciding factor. Anjali was full of apprehension. Rahul liked Gabriel, how much she couldn't say. But having him as a brother? He might not be keen on that at all. And how fair was it to ask a 10-year-old to make such a major decision?

Rahul got into the car and they fell silent after their

hellos. Anjali started driving home, trying to keep her mind on the road.

"Ma, will Gabriel come to Canada?" Rahul said suddenly.

"What?

"Will he?"

"Where did you hear that?"

"Mary told me."

"I don't think so," Anjali said in a singsong voice.

Rahul turned his head and looked out of the window.

"Rahul!"

He was bad at lying, but he tried to from time to time.

"You listened at the door, didn't you? When I was speaking to Mary, or was it Vandana or Jeremy?"

"The door was open when you talked to Mary!"

"That's true."

Might as well plunge in, Anjali decided. "Would you like to go for a milkshake?"

"Yeah!"

She took a sharp turn into a side street. A few minutes later she was parked at Mandy's Ice Cream and Juice Corner —a roadside stall painted with Mickey Mouse images, with yellow, plastic tables and chairs arranged in a semi-circle.

Rahul got a chocolate milk shake, a small one at Anjali's insistence; Anjali got a pineapple juice. They carried their drinks to a table.

"I meant to talk with you, *beta,* son," she said.

Rahul looked intently at her; the Game Boy was nowhere in sight. He was playing with it less these days, at least in her presence.

"Would you like Gabriel to come to Canada with us?" Anjali asked, wishing she had had more time to prep.

Rahul remained silent.

"I know you need to think about it seriously. You don't have to answer me now," she said.

"Would Gabriel sleep in my room?" Rahul asked.

"At first, yes. But when we move to Jeremy's house next year, you can both have your own room."

"But two beds won't fit!"

"A bunk bed would."

Rahul looked enthusiastic.

"Would I get the top bunk?"

"I don't see why not."

"Where will Gabriel go if he doesn't come to Canada?"

"I'm not sure. I expect he'll stay at his aunt's place."

"His school is far from there."

"True, that's a long commute. But it could be done."

"Can't he stay with Father Emmanuel?"

"At the Jesuit residence? I wonder if that's possible. Maybe there's a boys' hostel or something. We could find out. And we could leave money with Father Emmanuel and send more money from Canada."

"He'll like my school."

"I think so. If he came. He's good at studies."

"School's not just studies, mom. It's lots of stuff."

"That's true."

"I could help him out."

"Yeah, for sure."

"He'll be very sad without Mary."

"That's for sure."

There were a few moments of silence. Then Rahul said: "I'd like him to come. You want him to, don't you?"

"It's what you think that's important, Rahul. You know he'll be your brother?"

Sucking noisily on his milkshake, Rahul nodded.

"You can take your time and think it over. It's a big decision. I don't want you to hurry into it."

"I think it'll be OK. Jeremy wants him to come, right?"

"Yes, he thinks it's a good idea. Vandana *mavshi* also agrees."

"I like Gabriel."

"And he likes you."

"I think so. I think he likes me."

This is amazing, all this emotional revelation, Anjali thought.

"It'll be difficult for him in Toronto. He will miss Mary and Edith and Aissa and John and his school and everything," she said.

"It's sad, but he could visit here."

Like you visit your father in India, Anjali thought.

"If he comes with us ... I don't know ... do you want him to come?"

"Yes," she said simply.

"It'd be tough for him here."

It'll be tough for him either way, she thought.

"Let's take him with us."

"Are you sure?"

Rahul nodded. He put the glass down; he had finished his milkshake.

"We have to think about ourselves together as a family. But we also have to really think about how it would be for him," Anjali said.

"I could show him stuff. He'll need a bike, a good one. His bike's crap. He really likes my bike."

"So you think he'll be okay in Canada?"

Rahul nodded, a little tentative.

"We can't be sure of that. But we can think it through and try our best," Anjali said. She did not want to unload her fears on Rahul, but she wanted him to appreciate the seriousness of the move.

"There's no one here to really look after him," Rahul said.

"It is very mature of you, Rahul, to think like that. I'm really proud of you."

Rahul blushed. "We could get him a skateboard," he said quickly. "You should have let me bring mine. And he'll need a snowboard, too."

"Oh my god, winter! That'll be so hard for him." She had not thought about it. How short sighted!

"Quit worrying, mom."

"It's very serious, Rahul. I am very worried."

"I know. But he'll get used to things. You did."

"That's true, but I was an adult. I was able to think through things and speak up and ask questions."

Rahul shrugged. "Gabriel's good at that. And there's people like him in my class."

"That's true. He won't be the only first generation immigrant. Nor the only person of colour."

Rahul looked around restlessly.

"And he'll be in mourning too, with his mother passing away. He'll miss her so much. That'll be the hardest," Anjali said. She wanted Rahul to face the facts, hard as they were.

"He'll be very sad," Rahul said.

"So much will depend on us—on you Rahul, and on me, and Jeremy."

"We'll help him. And Jeremy will take us to the games."

Suddenly Anjali had a vision of a house full of men—sweaty t-shirts cluttering the laundry basket; big, muddy boots in the hallway, video games and gear littering the living room floor; hockey on the TV screen. I wonder, she thought, a half smile forming on her lips, if I am the one who is going to have the hardest time adjusting.

"Helping him does not include bossing him. You'll remember that, won't you?"

"Aw, come on, mom. You're the boss."

"Don't be cheeky," she said, happy he was being like that.

He was five when she had first told him that some people were poor through no fault of their own. They were not stupid, or lazy. If someone did not speak English it meant they spoke another language. If someone could not read and write it meant they had not had the chance to go to school. Just because he was well off and went to school and spoke English, he was in no way superior to anyone else. She repeated this every so often with minor variations.

"The bunk bed would work," Rahul said.

She nodded.

"And I'd sleep on top, right?"

"Sure."

Something else occurred to her. "Rahul, you know that West African kid in your class?"

"Lawrence?"

"Yah, him. And that girl, from St. Lucia I think she is?"

"Mariam."

"Was your teacher or anyone else ever mean to them? You know, because they're black?"

"No," Rahul said, looking offended.

"Well, these things can happen. You know about racism."

"Not in my class," Rahul said decisively.

"And you, Rahul? Have you ... has anyone ... in Canada?"

"No, Ma."

"Good, that's good to know," she said, wondering if he was really being truthful.

They sat in silence for a few moments.

"Oh Rahul, sweetie, I do want Gabriel to come, but I am scared too," she said.

"Don't worry, Mommy," he said softly.

When had he last called her Mommy? She gathered her son in her arms, her eyes moist. Rahul hugged her back. He was a really good hugger when he wanted to be.

When Anjali came home from work the next day, Gabriel was at the tomato patch in the kitchen garden, picking some tomatoes that would go in their dinner salad.

"Gabriel, could I speak to you when you're done?" she asked.

He nodded.

"I'll be sitting on the veranda."

Something Rahul had said at Mandy's Ice Cream had given her a cue about how she would breach the topic of Canada with Gabriel.

Making her way through the garden to the front of the house, Anjali sat down on the veranda steps. She could smell freshly cut grass; Fudu had been at it earlier that day. He used rusty garden shears, with which he also trimmed the hedge from time to time.

Gabriel appeared five minutes later. He sat down on a lower step, at an angle, half facing her.

"How's school?" she asked.

"Good."

"I would like to tell you a story, my story. It's about how I went to Canada."

Something quickened in his eyes, and then died. That word, Canada, fairly meaningless to him until recently, must have all sorts of connotations now.

"I went there to study. Did you know that?"

"No."

"It was very different in Toronto. Not at all like home. Everything was different, how the buildings looked, what the people wore, how the water tasted. Small things and big things. Some of the new things I liked, some I found really strange. There was a lot to discover. I had never heard any African music in India, for example. But in Toronto there was a lot of it, and world music, too."

"Did you like it there?"

"Yes, I did. I hadn't realized when I lived in India that all the world had flocked there, to Toronto. I liked that. I liked talking to people who had come there from somewhere else.

"As I lived there, I started to get used to the new things, and some of the things that I did not like, I learnt to live with. Now I think of Toronto as home."

"What didn't you like?" Gabriel asked.

This is good, this may work, Anjali thought. He's asking questions.

"Well, I had to talk in English all the time. I missed my mother tongue and other Indian languages."

She could sense that Gabriel was listening intently.

"I missed my family—my mother, father and sister, especially my sister. I also missed my grandparents and my friends. Missing my family and friends was definitely the worst of it. I thought about my uncles, aunts, cousins, and my neighbours. I was in touch with a lot of people all the time, in India."

"What did you do?"

"I would call home when I could. But it was expensive. My family called me as much as they could. I used to write letters, long letters describing everything. You can do that, too. And you can send photographs, just as Rahul does now."

She had connected her history to his future. She wondered how he was taking that. It was hard to read his expression.

"Did they write?" he asked.

"A few did. But you must not mind if people don't. Most people are bad letter writers. You must remember that your family still loves you. Rahul never writes to his father, but they talk on the phone. You'll be able to call Edith, Aissa and John from Toronto. We'll figure out a way."

Gabriel cast his eyes down. Maybe she was going too fast, leading him like this into a possible future.

"I went to Canada in summer, and then it was fall, so beautiful! The leaves changed to such lovely colours. They were red, yellow, orange and brown. Later, all the trees dropped their leaves. Well, not all. The evergreen ones were fine, just the deciduous trees shed leaves.

"It was sad to see all those bare trees. I had never seen trees like that before. I felt very strange, as if something was wrong. But soon it was winter and it snowed. Some of the snow stayed on the branches, and the trees looked pretty. They started looking normal! Then I was happy I went. Doesn't mean I don't find it hard. One of my uncle's is not keeping well. He's been bedridden for a year now. It bothers me that I can't see him. But on the whole I think I did the right thing."

Gabriel was holding her gaze now, his eyes bright.

"Would you like to see some photos?" she asked.

He nodded.

Anjali went upstairs to her bedroom. Things seemed to be going well! All those questions, she had not expected that.

She returned with the little album she had brought with her and sat down with him.

They were all there—Indumati and her father Haridhar, her grandmother whom they had lost, her surviving grandparents, Jeremy, Vandana, Himanshu, Vandana's husband, her friend Rani and her daughter, Mala, Francesca and her husband and two children, a boy and a girl, Jeremy and his mother. She slowly turned the pages, pointing, talking.

"That's fall." She had taken some photographs in High Park, and at a cottage that Jeremy had rented in the country, one year, inevitably on a lake.

They were skating on the ice now; they had made a beginning. The surface wasn't cracking, but neither was it solid. She would have to build slowly on this, their first conversation. She must encourage Rahul to speak with Gabriel about school and friends and life in Canada, but without boasting.

"Oh, and another thing you'll like. There are nice libraries in Toronto," she said.

She wasn't going to ask him how he felt, what he thought. Not yet. She had to lead up to that.

She had walked about in the garden one morning, when she had first arrived in Venimeli, before anyone was up. The fresh air and the clear sky had brought uncluttered gladness. On the lawn she had spied a little periwinkle that had just bloomed, just that little one, a delicate mauve. She had marvelled at its guilelessness and fragility. It had opened itself to the world, there, in the dewy grass, held up by its little stem.

She could defy her fears, couldn't she?

She would have to be strong. They would all have to be strong together.

Gabriel continued leafing through the album, his head bent. Anjali wanted to reach out and stroke his crinkly hair. How did you develop physical ease with a child you had not carried inside you?

Someday she hoped to find out.

CHAPTER 20

Graceland II

THE MAIN OFFICE of the Apostolic Church of Christ Our Saviour was housed at the back of their big church in Lekeme. An evangelical order that originated in Nigeria, it had come to Kamorga in the late 1930s. Grace was early for her meeting with Pastor Martin. Once he knew she had arrived, he would hurry through other business to receive her. But she couldn't resist the empty church with its simplicity and silence. She went in and took a seat at the back.

How large the organization had grown from its humble beginnings, she thought, and how its benevolence had radiated outwards, embracing more and more people.

It was her mother, Efia, who had gone over to the Apostolic Church of Christ Our Saviour (ACCS), following in the footsteps of her elder sister, Sisi. In doing so, she had defied her husband, for once. Godfrey Dia had continued with Our Lady of the Rosary, the main Catholic Church in Kamorga, a frequent if not regular churchgoer.

One Sunday morning when Grace was ten years old her mother and aunt had taken her to the ACCS, which was not located in the business district at that time, but far, far away. Later she had learnt that the suburb was called Bulago.

They had driven in the spacious family Ambassador through crooked, bumpy streets without any trees or flowers, passing small, sorry-looking houses. Here people were all out in the street, the women cooking odourously on open fires, children running around, men sitting on rough wooden benches outside dingy shops, drinking. Teenage girls bearing babies on their hips, boys with caps pulled low over their eyes smoking and gathering in groups at street corners, someone bouncing a football, someone carrying a battered cricket bat. Grace watched, fascinated, her nose pressed to the car window.

Every now and then they would see families in more formal attire, walking single-file. Their cheap faded clothes were well washed and ironed. Grace was conscious of her lily white, starched, frilly dress with its pretty pink trim and pink bow. There were pink ribbons in her hair and she wore spotless white socks and shiny white shoes.

She thought that these people were going to church, for every so often they would pass one, though these churches were nothing like theirs, which was stone, with a steeple, a clamorous bell and a lovely statue of Mary with the infant Jesus in her arms, right up front.

These churches were plain brick structures, sometimes with a rude wooden cross-perched on their flat roof. Their names were written on a plywood board in crude letters, the board nailed to the front wall. They often had cardboard signs stuck to a window or a post, which said things like:

"Finding the Real Jesus: Life's Greatest Discovery!"
"Jesus has the power to break life controlling problems."
"To ignore our Creator is the height of folly."
"Church Is A Hospital For Sinners ... Not A Museum
    For Saints."

She was struck by these sayings, especially the last one; it seemed particularly edifying, suggesting that sinning was not unlike falling sick. It seemed to somehow push sinners up a notch and pull saints down from their lofty perches. It was an unusual idea, quite different from what the priest at their church had conveyed through his sermons.

As their car glided through Bulago, she looked at her mother and aunt for a sign of what was to come. They hadn't told her where they were going. Her aunt's eyes were closed, her lips moving silently in prayer. Her mother, on the other hand, was fully present to the world. She smiled at Grace and took her hand in her own. Grace nestled up to her, keeping her eyes fastened on the world outside the window.

The car took a turn and came to a halt on a stretch of land, a sudden opening in that densely packed area. A medium-sized wooden structure stood there, amid browning grass and droopy plants. Grace looked for a saying and spotted one: "God loves you when no one else will." How beautiful! That night she had written it down in her diary.

"The Pastor will see you now," a young woman, who had sidled up to her, whispered in her ear. Grace was startled. Where had she come from? Reluctantly, leaving behind that hallowed space, she made her way to the Pastor's spacious office.

"Grace," Pastor Martin came up to meet her and took her hand in a firm handshake. Soon they were both seated.

"We need your help. We have in mind a project for our youth. You're going to love this one!"

Grace rewarded the Pastor with her full attention.

"We want to start a cultural exchange program. Our youth will spend their summer holidays with ACCS families in Nigeria and Cameroon, while their children come here. They'll do community service and take part in church activities, of course, but we will also have classes. History, crafts; whatever our volunteers are ready to teach, they'll learn. We will house them in our boarding school. Most of the children will go home for holidays; the rooms will be free."

"You're right! I love it! We need to know each other directly, certainly the young. Too much of what happens here happens through foreigners. I can think of my own Nairi and Agnes benefiting from this."

"And your boys too, perhaps? Doesn't Joshua's niece live with you too?"

"Yes, Miriam does, since her parents moved up north."

Pastor Martin beamed. "I knew you'd get it right away. I want you to form a committee to take charge of the fundraising. What do you think?"

Grace nodded.

"Who else could we have gone to?" he said.

"We'll approach companies and individuals," Grace said. "Our European counterparts could chip in, if needed. Should we ask the parents for something?"

"Yes, definitely. Not the poorer families, of course."

"We should have started something like this in 1960! But it's never too late."

She was referring to the year when Kamorga became independent, a year when no less than 18 African countries sprang to freedom.

"How old were you then?" the Pastor asked, his eyes twinkling.

"Fourteen."

"Well, I'm glad we waited!"

They laughed; the Pastor's booming, echoing laugh lasted longer. They went on to discuss some of the details of the cultural exchange and who might be on the committee, before Grace said goodbye.

She stepped out of the building in high spirits. How glad she was to be with the ACCS! The rousing sermon of the diminutive pastor with a deep, compelling voice and the passionate singing had won her over on that very first day in that small church in Bulago. It had been packed; the atmosphere electric. She had not understood the sermon very well. For one thing, his Morga was quite different from hers. But she had grasped that the pastor believed every word that he uttered, and spoke straight from his heart. Never before had she felt so welcomed or so inspired.

And how freeing it was to belong to a Black church, not having to look up at a statue of Christ whose skin was painted white, hair golden and eyes blue. Did her father not see how absurd that was? How could he have ignored the importance of a church that didn't sidestep their traditions, but rather, integrated them with the Word of God? Perhaps he looked down on the ACCS merely because his younger wife had gone and done something of her own true will.

Going to church was a duty Godfrey Dia performed because society demanded it. But Grace needed a heroic church that called to her highest potential, making this call from the midst of a caring community that held together through thick and thin.

"Morning," Goodluck Ironsu said, rousing Grace from her thoughts.

"*Hoori. Kabari ani?*" Grace responded.

She was outside the Church now, facing an indistinguishable government building from which Ironsu had just emerged.

"What's the Pastor saying? You saw him, eh?" he asked.

"Oh, nothing special."

"So, good thing Peter got his way, isn't it?" He said with a smirk.

"What do you mean?"

"Come on, you know what I'm saying."

"I don't."

"Too bad! Sometimes it's good to get off the pedestal and look at the real world."

"What's he done? You have to tell me, Ironsu!"

"You could ask him. Meeting with the PM this afternoon. *Aaheri*, bye Grace."

Goodluck stepped into his car and the driver fired the engine.

Grace stood stock-still, staring at the vehicle as it moved on. What a hateful man! A real busybody.

She went on her way, her mood soured.

Peter's words came back to her: "She's been lying down with dogs, that Anjali, and she'll get up with fleas. She's chumming up with Fatimah, that Aanke woman, giving her all the wrong ideas. Agitating for land and whatnot."

"Really?"

"It's been going on for some time. Surprised you don't know."

"What do you mean?"

"I mean she's interfering in what's not her business. I think you should tell her to lay off. Yes, that's what you need to do. This is not her business."

Christ Almighty, what had Peter gone and done this time?

CHAPTER 21

Amadu's Wedding

"**S**HE'S SO BEAUTIFUL!" Anjali said.

And so she was.

Ebun sat on a low carved wooden chair in a fitting bodice and a full skirt that reached her ankles. Over her head, a masterpiece of elaborate braids piled high, was a transparent red veil, which fell in folds to her shoulders. A red hibiscus was pinned over her left ear. She wore large, white metal earrings, and a few necklaces, as well as bracelets, rings, armbands and anklets. Red and white dots marked her temples and chin. Her eyes were kohl rimmed.

Rahul too was staring at Ebun. "Mama, she looks kinda like Naomi Campbell," he said in awe.

"Once you taste pineapple you'll never go for any other fruit," Elizabeth said. Bending towards Anjali, she whispered: "Her bride price would have been very high, but given the situation of Fatimah's family, I expect it was deferred."

"Amadu's a catch too!" Anjali whispered.

"Of course. I believe Baaba Kaarya had the third highest status among the Aanke chiefs, and Abubakar would have a high rank as well."

Anjali smiled at the classification. Inevitably, there was a hierarchy among the Aanke.

They were in Abubakar's spacious compound. The space around the large hearth was sheltered from the sun by a white cloth canopy, while reed mats covered the ground. There were no fires burning here; the communal feast was being prepared in Fatimah's compound. Anjali guessed that there were about 200 guests, though only about 50 fitted under the awning. Anjali was hot in her heavy, silk *saree*. The numbers are about right for a small, Indian wedding, she thought.

"Can I take pictures?" Rahul asked.

"Only if you keep out of everyone's way," Anjali replied.

Rahul leapt to his feet and signalled Gabriel.

I wonder how Amadu courted Ebun, Anjali mused. This was an arranged marriage of sorts; courting would have to be formal and discreet. Her mother and grandmothers had had their marriages arranged, yet they were courted, she was sure, only after the wedding, not before. Perhaps that would also be true here.

As a student on a tight budget, Manish had courted her with samosas he bought at an Indian store that was not close to the campus. He also kept his fridge stocked with tamarind chutney. The tangy chutney, her favourite, had been the clincher. Anjali had returned again and again to his unkempt student pad that he had shared with two others. Jeremy had wooed her with tickets to the Opera and the Stratford Shakespeare Festival.

The wedding ritual got underway a little before noon. The musicians stopped playing as the groom was ushered in. Amadu, dressed in a white embroidered kaftan and a knitted red skullcap, had kohl rimmed eyes too, and white dots on his face. People moved aside so that Ebun and Amadu could stand facing each other in the middle of the space.

The bride and groom looked gravely at each other and bowed. Then they turned to the guests and executed a series of bows, taking a slow turn around themselves. Facing each other again, they moved slowly around in a small circular formation, bowing to each other, then standing still for a moment, then taking a small step to their right and bowing again, always face to face. Anjali knew that this was a Sufi way of greeting one another, and including God in that greeting.

After they had completed the circle, Amadu moved to Ebun's side and they bowed reverentially to Abubakar and Sabra. Abubakar and Sabra moved back and their place was taken by Lahmey and an old lady, who was dressed much like Fatimah. Masumi, Fatimah's mother is here, Anjali thought. It made sense that she would come down from the Highlands for her youngest child's marriage. They must all feel Baaba Kaarya's absence keenly today.

The familial bows completed, Amadu and Ebun were left standing in their midst, now man and wife. The drummer struck a single note. People closed their eyes, and holding up their arms, started praying silently. Some moved their lips. Anjali closed her eyes too and a prayer to Lord Ganesh, remover of obstacles, came to her.

When she looked around, many people were still praying; Elizabeth, Rahul and Gabriel had their eyes closed. She was touched to see that Rahul's hands had come together in a *namaste*. Neither she nor Manish had paid much attention to Rahul's spiritual upbringing, though Anjali celebrated the major Hindu festivals. Maybe he had learnt something from his grandmother, Manish's mother.

Minutes later, people were talking, laughing and embracing, and the musicians started playing a happy tune. Elizabeth, Anjali, Rahul and Gabriel joined an informal queue and started moving towards the couple.

"Do you know what they are thinking when they bow?" Elizabeth said. "They see each other as creatures of light. Lovely, isn't it? There was another ritual last night. Everyone went to Yasa Madafi's shrine and lit candles, and prayed and sang together,"

The beauty of the chaste wedding ritual had brought Anjali the kind of peace and joy she rarely experienced. She hoped she would feel as good at her own wedding, their wedding, her and Jeremy's. They too would have a simple ceremony.

Soon they were greeting the couple, giving them gifts. Anjali introduced Gabriel to Amadu, Ebun and Fatimah, who was now standing next to them. Bending down, Fatimah addressed welcoming remarks to him; Gabriel blushed with pleasure.

Nathan and Julie joined them for the feast that followed. They all sat on the ground on the reed mats and ate off reed plates.

"I'd like to talk to Masumi," Anjali said to Elizabeth, who was sitting next to her.

"I'll go with you."

"Seems that the position of Aanke women isn't so bad," Anjali said to her in a whisper.

"In the past the Aanke used to be matrilineal, I think," Elizabeth whispered back. "Maybe that's why. You know they have polygamy, though not in Fatimah's family for some reason. And it is less common with the younger generation."

Anjali had been surprised at the number of middle-class, Muslim men in Venimeli who had second wives. As for the Christians, it was common for them to go straight to bars after work, and flirt with women there, or have a fling. Then there were the sugar daddies who lured girls as young as their daughters with gifts and money. Teenage pregnancy was high; some non-profit organizations were fighting for pregnant girls to continue in school. It was common, especially in rural Kamorga, to expel them from school when they got pregnant. Anjali had noticed that many of the African women she knew in international development were divorced. She was happy with the seemingly equal relationship between Elizabeth and Kamau.

The guests began to disperse after lunch and Gabriel and Rahul ran off to play with Jelani and some other boys, while Anjali and Elizabeth sat down with Fatimah and Masumi. Masumi smiled mightily at Anjali. She is so charismatic, Anjali thought. Fatimah introduced them to her brother-in-law, Oluwe, the husband of her eldest sister, who had accompanied his mother-in-law to Madafi from the Northwestern Highlands.

Masumi seized Anjali's hand, and reached out for Elizabeth with the other. Then she spoke in Bisseau.

"She says thank you very much for all your effort to get us land. She prays every day that we meet with success," Fatimah said, translating into Morga.

Masumi continued in Bisseau, with Fatimah translating. Things were not going well in the Northwestern Highlands, they learnt. Good land was mostly all taken, and the land that the Aanke had managed to secure to found Alfajiri was not very good. It was also not near other Aanke villages, so they could not count on that support as much as they had hoped to. More young men had left to work in Georgetown or Meseri, towns that were the transport hubs for minerals since colonial times. After independence, other industry had also developed there.

Fatimah had not told them all this.

"I believe that one day all the Aanke from Ferun will be united again, working the same land together, close at hand here, close to Yasa Madafi's sacred shrine," Anjali said, surprised that she had rendered all this in fluent Morga.

Fatimah took her mother's hand as she translated this, and Masumi bowed her head low. Anjali found herself silently praying: "Lord Ganesh, please give Aanke the gift of land."

Amadu came by just then. "You staying for the dancing, huh?" he said to Anjali.

"Luckily I am."

Giving her a thumbs up, he walked away.

Nathan had a meeting in Venimeli the next day. He and Julie would drive Rahul, Gabriel and Elizabeth back to Venimeli. Anjali had driven down in a rented jeep and decided to stay overnight at Nathan's house and go directly to the field office the next morning to finish her research.

CHAPTER 22

The Fence

ANJALI SURVEYED THE room with satisfaction. When she had first walked in, months ago, she was confronted with stacks of crumbling, warped-looking cardboard boxes, lined up against the walls. Here was a graveyard (or was it just a retirement home?) for files starting in 1981, the year that Frank Maier had started HELP, inaugurating the head-office in Toronto, and setting up HELP's first international office in Venimeli.

All the paperwork was dumped in Makaenga because the field office had more space. Inside the boxes sat faded folders containing yellowing sheets of paper held together with rusty staples; the moth eaten ones had made her gag. There were minutes of meetings, memos, evaluation reports—draft, interim and final; annual reports, concept and position papers, proposals, planning documents, correspondence between the three African offices, as well as correspondence between Venimeli and Toronto.

Earlier attempts at classification had been sporadic, at best, and the room contained not only paperwork, but all sorts of junk, including discarded and broken down equipment

—typewriters, fax machines, paper punches, a never used paper shredder. On her first visits Anjali had methodically sorted, classified and cleaned up.

She was proud to have tamed that chaos, and the report of her findings was nearly done. She would feed it to a local consultant who would interview Anne and the local staff and write the final version.

She was going to miss the research work—going carefully through the files, photocopying relevant sections, taking meticulous notes; then reading, writing and analyzing. She didn't have to deal with people problems, only with unsystematized data that would yield a set of conclusions after careful consideration. The process had given her an insight into what had worked over the past years, and what needed to change.

No wonder Hassan relished being an academic!

An image of their last meeting flashed though her mind: their fingers intertwined, his lips on her hand.

She had set up a meeting with him to discuss the IDP Committee. Overall, the Committee was working out well, and they already had a rough draft of the IDP policy, which everyone needed to read and comment on. Getting agreement on the exact wording was going to be tricky. That was always the case. She had hoped that Hassan would be able to provide some tips on generating consensus. She also wanted his opinion on the draft policy.

All through lunch there was a distinct undertone of intimacy, but neither had said anything. After the meal he had driven her back to the office and parked at the mouth of the lane. They had chatted a bit, not wanting to part just as yet.

Anjali was assailed by a sudden, sharp longing for him.

She had looked away, but not fast enough, for he lay his large, dark, hand caressingly over hers. Their fingers danced, then held fast. He bent down, passionately kissing the back of her hand. She pulled it quickly away, a shock running through her, going right down to her toes and to the top of her head. Their hands belonged once again only to themselves. Or did they? She felt her skin tingling under the imprint of his lips, would feel his lips on her skin for some time.

"Let's go out again, Anju, please," he said huskily.

She opened the door and got out, without speaking, without looking at him, and walked away. The devil! That's why he had not parked in front of the office gate but a little distance away. But who was she to blame him? Wasn't she, after all, being devilishly provocative?

Last night, after the wonderful communal dancing at Madafi, she had lain in the guest room of Nathan and Julie's house, drenched in longing. How she had missed him! She had almost called Hassan at two in the morning. But the moment of madness had passed. They had taken to calling each other more often; talking at random, unable to say what they really wanted to say, unable to stop calling.

What was she going to do? It couldn't go on like this; they had to stop; she had to make them stop. Somehow.

Anjali headed towards the HELP canteen for lunch. She was a bit tired, and quite hungry.

Soon she was passing the primary school, the walls decorated with anatomically correct illustrations of human organs—heart, lungs and brain; a map of Kamorga, and portraits of the Fathers of the Nation. Other schools she had seen also used their walls to edify their students. They served a purpose in a country where textbooks were hard to come by.

Then came the kindergarten, endearing, with its red tiles and a crude mural of children playing amid a landscape of flowers and butterflies. The local artist who had done it was not a master of proportion or human form, but his optimistic vision added a touch of gaiety to the surroundings.

Anjali was tempted to look in on the children, but she was running late. Nothing was as gratifying as seeing those small, upturned faces, sunflower-like, bright eyes against black skin, shy smiles, eyelids momentarily tilting down, then lifting up again. After all, it was images of children, thin and ragged in one photograph, healthy and happy in the next, that had caused Westerners to reach deep into their pockets.

At least the adoption is going well, she mused. The Kamorgans, Elizabeth and Hassan included, were in favour of the adoption, and her mother had called to say that she believed it was the right thing to do; she was looking forward to seeing Gabriel.

Following Father Emmanuel's advice, Anjali had applied for the legal guardianship of Gabriel. Katherine Grey at the Canadian High Commission had been very helpful as well. There had been a ton of paperwork; but what was paperwork to Anjali? She lived and breathed paperwork!

All the same, she was a little worried about Gabriel; he seemed out of sorts these days. He avoided looking directly at her, whereas in the past he had always held her gaze. What had not changed was the reading. If anything, he seemed to devour even more books. Nothing had changed between Rahul and Gabriel; they continued to play together. This reassured her somewhat.

Well, they're both dealing with big issues, she thought. If only they would speak to her about them! She could not discuss any of this with Mary; Mary, who was plainly losing her strength day by day. She longed to speak with Martha, even though it was Martha who had asked the toughest questions about the adoption. But when they met they were never alone. So she had ended up confiding in Hassan instead.

"Anjali!" She heard pattering feet. Turning, she saw Jelani running towards her.

"*Kabari ani*?" she said automatically as he got to her.

"There is trouble. Fatimah is waiting for you," he said gravely.

Oh my god, something is very wrong, she thought. Her Morga lessons had included some cultural notes; you never said, "there is trouble" unless the situation was dire.

She hurried after Jelani to the entrance of the HELP compound to find Fatimah standing by the gate.

"Come quick. Use the car," she said.

"What happened? Where are we going?"

Taking her arm, Fatimah guided her firmly to the car. She gave directions when they were all seated. As the car rolled forward, Fatimah said: "Earlier today a man from Madafi was cycling by the land, our land. He saw men there, six men, who were putting up a fence. He went up and saw that there was a large board on the ground that said: 'Tizilale Cooperative Farm.' He asked what was going on. The men weren't too friendly, but they told him they were working for a company in Venimeli."

"No!" Anjali said.

"The man asked for the name of the company. They wouldn't tell him. He sat down with one of the men, shared a cigarette, and they talked. The company is Radius Properties."

"Radius Properties?"

"Yes. When the man came and told us all this, Amadu got really angry. He said he was going to break the fence down. He is on his way there, with a few of our men."

"What about Masumi? Abubakar?"

"My mother, Abubakar and Lahmey went early this morning to meet a relative who lives a little out of town."

"And Amadu wouldn't listen to you?"

"No! I've never seen him like this. He also ignored other elders who told him to stop being foolish."

"Do you know what's going on?"

"We've never heard of this Cooperative or this company. Have you?"

"No."

Anjali focussed on driving; she had driven on such rough terrain only a couple of times before, and not that recently. And certainly not in a rented car. It was a jeep, but still.

Such misfortune in the wake of such a lovely wedding! Poor Amadu! She hoped the community would not cast a superstitious eye on the turn of events, perhaps blaming the bride for what happened.

A little ahead, Fatimah asked her to get off the dust track and drive through the bush.

She's kidding, this car can't make it! Anjali thought, but she kept driving.

The jeep shuddered horribly but did not stall. It was a sturdy German make. Anjali felt anxious all the same. Mercifully, they did not have to go far before they saw a group of men armed with long spears. Anjali drove right up to them. The car stopped with a thud. As they got out, the men turned around.

"*Kabari ani*?" Anjali addressed Amadu, moving towards him.

He merely shook his head.

"Tell me what happened, please," she said softly.

Amadu blazed with words. He repeated everything Fatimah had already told her, then continued: "First they took our land from us. Such fertile land, you can never imagine how fertile it was! We didn't want to move; they forced us. We thought they would give us money; they pretended they were buying our land. It's not a lot of money for them. It's nothing. But they have denied us everything. It gets worse every day. How long can we keep still? Why should we do so? It is the end of peace and the beginning of war."

The man standing next to Amadu nodded. Anjali noticed that he wore a belt that had a short knife tucked into a sheath.

"You are absolutely right to be furious, Amadu," Anjali said. "It's too much. With the government you have only known injustice and bad faith." She looked around at the men; they were eight in all. "But how will breaking the fence help? The government has the police, the army, on their side, don't they?"

"It won't help in the long run, we know that. But we must teach them a lesson. The other way hasn't worked."

"There is yet another way—the law courts," Anjali said.

Amadu snorted; some of the men laughed. "As if we would ever win! The law is not on our side."

"But look, you're not attacking the real enemy, but some poor men the enemy has hired to work for him." Amadu shifted from foot to foot. "Let's first find out who is behind this, and let's go after them."

"How can we know?" one of the men asked.

"You know that Elizabeth's husband, Kamau, works at the *Kamorga Times*? He is a good journalist and he could find out who owns Radius Properties, what is this Tizilale Cooperative."

The men started talking among themselves in Bisseau.

Anjali waited for the voices to die down. Then she said: "And that is not all. Kamau works with Milton Saneo, who's the best investigative journalist in Kamorga. He writes in Morga too, not just English, doesn't he? Amadu, you must have read him."

Amadu nodded. The men started talking among themselves again.

Meanwhile, Fatimah came and stood shoulder to shoulder with Anjali and addressed the men in Bisseau.

"That's all very well," Amadu said. "We need to find out who is really behind all this, but we want to show him right now that he can't just spit on us."

More loud, excited talk in Bisseau followed.

Anjali stepped still closer to the group.

"Look, so far your women and children have been safe. They only put Amadu in prison. Yes, I am sure that was the work of the same person. But if you break the fence you'll all go to prison. God knows how long they'll keep you, and under what conditions. They may also pick up other young men from Madafi. In fact I'm sure they will. The most dangerous part is that they will come to Madafi. They will come into your homes. It's important to keep them out of Madafi, don't you think?"

She had played her master card; Amadu's expression changed. There was more talk; but she knew she had won the day. Fatimah looked gratefully at her, then stepped amidst the men and said something.

They talked among themselves for 15 minutes. Anjali stood straight and tall, looking from one to the other. She was ready to grab Amadu's spear if it came to that. Things were not going to get any worse. There was not going to be any head-on confrontation. They just had to return to Madafi, peaceably.

Finally Amadu turned to her. "You're going to talk to Kamau? When?"

"I am going to drive back to Venimeli, go straight to the office and get hold of Elizabeth. That's what I'm going to do. She'll know how to get hold of Kamau at once."

They turned in the other direction then and started walking, still talking loudly among themselves. Fatimah stayed behind with Anjali; Jelani followed the men.

How had she managed to come up with so much Morga, Anjali wondered. But she had! She had suddenly become fluent in a language that she had struggled with all these months! Frank Maier had been so right to insist that HELP field staff had to speak the local language.

CHAPTER 23

An Education Interrupted

DRIVING SLOWLY, CAREFULLY, she took Fatimah back to Madafi.

"We'll get to the bottom of all this, Fatimah. I promise we will."

Fatimah said nothing. She sat with her head bowed. Anjali had never seen her like this—depleted and dispirited.

"No children," Fatimah said suddenly.

"Fatimah!"

Anjali knew that Fatimah and Lahmey had recently undergone a fertility screening at the clinic.

Fatimah remained silent.

"Look, it's going to turn out right. We're not going to give up, OK?"

Fatimah looked at her then and nodded. "Yes," she said mechanically. "Mandi mana."

They drove the rest of the way in silence. When they reached Madafi, Anjali asked: "You think things may flare up again?"

"I don't think so. Masumi, Abubukar and Lahmey will be back soon."

Anjali could not see even the volatile Amadu defying out-right his regal mother, nor Abubakar, whose happy-go-lucky style had real authority behind it .

"Lahmey almost never speaks out; but when he does, everyone listens," Fatimah said.

Anjali nodded. "I think it's better if Masumi stays for a few days," she said.

"She was planning to."

Anjali took Fatimah's hand. "However long the night, dawn will break," she said. She did not usually remember lo-cal proverbs, but this time she did.

"It's going to be all right, I think," Fatimah said slowly, as if she was coming out of a daze.

"Courage!" Anjali said. She held up her fist.

Fatimah smiled faintly. That will have to do for now, Anjali thought.

Back on the road to Venimeli, Anjali was, once again, in Vishwas Bhau Colony.

There had been 23 women enrolled in the literacy class that she and Vandana taught; fifteen of them always at-tended. There were two other classes like theirs, with other volunteer teachers. Gangu *bai*, Radha *bai*, Aruna *bai*, Chhaya *bai*, Viju *bai*, Rupa *bai*, Manda *bai*, Parvati *bai*, Medha *bai*. She tried to remember the others. Anandi *bai*—large, che-rubic and happy-go-lucky as her name suggested. And the two young sisters, Sindhu and Narmada, both named after rivers, one so shy it was hard to get her to say anything at all, and the other very serious, who had started keeping a jour-nal, writing in a large, childish scrawl.

They were all at different levels. Some had two or three years of schooling but were not literate. And others whose skills had rusted from disuse. Some had never seen a blackboard in their life. They came sometimes with a baby or a younger child, bringing with them a chipped slate and chalk, a half-torn exercise book, a chewed up pencil and a stub of an eraser. Anjali suspected they had taken these things from their school-going children. She asked Indumati for money so she could get them proper supplies. They usually brought something for Anjali and Vandana to eat—*rava laddus, kanda bhajias.*

A student would suddenly disappear, without warning, for weeks on end.

"*Gavala geli aahe.* She's gone to the village," they would say, and no more, as if that explained everything. Why had she gone away, where exactly, and when would she return, no one told them. Nor did they ask. The gone-to-the-village women returned with food for Anjali and Vandana—a giant jackfruit or a bag of fragrant rice. In their village, their brothers, sisters, parents, relatives, someone in their family, cultivated a small piece of land. Anjali had been struck by this, this link they all seemed to have to a village, to land. She envied them for it.

"I can't believe they're giving us all this," Vandana said to her. "Should we take it? Do you think it's right? They're so poor."

They had told them not to give them anything, but the women refused to take no for an answer.

"They're generous," Anjali said. "I think they'd feel insulted if we refused. I guess they are kind of paying us back."

They took the gifts back to Sakhu bai, who smiled knowingly and turned them into delicious dishes.

The women also enjoyed teasing them, saying that they needed to stock up for their weddings, telling them there were many eligible bachelors to choose from in the Colony.

Anjali would find out later when she started working in international development that the poor were less calculating than the middle-class, more spontaneously giving.

When Anjali tried to picture the villages that the women were so drawn to, a recurrent image came to her—a field, and a plough pulled by an ox, with a farmer in a white *dhoti*, a long piece of cloth twisted into a turban on his head, walking behind, a stick in his hand to keep the ox in line. The landscape behind him remained indistinct.

Bombay was an illusion of sorts, albeit a very strong one. Just behind this seaport lay a hinterland—vast, dry, dusty. Their home state, Maharashtra. Anjali and Vandana were always conscious of "the village," though they had never actually been to one. When they complained about the monsoon—the torrential rain, the damp, the mould, the mud, the overflowing gutters, their grandmother shushed them. "It's good for crops. Good for farmers. Don't curse the rain. Thank God."

There was always the village somewhere in their consciousness, the village with its fields, crops and food.

"*Lagne bigna nantar kara,*" Gangu bai said to them one day. "*Changle shika ani jaagaat kahi tari karun dakhwa.*" Get married later. Study well and do something worthwhile in the world.

How proud Gangu bai had been because she could sign her name!

"Soon you'll be able to do much more than that," Vandana had said.

But Gangu bai went around telling everyone over and over that she could now write her name, pulling out a piece of paper tucked into her *saree* blouse as proof of her prowess.

Anjali could imagine her lined up for a service, or a government handout. When her turn came, the woman behind the desk would incline her head towards the inkwell, indicating that she put a thumbprint on a piece of paper. But Gangu bai would toss her head and ask for a pen, signing off, with a flourish. How grand she would look as she made this gesture, this gesture that made her practically as good as the lady behind the desk: the one in charge, the one in power.

After the demolition of Vishwas Bhau Colony, Indumati's friend, who had started the literacy project, wanted to take action against the municipality. She wanted to get the organizations working for slum dwellers and their rights involved. She wanted justice done for the Colony residents. Indumati, who was Head of Department at the prestigious Tata Institute of Social Sciences by then, had provided her friend with contacts and suggestions. The friend had tried, called this person and that, but nothing had come of it. She had decided against a court challenge, saying she did not have the energy for a long drawn out legal process.

Meanwhile, the women, men and children of Vishwas Bhau Colony had dispersed, and a few months later, the land was bought by a developer.

Anjali had written a letter to *The Times of India*, chronicling the demolition, talking about the literacy project, urging for the recognition of slum dwellers' right to land, to the houses they had built with their own hands. It had been published. She had preserved a copy in a folder, along with other articles about slums, land rights, corruption in the construction industry.

Some more time had passed, then an apartment complex had risen confidently on the grave of Vishwas Bhau Colony.

Study hard and do something worthwhile in the world,

Gangu bai had said. Anjali was going to join the Indian Administrative Service; Vandana would work in the villages as a doctor.

Since then, the rumblings of the demolition had become a distant echo, and their lives had taken a different turn. A chance meeting with a professor from the University of Toronto at a conference in Bombay, as an undergraduate, student volunteer, had ultimately brought Anjali to Canada, on a scholarship.

The rumblings of the demolition had receded, but the stark reality of dispossession and the lessons learnt remained potent. Moving to Kamorga had brought Vishwas Bhau Colony back in sharp focus. She had joined HELP because it catered to basic needs, providing access to education, health and vocational training. Without these fundamentals, what hope was there for the poor? It was uphill even when they had these, but at least they had a chance of improving their lives.

Non-profit organizations treated poor people like human beings. They believed that they lacked opportunity, not ability, while the rest of the world just passed them by. Or worse, exploited them.

Basic Needs. Land was a basic need for a farmer.

Who had snatched their land away from them? Not the government this time. But someone powerful and filthy. She was going to ferret him out, with Kamau and Milton's help.

When Anjali got back to the Venimeli office, Elizabeth had news for her. Mathew had called. Anne's mother had passed away and she would be heading back to Kamorga the following week.

CHAPTER 24

Combustion

FOUR DAYS LATER, Kamau had news.

"He'll meet us today at Mama Penda's for lunch," Elizabeth told Anjali at work that morning.

"Wow, already! He's fast!"

"It's Milton who works fast."

"What did Kamau say? Will Milton meet us too?

"Milton's too busy. Kamau won't tell me anything. He fancies himself as Sherlock Holmes, or something." Elizabeth rolled her eyes.

Anjali laughed. It felt good to laugh; she hadn't done that for a while.

At 1 o'clock the three of them were seated at Mama Penda's.

"Crime leaves a trail like a water beetle," Kamau said, grinning. He looked very pleased with himself. "You were right, Anjali. There is no Tizilale Cooperative, at least not any more. There used to be one, it's registered and all that. But it hasn't really worked for about 10 years."

Kamau paused.

"There is a Radius Properties, and it's a little known subsidy of Peter Dia Associates."

Anjali saw Elizabeth start up.

"Peter," Kamau took a dramatic pause, "is Grace's younger brother. He has a number of businesses, including real estate."

"No way!" Anjali said.

"And guess where the Tizilale Cooperative used to be when it did exist? In a village not that far from here. Grace's father Godfrey had a lot of land there. It's his ancestral village. Most of that land's been sold off now. Peter knew about the Cooperative, obviously, and decided to use it for his own ends."

"So Grace knows all this!" Anjali burst out.

"Not necessarily. Peter's her darling brother; she dotes on him. Radius Properties led us to Dia, but not easily. The connection is not direct. The Cooperative we traced to Semparu, that's Godfrey Dia's village. And our source in the Ministry of Agriculture said that Tizilale Cooperative had put in a proposal under the Cooperative Land Distribution Scheme, and it had been sanctioned."

"Do you know when he sent the proposal?" Anjali asked.

"Our source could not give an exact date."

"I'm sure it went in after our proposal!"

"Very likely."

The waitress brought a plate of plantain curry rice for Anjali. It was the only vegetarian item on the menu, so they didn't ask her what she wanted when she came here. She took the order for the other two.

"What did the proposal say, exactly what?"

"It said that the 78 families that formed the Tizilale Cooperative would start a commercial farming venture on that land. Part of the land would be used to grow hops for export. That's where Radius Properties comes in. They have the export connections. It said that the farmers in this Cooperative were very poor and the land they presently cultivated was badly degraded."

"Hops? That's original. I thought you can't grow them in the tropics!" Anjali said.

Kamau shrugged. "It's a scam—rich developer like Peter getting land cheap to do commercial farming, then exporting the crop. Or maybe he will grow something else there. Who's going to check?"

"It's disgusting," Anjali said.

"That's true, but that's how it is. My editor says we can't run the story, at least not right now. This is hardly the first time Peter's played dirty. He's a dangerous guy. He's hired toughs to beat people up, and even got a couple of men killed, they say."

Anjali stared incredulously at Kamau. "And Grace doesn't know all this?"

"Peter's a good liar, and Grace wants to believe him, so she believes him. That's my theory."

"Couple of years ago it was Peter's 35th birthday and Grace hosted a grand party," Elizabeth said.

"It's possible that Peter will come under fire one of these days," Kamau said. "He'll step on the wrong toes. That would be our chance to get this story out. Milton's excited about other possible misuses of the Cooperative Land Distribution Scheme. He had an idea that not every proposal approved was clean. But we thought they had left it alone, more or less. It's so high profile. He thinks it's worth looking at all the proposals that have gone through."

"If we hired a lawyer and gave him all the information we could go to court and get the land back. It would be a long process, but worthwhile," Anjali said.

"Not a good idea. Peter's too dangerous, and given his connections, most people would want to stay away," Kamau said.

"We can't just let it be!"

"Maybe take it up with someone high up at the Ministry of Agriculture, or go to the Cabinet, if possible. Though I doubt we can change anything. Who knows who's in his pay? This kind of thing is better settled out of court. Like I said, Peter is very well connected and he can play dirty. Very dirty."

"What about Grace's husband, Joshua?" Anjali asked.

Kamau looked puzzled.

"He's an MP," Anjali said. "And isn't he the General Secretary of the People's Democratic Union? If he is involved, we could threaten to expose him, couldn't we?"

Kamau shrugged. "Nice in theory, but he has a pretty clean rep. As far as these things go. When he was younger he even did some human rights work. He's a lawyer by training. I think he stays away from Peter. Most people do."

Anjali said nothing.

"I'm afraid this is the end of the line," he said, looking uncomfortable. "Milton will investigate, there's no stopping him. If he uncovers other misuses of the Scheme, we will run the story, or even a series. Peter may get exposed then. But the land in Makaenga, the Aanke land, I think that's over."

Anjali opened her mouth to speak, and closed it again. For a while they ate silently, Anjali picking at her food.

"Milton should look at how people who apply for the Scheme get the Land Certificate. That wasn't easy for us at all," she said.

The Land Certificate used existing land surveys and other government documents to provide details of a particular piece of land—size, exact geographic location including latitude and longitude, main features, current land ownership and availability, and an estimated land price. This was specialized and expensive information, but according to the Cooperative Land Distribution Scheme, it had to be provided free of charge by the relevant rural municipality. Their application had got delayed because it had taken so long to get the Certificate. Julie had used a contact she had in the Makaenga Municipality, through one of her expat friends, to finally reel it in.

"I don't know how you got it without paying anything," Elizabeth said.

"Not that it did any good," Anjali responded dryly.

"Fatimah can write another proposal. Thanks to you she knows how to do it," Elizabeth said.

It's nice of Eliza to boost my ego, Anjali thought. But it's no use. Their efforts had come to nothing. She was too stunned to say anything more.

When they parted, she thanked Kamau profusely.

"I wish we could nail the son-of-a-bitch," Kamau said. "But ..."

"I understand. You have to live here, and Peter's dangerous. I would not want any harm to come to you or Elizabeth. Or Milton."

"Milton's a crazy man. He will come to harm, one of these days. He's done all those exposes on the mining industry. There's more than one person out there who wants him silenced. We've been telling him to get out of here, go abroad and do a Masters or something, but he won't listen."

Anjali nodded, only half listening. Kamau hopped on his scooter and took off, and she and Elizabeth started walking back to the office.

Anjali saw Vishnu's figure slumped against the crumbling wall. No, it must not happen again. They could not give up without a fight. She would speak to Grace; she would confront her. Grace must know about this. She may have led Peter to the land. She seemed to have something against the Aanke from the start. She had opposed giving them regular status as HELP beneficiaries. Maybe it wasn't tribal rivalry; maybe it was something else. I must find out what she knows, Anjali thought. We cannot have a Board Chair with such an unsavoury alliance.

But even if she was clean, as Kamau seemed to think, Grace needed to know what was going on, what her brother had done.

They were now in the foyer. Nailed to the wall here was a wooden board, with several hooks, and dangling from them were various keys. Pausing, Anjali took the office car key off its hook. Elizabeth had gone a couple of steps further and turned to see where she was.

"Where are you going?" she asked as she saw Anjali at the front door.

"To see Grace," Anjali said over her shoulder as she hurried to the car.

There was a moment's silence, then Elizabeth followed her: "Wait! Don't go!" she called out urgently.

Anjali was already out of the front gate. Kibwe was nowhere in sight. She got into the car and fired the ignition. The car purred and jumped forward.

Before she knew it she was on the main road and going in the general direction of Masakeni. She drove single-mindedly, hardly conscious of the fact that she was driving through disorganized city traffic. She was not nervous and she had forgotten that her International Driving License wasn't with her.

When she got to the edge of Masakeni she would pull up on the side and take out a book of addresses that was kept in the glove compartment. Grace's address would be there.

She had to ask for directions in Masakeni, but it was not too hard to get to Grace's house. There was a low wall around it and a doorman sitting outside a wrought-iron gate. Anjali parked outside.

"I've come to see Grace," she said to the doorman in Morga.

"Madam is not at home."

"I'll wait. She's expecting me."

This was good; she had some time. She needed to think through what exactly she would say; how she could get Grace to spill the beans. Grace was forthright; that was one thing that could be said in her favour. But she was obviously not rational when it came to her brother. Still she had a sense of what was right and wrong. Perhaps Anjali would be able to leverage that to her advantage.

The doorman had led her up a long driveway, through a veranda, into a large sitting room.

"You wait here?" he asked in English.

"Yes, *mandi mana*," she said.

She paused before a worn lion skin nailed to the white-washed wall. There were spears, shields, rifles and a well-stuffed rhino head. She couldn't take her eyes off it.

A woman dressed in a colourful print dress appeared with a tray in hand. On it was a glass of water.

"*Mandi mana*," Anjali said, accepting it gratefully. She hadn't realized that she was very thirsty.

"Tea, cold drink?" the woman enquired.

"*Nigiyo*, no," she said.

The woman left. It seemed that the doorman had told her she'd come to see Grace.

Anjali was surprised that no one seemed to be around. The children? In any case it would be better to see Grace alone.

Her eyes went back to the rhino head. What a powerful beast, she thought, and it had ended up here, stuffed up, on someone's wall. She felt very awake, every part of her felt alive.

The first thing was to understand Grace's role, take in what she was willing to reveal. That was what she hoped to accomplish that day. After that she would bring pressure on her to get the land released. Here she would need advice from all her friends. She would do whatever string pulling she needed to do. No one was invincible; Grace had a reputation to protect.

She sat there for a while, and her mind went strangely quiet. She wasn't sure what the time was when she heard the sound of an engine. Through the window she saw that a car had appeared at the gate. It wasn't Grace's Nissan Sentra, nor was it the HELP van. Getting up, Anjali went to the door.

The driver parked the car half way up the drive, a little on the side, and got out. Anjali saw him in profile—tall, large and ... there was a slight resemblance to Grace, and he was younger than her. Anjali's heart started beating faster.

"Hello," she said, striding up to him. "Peter? Are you Peter Dia?"

She had come right up to him before he noticed her. He surveyed her from head to toe. He had a close shaven head and was powerfully built; he reminded her of the rhino. The expression in his hooded eyes, under thick eyebrows, was not friendly.

"Yes?" he said coolly.

"I am Anjali. Anjali Bhave Bhagat." She felt stupid, awkward, as he looked on impassively. "Acting Executive Director of HELP."

He looked her up and down again, scornfully, managing to demean her. She realized that the afternoon sun was quite fierce. She wanted to wear her sunglasses, but that would not do.

"What do you want?" he said gruffly.

"I came to see Grace. But I have business with you too."

"What business?"

"I know that there is no Tizilale Cooperative," she said.

Suddenly he went as cold as an alligator. Anjali felt an involuntary shiver. "I don't know what you are saying," he said. He made as if he was going to walk up the path but she would not stand aside.

"You do know what I am saying. You pulled a fraud, Peter. And you'll have to answer for it." Anjali folded her arms in front of her and looked him full in his face.

Anger flashed through his eyes. For a moment she thought he was going to hit her. She prepared to duck, but he did not. Instead he said: "What are you doing here?"

"I came to see Grace. I told you."

"What are you doing here, in Kamorga? Why did you come here?"

"I told you who I am."

"HELP. Director, HELP," he said contemptuously.

"Yes, exactly."

"Why you build somebody else's place while yours is falling down? Why you don't run your own place, huh? Like the other one did?"

"I've been doing my work, if that's what you mean. This is my work too. Land is a basic need for farmers. And HELP's mandate is fulfilling basic needs. The Aanke need land and they applied for it under the Cooperative Scheme ..."

He interrupted her with a loud laugh. Then he took a step forward, forcing her to take one back. She would feel his malevolence now, his sheer force, bearing down on her.

"What do you know about the Aanke? The Aanke were just people in the bush. They didn't know anything. My people come from Sudan. There the Aanke worked on our land. They were like our slaves. We gave them work, we gave them food. We gave them everything, you understand? Otherwise they'd have died. Now they want land. But it's not their land. It is not their land." He pronounced the last sentence with great emphasis.

"This is not Sudan. And this is 1991. Whose land is it then? Yours?"

Peter shook his head.

"A stranger has big eyes but sees nothing. You read books written by white men, and you think you know everything. You study in some university in America and think you can come here and tell us what to do. You understand nothing, Anjali, nothing. Why are you here? Go back. Go back to Canada. Go back to India. Go!" His voice was low and menacing.

"And if I don't, and expose you instead?" she said, her eyes flashing.

"This is not your country. This is Kamorga. Funny things happen here. People can do magic, strong magic. One day a boy is good. Next day he is sick, very sick. Sometimes he can even die."

"What?" said Anjali, her heart roaring in her ears. "What are you ..."

"Get out. You're not needed here. Think about your family and get out. While you can." He turned around and went up the driveway, into the house.

Anjali stood, rooted to the ground, staring after Peter. Then she hurried to the car and started driving. She felt shaky, her confidence to negotiate the roads on her own gone. She thought of parking the car somewhere and taking a taxi. She longed to get out of the car. But no, she must drive on, and reach the American International School of Kamorga.

The American International School of Kamorga. The destination provided purpose, and she seized it. Concentrating on driving, she refused to be distracted by her panicked, racing thoughts.

Soon after entering Jamesville she spied a public call centre. She called Esther and told her that she would not be coming in; she was unwell. Then she asked for Elizabeth and told her she would call her that evening.

"Are you all right?" Elizabeth asked.

"Yes fine, thanks," she said, and hung up.

She got back into the car and drove towards Rahul's school. She was going to pick her baby up and bring him home.

Through the difficult, early months in Kamorga when Rahul had practically stopped speaking to her and had eyes only for the Gameboy, there was one scene that she went back to, again and again.

Rahul was four, bundled up in a red and navy blue winter coat, a red toque and a blue scarf. She had taken him to High Park that day. They had gone for a walk and were on their way home, going towards the car park, when it started snowing. Picture perfect snowflakes drifted lazily down from the sky; some paused, levitating, before they fell to the ground—the season's first snow!

Rahul stopped in his tracks, his face transformed with wonder. Anjali watched, her heart so tender that even a snowflake could have left a mark. Rahul stuck out his tongue. He stood still, patient. Time passed. The snowflakes slowly swirled; none landed, till suddenly, one alighted on his tongue. Turning towards her, he gurgled with joy. Anjali collapsed on the ground next to him and took him in her arms, kissing, murmuring endearments. When she released him he stuck out his tongue again. Kneeling beside him, Anjali did the same. Nothing happened. Then, suddenly, a snowflake alighted on her tongue. Oh, how light its touch! Barely perceptible! But there was a little cold tingle when it landed.

As a child she had believed in fairies; waited at the window, eyes closed, for a gossamer wing tip to brush against her cheek. She closed her eyes and felt another flake land, and melt, slowly, teasingly. When she opened her eyes she saw Rahul lying back, content, the snow accumulating on his clothes and face. She scooped him up and they made their way home, to drink hot chocolate, sitting by the kitchen window, still entranced by the falling snow.

How could so much hope spring from such a small source?

Back home, with Rahul safely ensconced in his room, Anjali was taken over by massive rage. How dare Peter threaten and intimidate her! Bastard! He just had to be exposed; he couldn't be allowed to get away. Not this time. Not again. The people in Vishwas Bhau Colony had lost everything, and the very same thing was going to happen to the Aanke.

But the anger was also personal. The hatred that gnawed at her gut demanded revenge. She pictured him lined up before a firing squad.

She didn't just want him stopped. Merely humiliated. Thoroughly punished. She wanted him dead.

CHAPTER 25

Collision

THEY SAT UNDER the ragtag blue plastic awning, Anjali and Fatimah. Fatimah and Anjali. Feeza's three-month-old slumbered in Fatimah's lap. At least she has her grandchildren to comfort her, Anjali thought.

It was Saturday afternoon, and Anjali had driven up to Madafi by herself, in the office car. They had had a couple of exchanges on the phone since their last meeting. Fatimah knew everything, including that Peter had threatened Anjali. She had said that the Aanke would have a community meeting to decide what to do next.

Anjali was here to find out what had happened. She hoped, had in fact convinced herself, that the community would decide to take legal action. But as they sat together, talking, she wasn't getting a straight answer from Fatimah.

Anjali had talked to Nathan and Julie, Hassan, Martha and Richard, and Jeremy. The advice from everyone was the same—she should not take Peter on. A legal battle would take months, likely years, and result in Peter's victory. As for talking to Grace, they didn't believe that would accomplish anything either. The government had granted the land to the Tizilale Cooperative and they weren't about to take it back and admit that there had been a mistake. Who knew what strings Peter had pulled? Anjali should be careful and leave the country at the earliest, that had been Martha, Nathan and Jeremy's advice. Anne had come back a couple of days ago; they had not had time to talk properly yet, though she knew about the loss of the land.

"You won't be here for long!" Fatimah said suddenly.

"I'm not tempted to linger. I have a month and half left in my contract, but Mathew is OK if I return sooner. The hand-over won't take time. And with Father Emmanuel's contacts, Gabriel's papers are being processed fast. They will courier them to me when they're done and I can start the Canadian process. We've also applied for Gabriel's passport."

Fatimah nodded approvingly.

"But what do you want to do, Fatimah? What do the Aanke want to do?"

Fatimah looked away. Fussing with the baby's clothes, she said: "We want to do another proposal. We are looking for land. Margaret Aguwe, you remember the officer who was handling our file?"

"You've talked about her."

"I went to see her. She told me we should try again."

"And you trust her?"

Fatimah said nothing.

"I suppose it's worth trying," Anjali said guardedly. "But if you're not here ..."

"But I'm not going tomorrow! And Nathan and Julie could help you. Just show them the copy of our proposal."

"We have found some land in the Northwestern High-lands, not that far from Alfajiri, that may be good. We had so many problems in Alfajiri that we had stopped thinking about

having land there. But most of our people are there. Abubakar and Amadu will go soon to look at the land."

"Why not?" Anjali said.

"It won't be as good as the land here but it'll be OK. Even
if we don't get new land, we will move there. We can to do
something in Alfajiri, but nothing here." She held her Tawiz
for a moment.

She did not tell Anjali that they wanted to go back to a
rural setting as soon as possible because they were afraid of
the adverse effects of urban ways on the young, especially
the young men. Instead she started giving Anjali news about
various family members. Anjali listened with half an ear. So
this was it? It was over? Just like that? She expected a discussion, an attempt to analyze what had happened, expressions
of regret, words that brought closure.

"Please come for lunch before you leave Kamorga," Fatimah was saying. "With Rahul and Gabriel."

"Sure."

She accompanied Anjali to the car. Hawa came with
them, carrying Anjali's purse.

"You're going back so soon!" Hawa said mournfully.

Despite her disorientation, Anjali was touched. "It always
feels like that. Time passes fast. But I'll be back for Gabriel."

As she drove away, the sense of unreality that had taken
hold of her began to loosen its grip, gradually, to be replaced
by regret, and a touch of anger. Did her sole value lie in writing proposals? Fatimah should have been sympathetic about
Peter's threats, much more sympathetic!

They don't want to antagonize the government because
they hope to get another piece of land through the Cooperative Scheme, Anjali thought. That's why they don't want to go

the legal route. And they want to move to the Highlands as soon as they can. So why was she thirsting to start a legal process? Didn't she owe it to Rahul and to Jeremy to return to Canada as soon as she could? Owe it to herself as well?

Peter was right about one thing: she had not really understood Kamorga. The barriers were strong—not thick walls but obfuscating veils. She lacked cultural understanding, something that Anne had, even though she was a foreigner. But then, Anne had been in Kamorga ten long years; Anjali had been around for less than one.

Africa was 11,657,000 square miles of land, she had read somewhere. Land, land and more land, stretching in all directions, from the dust track on which she was driving to infinity.

So much land and yet all this land hunger, a bottomless need that had always been there. India, Canada, Kamorga—everywhere the same thirst for land and the same practice of getting hold of it through any means possible, hoarding it, wrenching it away, denying it to needy people.

In Bombay they had reclaimed land back from the sea, dredged it from salt marshes, but there still hadn't been enough. Millions slept under the sky every night, still others under plastic stretched over poles. But even those cardboard and tin huts were razed to the ground, poles wrenched from under the plastic awning, lives callously tossed asunder.

In North America there had been the greatest land grab in history. An entire continent, inhabited, seen as "empty land" and taken over: unfair treaties signed with the natives, treaties signed and ignored, no treaties signed at all, the original inhabitants of the land put on reserves, their children shoved into residential schools and barred from speaking their mother tongue and practicing their ways; abused. The horror! The absolute, incredible, palpable horror of it, the fallout everywhere—native men begging on the street, lying drunk, native children sniffing glue, native women turning to prostitution and drugs, "disappearing," native men filling North American jails.

In Africa, the colonial powers had come and gone, but their legacy shone bright. And African politicians often carried on with the exploitation. People without a roof over their head or a way to earn a living. People without basic services —water, toilets, public transport, electricity—to speak nothing of healthcare and education. People driven away from their traditional lands, working as labourers on someone's export-oriented farm, or in a mine whose wealth ended up abroad.

And on that vast surface crawled tiny worker ants who were yoked to a non-profit organization of one kind or another. CBOs—Community Based Organizations, charities— linked to religious groups or otherwise, organizations spun from trusts, organizations linked to universities and other institutions; cooperatives, collectives, coalitions and networks; NGOs—non-government organizations, organizations that were the vision of one courageous and caring person, family or community—local or foreign. Drops in an ocean of need. These organizations were not infallible, forced to categorize people into regulars and irregulars, like HELP. Helping some while ignoring others, from lack of funds, mostly. Some were corrupt, some wrong-headed, others merely inefficient. But nearly all of them were well intentioned.

Made up of people who ferried a speck of sugar or a grain of rice from one place to another, who tried to move mountains by digging molehills. People she admired. People she could relate to, whom she preferred vastly to the cynics and "despairers" who threw up their hands and said—there was no alternative. Nothing could ever change, nothing would, life would only get worse and worse. Hence there was no use trying. The world was a nasty, brutish place, and so be it.

If you tried, at least you felt that you had not lived in vain.

Mary had tried too. She had acted. Secured a future for Gabriel, despite the limitations of her situation.

Anjali imagined the land stretching, folding, rising; forming mountains and drying out into deserts. The mighty Sahara wasn't that far off. Land covered by forest and crisscrossed by rivers, enlivened by savannah and fertile, flood plains, trampled by humans since the time when homo sapiens first emerged, to become a species always on the move, restless, questing. But for all their wandering people wanted to attach themselves securely to a piece of land and call it their own. Own it forever and pass it down to their children and grandchildren.

It wasn't so bad, this need to build a home, create a garden, to have a speck of dirt on the planet to call one's own. How attached she was to Anne's garden in Venimeli! What was reprehensible was the need for more. More. More. The immense greed that pushed the prices up and up, and market manipulations that sent them into a tailspin. The fact that some people went to any length to have that land, crushing lives, regarding others as less than the earthworms that silently till the soil.

She had come face-to-face with that naked greed and power and disregard for human life for the first time, when she had stood before Peter. His contempt had burnt through her skin, had found her internal organs and squeezed them. She was a pawn he would have trampled if she stood in his way.

She was used to dealing with abstractions—feudalism, patriarchy, big government; globalization, neoliberal policies, corporate control. She had studied what the oppressive weight of these forces had done, was still doing, to people, and to their world. She had read innumerable reports and sat through countless conferences where well-dressed professionals had explained how these forces had twisted the lives and broken the hopes of the poor, of people at the margins, as they were called. She had met some of the "victims," transformed into "stakeholders" by development projects.

But it was the very first time that these forces had assumed human form—become a figure that threatened her directly, palpably. She had not entirely crumbled under that gaze, but it had shaken her. She had come to realize how puny she was, how limited her resources, particularly here in a country not her own. Her colleagues and family and friends had pointed out her powerlessness. What a chorus of middle-class cowardice she had encountered!

Cowardice or practicality?

There was certainly a strong message there to save one's own skin, and that of one's progeny. There was consensus that she put her tail between her legs and flee. Fatimah and the Aanke too had gone along with this idea. No wonder then that these unjust systems persisted and grew stronger.

But could she blame these subsistence farmers for not going to battle? People with much more power had acquiesced all too easily.

Would my situation be different if I had crossed paths with the mafia in Canada or goondas, underworld thugs, in

Bombay, Anjali wondered. She would surely have been able to do something about it, though once you left that narrow strip where the rule of law held sway; the criminal wilderness that confronted you was the same anywhere, more or less. The zone, the grey area, between civil and uncivil was thin indeed.

For a moment she was back in the brick enclosure at Vishwas Bhau Colony, white plastic sheets stretched across the exposed parts to keep the rain from lashing in. It hammered against them, as they all sat close together, in the centre of the shed. Instead of dictation, which they had planned on earlier, she and Vandana had given the women a writing exercise. They were hard at it, their heads bent over their exercise books. Anjali was a bit cold. Her damp clothes clung to her. Despite the umbrella she had come with, the pelting Bombay rain going in all directions at once had got her. She looked at Vandana. Her sister smiled. Sliding closer, she put her arms around Anjali.

Suddenly she wanted to go home. She ached to see Jeremy. To be with Vandana. Maybe her time here was done after all.

Soon Anjali was traversing the barren stretch of land that she used to dread. She had driven through it without unease this morning. All she had felt was awe at its strange, desolate beauty.

Maybe one of the reasons Fatimah seemed to take it all so calmly was her faith? Suddenly Anjali was jealous. Faith could be a bedrock; she had heard that somewhere. Fatimah had faith and she had community. Despite being uprooted from her home, she was buffered by her faith and supported by her community. I have neither, she thought. In moving here I lost my friends, my family, my colleagues. And my faith in international development is not as strong as it used to be. I don't have anything solid to hold on to.

A large truck loomed large in her rear view mirror. She had noticed it following her for some time, at a distance. It was the first time she had seen this kind of truck on this road. It had speeded up, and in what seemed like seconds, it was bearing down on her, hooting its horn.

What the hell, she thought, there was place for it to pass. She waved her hand to signal that the driver could go ahead. She could not actually see him because the chassis was high, and her back window and the truck's front window were both dusty.

The truck hooted again and came so close that it must have scratched her fender. Anjali's heart started to beat hard and her grip on the steering wheel tightened. She sped up; so did the truck. The car was bumping now; the speed she was using on the dust track was far from ideal. He was still right behind her, far too close for comfort.

Should she swerve to the other side of the road? But she didn't really have the space to do that. Not unless he backed off, at least a little. What the hell was going on?

She felt a rude bump, metal hitting metal. The car rocked. He was actually trying to run her down!

Anjali swerved hard so that her car was off the road, skidding down the slight slope at high speed, headed straight for some bushes. She swerved again, managing to avoid them, and the car shuddered to a halt, her head banging on the steering wheel. Her vision blurred for a moment, then cleared. Her left temple started throbbing.

Looking back, she did not see the truck. Was it gone? Shit, she hadn't got the number!

Reaching for her water bottle, she drank greedily, spilling some water on her shirt.

She turned the key. The engine spluttered, then died. Anjali put away the water, her mouth dry. Her hands gripped the steering wheel again. She tried to restart the car with the same result.

She sat still for a few moments, then she opened the door and got out. She walked around the car, examining the tyres, testing them with her feet. They were OK. The back fender had a dent. Everything else seemed OK.

She got back into the driver seat and pulled the lever to open the hood. Perhaps the car just needed to cool off. There was a bit of water in the bottle; maybe she should check if the water in the car needed a refill. Then again, if she had to walk ...

If she had to walk! She got out of the car and leaned her head against the open hood, breathing in the dust and metal and grease. If there was something wrong with the engine she would not be able to fix it.

If she had to walk, was it better to go backwards or forwards? She closed her eyes and pictured the road. It seemed to her that she should walk backwards.

Anjali got into the car again. She tried the engine. It spluttered to life and then stalled. She got out of the car and shut the hood. She got back in to get her purse, hat and sunglasses. With the door open, for the heck of it, she started the car again. This time the engine kept running.

She shut the door and engaged the gear. Slowly, carefully, she took a wide turn. Moving into higher gear, she managed to gain the road. She decided to keep going in the direction of Venimeli. Huts would appear in 15-20 minutes and if the engine stalled further on there would be a village where she could stop for help.

She was trembling now, now that she might be safe. She wanted desperately to play the Kishori Amonkar tape but decided against any extra moves. Better not tax the battery. All thoughts left her; there was only the steering wheel, the road, and the determination to get to the end of it.

CHAPTER 26

Either Or

ANNE GREETED HER from the veranda when Anjali got
back home.

"Hey, I'm home for dinner today. And you?"

Anjali nodded.

"What happened?" Anne got up from her chair, looking
concerned.

"Tired. Just back from Madafi."

"You look shot. Want to take a nap?"

Anjali hesitated.

"I can pick Rahul up. Happy to," Anne said.

Anjali handed Anne the keys. "Thanks. The car seems a
bit off. Someone bumped me while I was at a traffic light."

"Oh no! I'll have it looked at too."

Giving Anne a grateful smile, Anjali escaped upstairs
and climbed into bed. When she woke up, she took a shower
and came down. Anne and Rahul were both home and ready
for dinner.

They talked about baseball over dinner, allowing Anjali
to make a slow recovery. Peter had tried to kill her! No, he
had probably wanted to give her a big scare. She had no doubt

that it was his doing. He was keeping track of her movements. It wouldn't be that hard for him to set one of his trucks after her. That said, he'd have had to act fast. Kamau had listed his businesses and trucking, she remembered, was one of them. What a pity she hadn't got the number!

All through the journey back to Venimeli her focus had been on the car. Would it keep running? When she made it to the outskirts of the city, the adrenaline had drained from her to be replaced by a deep fatigue. That short drive back to Jamesville and home had been the most challenging part of the whole ordeal. She still felt a little tired but her brain was ticking away again.

After dinner, Rahul and Gabriel set up their books on the dinning table to do homework.

"They are so sweet together! I am so glad Gabriel will be a Canadian soon," Anne said.

They sat out on the veranda. Anjali was happy to let Anne talk about her mother's last days and some of the changes at the Toronto office.

"Had lunch with Grace today," Anne said.

"Did she say anything? About me helping Fatimah?" Anjali asked at once.

"No, but Mathew gave me her letter complaining about it. You know she wrote him."

"And?"

"He said he'd ignore it, unless she took it up again. But she didn't."

"He certainly hasn't said anything to me."

"Such a pity that things went badly between Grace and you. I don't know what happened."

Anjali didn't say anything.

"Grace can be demanding," Anne said.

"The worst thing was that she would undo everything I did," Anjali said.

"With me she always wanted to talk and give advice, and that I didn't mind."

"You were already at HELP when she joined the Board, so it must have been different. Guess I made mistakes, though I don't know what they are."

"Frankly, I was surprised when I heard that you had taken up Fatimah's case so seriously."

"Why surprised? The Aanke lost everything. That's why I wanted them to have land."

"It's very hard, Anjali. It really is. I do understand how you felt. But you know HELP's mandate. It's not within our power to give them land. If you had taken Grace in your confidence from the start, it may perhaps have gone differently."

"Oh no, I think it would've been worse. The same thing happened in India, in Canada. People lost their land. It happened everywhere. In Vishwas Bhau Colony too. I've told you about that."

"It was wonderful, how you volunteered in India. But it's not up to us to give the Aanke land."

"We can just hand out band aids, right?"

"I wouldn't say that. We give people an opportunity to educate their kids, learn a trade, become healthier. That's something."

"And when we leave?"

"Who's going away? We're going to stay. I know I am."

"What we're doing is good, but it's not enough."

"You're right. But it's a hell of a lot better than nothing."

"But the land ..."

"There are social movements forming, labour movements, actions led by civil society networks. They may give people land."

"Fatimah needed help writing that proposal."

"I know you thought of it as just giving some information and advice. No big deal. But it's not seen that way here. If they feel we're interfering, this government, all these African governments, they won't let us stay."

"I thought I was following HELP's mandate."

"And you're right there as well. But the Cooperative Land Distribution Scheme is a government scheme. They're very proud of it. A HELP employee pushing it, even indirectly, would be seen as a problem. Rigid, old fashioned and paternalistic—but there it is."

"I think Grace's objections were more personal. She called Fatimah and Amadu names for no good reason."

"Oh?"

"Is there an enmity between the Kakwa and the Aanke?"

"Could be. The ethnic groups here are not fighting outright, but they do have prejudices, sometimes strong ones."

"Remember how Grace never wanted the Aanke to have cards at the Makaenga clinic?"

"Only too well. She is such a stickler for rules, like a headmistress in so many ways. She does not think of them as IDPs. And strictly speaking, they're not."

"If she is so rule-oriented, it's strange that she turns a blind eye on her brother's activities, don't you think?"

"You mean Peter. Yeah, he's something else. Look, I'm not defending her or anything. I'm just trying to explain how your work with Fatimah could be seen here."

"Yes, I see that a bit better now. Though I don't agree with that point of view."

They sky had assumed darker hues and a large cloud, grey rimmed, was in plain view.

"This garden is such a blessing," Anjali said suddenly.

"I love it. And I'm glad you got to enjoy it. I worked in my mother's garden. She used to be such a keen gardener. It helped me to pull out the weeds. Mother would sit at the window and just look out at the garden for hours. I think it helped her too. I can never thank you enough for agreeing to come here."

"I am so glad it worked out like that. Guess I messed up too."

"Don't make too much of it. You did very well. You ran the office efficiently. Held that IDP committee together and now the policy is almost done. Those committees are like herding cats! You got Hassan to do that Iberu evaluation and wrote that proposal. We'll get the funding for the project extension; I'm sure of that. And you cleaned up that mess in Makaenga. I have wanted to make some sense of all that paperwork for years. Your situation was really challenging. I am so thankful you managed so well."

"Thanks, Anne. I am looking forward to the complete Lessons Learnt report. We should devote a day to it when we meet in Bangladesh."

"Yeah, makes sense. I think your past came back to haunt you. I've been in this business for over 25 years and all kinds of things have come up."

The past isn't just in the past, Anjali thought. It's right here in the present. The past would always interfere. The women from Vishwas Bhau Colony would always be with her. Vishnu would always be with her. That's why she worried for Gabriel. She hoped he would be able to make a tolerable life in Canada, even as Kamorga lived on in him, perhaps making unreasonable demands.

"You don't know the whole story, Anne," Anjali said.

Then she told her about the confrontation she had had with Peter and the threat he had issued, and how the truck had tailed her and forced her off the road.

Anne drew a sharp breath.

"Oh my god, that's all so horrible!"

"I don't think it was his intention to kill me; just scare me half to death."

"Peter's tracking your movements! We must go to a security company first thing tomorrow. Hire a bodyguard. You have confirmed flights, right?"

"Not yet. But we have tickets they're holding for next week."

"And you're going to confirm them tomorrow morning?"

"I think so, though ..."

"You're not planning to stay! Not after all this!"

"I guess not. No need for security and all that though."

"I don't know. This is very serious. I am so sorry, Anjali. Ohh! It shouldn't have come out this way."

"I'm safe now."

"Thank god for that! I'm going to talk to Grace. I had no idea things were so bad. But I'm going to talk to her only after you and Rahul are safely out of here. If Peter's willing to go so far, then she needs to know about it."

"He's just a big bully. Wish I could take him to court."

"He's going to go too far one of these days. People like that usually do."

"That's what Kamau said, that he'll step on the wrong toes."

"Exactly."

"What do you think Grace will do?'

"Who knows? I think it's going to be a wake-up call. A serious one."

Anjali didn't say anything.

"I hope you're going to continue working for us," Anne said.

"Oh, I'll continue for sure, at least for some time. But I feel I have a lot of questions. Don't you have any doubts at all, at least sometimes?"

"I used to, a lot, but not any more. I'm far away now from those academic discussions about aid. I see the need here and I want to respond. I think we're learning all the time and trying to apply what we learn. We're helping advocates, feeding them information, even though we don't advocate directly ourselves. So in that sense we're involved in policy change. Perhaps the most important thing is that we bring new ideas; I'd go so far as to say new inspiration."

"You're wise, Anne."

"I don't know. I do know that I don't believe in heroics. Single-handedly slaying the dragon and all that sort of a thing. Makes for a good story, but it's not a good way to bring change. Real, lasting change. You have to try and tame the dragon, little by little, somehow. And you have to do it with other people, lots of other people and organizations, not alone."

"Back in the car I was thinking of NGOs as worker ants transporting a grain of rice from one place to another."

"A good analogy. Though there are innovators among our ranks too, and human rights defenders, and people who expose some of the outright vile stuff."

"Yes there are."

"You know those women you taught as a volunteer? You always regretted that they could not continue their studies, and how they lost their homes. There's tragedy there, and real injustice, but even what you managed to do must have had some positive impact on their lives."

Anjali considered the idea. Then she said: "Actually, I believe that too."

CHAPTER 27

Café Lafayette

ANJALI WAS GLAD that Hassan was late; it gave her some time to compose herself.

She was waiting for him at Café Lafayette, on the terrace, charmingly lit by the stars and the yellowish light that spilled out of the interconnecting doors and windows. The night was warm, and utterly gorgeous. The fountain on the lakefront was working, water cascading heavenwards, then rippling down, down, the light spreading translucently on the water. Around that effervescence, Lake Mathilda was enveloped in a dark, velvety void.

We reach out, stretching our hands towards the sky, and then we fall down, down, Anjali thought. Sometimes we collapse into a nerveless heap and almost disappear. But somehow we don't. With our last shred of determination, we gather up the scattered bits and pieces, patch ourselves together, and try once again. She felt awed by this commonplace yet remarkable human reality.

It was sometime in the late 1820s that Christoph Sommer, a German explorer, had crashed through the dense jungle to reach the shore of Lake Mathilda, right around here. No one seemed to know what the lake was called at that time, though it must have had a name. Christoph had reached a piece of inhabited land. The lake, teeming with fish, and the fertile land around it, supported a small indigenous population.

Anjali imagines Christoph, a gangly white guy, bush-scarred, hairy, accompanied by a posse of men, pitch black and smooth skinned. Suddenly, they are upon this immense body of water, shimmering in sunlight. What a sight it must have been to Christoph's fatigued eyes, to everyone's fatigued eyes—a benediction, a blue marvel stretching to the horizon.

Who else could have led him through the wilderness but his guides, people with local knowledge? Yet these people would not have been from the immediate vicinity, and could they have, perhaps, not known the name of the lake? Impossible! Such a large body of water would not only be named; it would have been the stuff of myths and legends. Its fame would have travelled over large distances; its existence known to many.

Christoph energetically strips off his clothes and jumps without ceremony into the embracing waters. Yippee, he must have said, how refreshing this is, this life-giving water, this bountiful inland sea. Here I will pitch my tent and rest awhile.

When Christoph emerged from the lake, he had already named it. He called it Mathilda, after his wife whom he had left behind in Hamburg or Dusseldorf or Berlin, someplace like that. The balmy waters had welcomed him and enfolded him in their arms, not unlike his wallflower wife left behind at home while he adventured. (But perhaps she was not so passive a creature after all, even though history had made no mention for her.)

Incredible, the eagerness of explorers to name places, as

if they have no former history, no claims, no ties. Whoopee, I name you East Africa Protectorate, you Capetown, you Central African Empire, you French Sudan, you Kenya Colony, you Spanish Sahara, you Upper Volta, you Lake Mathilda. I name you all, without fear or favour, for now and for all of eternity.

This is the point, the exact moment, where Anjali's anger about colonial arrogance turns to bewilderment. How could they have claimed land just like that? How? How could they have inscribed their own names on it with such impunity? White Man's burden, spreading God's Word, a search for gold, for spices, for loot, for Eldorado—she is familiar with all the theories, but she just doesn't get it.

Lake Mathilda—a name that had stuck. But how was it that right here on its shores, she had never learnt the earlier stories about this lake, didn't know its ancient name? Why was it the colonial version that had stuck, like a barnacle welded to a rock?

All the same, I admire you, Christoph, she thought. I can't help it. You, and others like you. You who braved malaria and leeches, the darkness of African nights, the density of her forests, the utter void of her vastness. You who trusted fate as much as the natives, and stumbled on through bush and bog and river and grassland to get here, and there, and everywhere. You who dreamt, and dared.

Hassan believed that one had to take a firm stand for or against the oppressor; a view that did not allow for grey areas. *But I am taking sides, Hassan, I am. Against the kind of oppression that leads to the obliteration of that other story, of those other stories.*

She felt a movement and turned to see him making his way to the table. Smiling, he sat down. They sat looking at each other, and did not speak until he had ordered a drink. She already had a glass of white wine before her, untouched.

"How are you?" she asked.

"Not bad. Marking exams. And you?"

"Winding up, or is that winding down?"

The waiter brought Hassan a beer.

"Look, I wanted to say something," she said. She drew a breath. "I care about you, Hassan, but I can't do anything about it. I hope ... I mean, I hope I didn't give the wrong impression ... I know I let myself be carried away, of course I find you attractive, but ..."

He had been looking keenly at her. Now his shoulders relaxed and he said: "That's one of the things I really like about you—your honesty."

"Am I honest?'

"Oh yes, you are."

Anjali remained silent.

"I am glad you spoke. It means a lot to me that you care a bit," he said.

"But you know that! You know I care a lot!"

He touched his hand to his heart. "I liked you on the very first day, at that little reception at HELP."

Anjali flushed.

"You didn't say anything," she said. She had noticed him right away too.

"I made some inquiries. Found out you had a boyfriend. And you mentioned Jeremy. I think it was when we had our second conversation."

"I don't remember that."

"I enjoyed our night out so much. And I'm happy we are here."

How little time they had had together. She looked at him openly, with longing. She wanted to melt into him, just as she had done out in the desert, in her dream, as he sat there, making love to her with his eyes.

Then they both looked away. Anjali focussed on the dark, still waters of the lake; he toyed with the menu.

"You've had dinner?" She had told him on the phone that she would see him after dinner.

"Not yet. What's good here?"

She had an image of his life as a bachelor, a little disorderly, but free.

"So many things. All the fish dishes especially. That's what Martha says."

He called the waiter and placed his order. Turning to her he said: "I remember what you were wearing on that first day. It was this long, white shirt, so light, so elegant."

"*Kurta*. It's called a *kurta*."

"You looked lovely, and serene."

Serene! She recalled how she had been when she first got here, hopeful and confident. But it was Hassan she wanted to talk about.

"Were you ever ... I mean, did you ..."

"Did I fall in love? Did I marry?"

"Yes." She looked gratefully at him.

"Yes, and yes."

He fell silent and reached for a potato chip.

"I met her when I was doing my studies at the University of Ghana. She was from South Africa. It was first love for both of us, so intense. Blotted out everything else. She followed me here. Not right away, but a year later. But it didn't work out. I have never really figured out why."

"It can be quite mysterious."

"Yes. I mean look at this. Someone my age, falling once again."

Anjali put her glass down.

"You're not that old!"

"Forty, that's old here."

He was four years older than her, and five years younger than Jeremy.

"You are not old," Anjali said emphatically. "Someone like you never is, because you're always growing and learning."

"Thank you. That's kind," he said. He held up his glass and she extended hers. The gesture lightened the atmosphere.

"And after her, the South African woman?"

"Her name was Hannah. Well, that didn't end right away. There was some back and forth for a few years. Then nothing much happened. I met a few women but no thunder and lightning. Then I turned 35 and decided to get married. Someone I had known a long time. Yvonne. We were distantly related. She was very young, just 25. Had finished her studies and was working as a secretary."

She had not expected this. It sounded like an arranged marriage.

"Guess you were lonely."

"Think I was. I was busy at the University. Was consulting as well. There was family pressure, though I could have resisted that. What I really wanted was to be a father. And I wanted to settle down, as they say."

He gave a short, dry laugh. Anjali felt a pang.

"But that's understandable," she said.

"I don't know, but that's what happened. We were happy enough. She was a lovely person, kind and gentle. She got pregnant and ..."

He stopped, a catch in his voice. Her hand reached her lips, nervously.

"She died in a car accident. Hit and run."

She seized his hand, so warm and alive, which had been idling on the table. This was too much; such good people dying so young—Mary, Yvonne. She wanted nothing more than to keep holding his hand, but she let it go.

"I am sorry," she said. "This is really terrible. I didn't mean ..."

"It's okay. You didn't know, and I wanted you to know."

They stayed and talked till the café closed, trying to convey all that had been meaningful in their lives in a handful of hours. She talked about Vishwas Bhau Colony and her life in India and then Canada. He described the horrors he had witnessed in the mining areas up north, how the companies didn't give a damn about the miners and how the government sided with them, allowed miners to flaunt all the laws. But Mahamud Siyahi, the youthful, fearless leader of the Mine Workers Front, a fantastic orator and a savvy negotiator and organiser, had given him hope that change would come. Their conversation was a complex symphony, now surging into wide, sweeping circles, now narrowing down to a point.

It was past midnight when he drove her the short distance home.

She turned towards him and said: "I'll miss you, back home."

"At least you'll be safe."

She was about to get out when he said: "I have something for you."

It was a little brooch, shaped like a bird on a branch, made of silver and ebony, the strong black wood that is native to West Africa.

"It was my mother's," he said. "My sisters got all the jewellery, except a couple of pieces."

"She's no more?"

He nodded.

She looked at the brooch that lay in his open palm.

"How did you know I love birds?"

"You told me about the crow," he said.

She hesitated, wondering if she should accept it; after all, it was an heirloom. She looked into his eyes and found there a confirmation.

"It really is for you," he said softly.

Then she was in his arms.

If she raised her head and they kissed, all would be lost.

Or perhaps, everything would be gained?

That night, afloat on her high, four-poster bed, she grounded herself by weeping for all the losses—too many to count, but not too many to mourn.

CHAPTER 28

The Snake

"**W**HEN WE LEFT Ferun my mother made a *Tawiz* for each and every one in the community," Fatimah said. "She filled them with the sacred earth of Ferun. I have made these with blessed earth from the shrine of Shaikh Misfar Yasa Madafi. They will protect you from harm."

Anjali's took in the shallow, wooden bowl that Hawa was holding out to Fatimah. In it were three necklaces, coiled like little snakes—one for Rahul, one for Gabriel, and one for her. They consisted of a little metal cylinder on a black cord. Anjali knew the *Tawiz* from India, amulets that typically had Koranic verses on a small piece of paper inside them. She liked Fatimah's animist twist on the original.

They came up one by one so Fatimah could put a *Tawiz* ceremoniously around their necks.

She is Masumi's daughter all right, thought Anjali. She has already assumed her father's mantle, and she will assume her mother's as well when Masumi passes away.

Rahul and Gabriel received their *Tawiz* gravely, bowing to Fatimah. Anjali was the last in line. She bowed as well. Then they embraced. Anjali could smell Fatimah's sweat, mixed with some kind of perfume, possibly amber. She would always associate that smell of labour, earthiness, coupled with adornment, with her.

This was the official farewell. Anjali had driven up that Sunday morning in the office van with Anne and the boys, with Kibwe at the wheel. Anne had insisted that they could not go alone. She was visiting Nathan and Julie while they enjoyed their feast at Fatimah's.

And a real feast it was! Everyone in the two compounds had been invited: Bisa, Abubakar, Sabra, Abubakar's second wife and their two teenage boys, an elder sister of Ebun who was visiting with her two children, Ebun herself, Lahmey, Amadu, Arza, Feeza and their children, and Hawa and Jelani.

On their arrival, Fatimah had greeted them with some good news.

"Nine families have got compensation!" she had cried out as soon as she had spotted Anjali coming in through the gate.

"How? When?" Anjali asked, advancing towards her.

"It came through last week. Two families here got the money, and seven in Alfajiri. And they are saying that we will all get the money soon."

Anjali wondered if this was a post land grab attempt to pacify and contain the Aanke. Too much conspiracy theory? Could a lumbering, uncoordinated beast that is a government department act so strategically? Perhaps it was just the usual case of one hand giveth while the other taketh away.

"I told Nathan," Fatimah said. "He wanted to call you. But I said, wait, she's coming soon. I want to tell her myself."

"How many families are still to get the money?"

"So 9 families now and 8 before, 17 out of 42; 25 still remain."

Anjali nodded.

"If we get the compensation in time, then Amadu will not come to the Highlands. He will stay here and sell chicken and eggs. *Inshallah,* god willing."

Anjali recalled Amadu telling her about starting a poultry business. When Anjali had first got here, he had been taking a course in small business development at the HELP Training Centre in Makaenga.

"*Inshallah,*" Anjali echoed.

Having ingested the good news, and a too large lunch, a Tawiz secure around her neck, the boys playing somewhere out of the compound, Anjali lingered with Fatimah and Bisa under the familiar blue awning. Bisa was half dozing, and Fatimah was quiet, smiling every so often.

Soon Anjali asked Hawa for a strong cup of bush tea. She had to rouse herself and get going. Their next stop was Nathan and Julie's house to pick Anne up, before heading back.

Suddenly Bisa seized Anjali's hands and heaped blessings on her in old-fashioned Morga, her voice quavering with age. Anjali did not get much of what she said, but she was very moved. Bisa took her leave and started walking, slowly, painfully, towards her hut. Anjali watched her go, feeling sad. Perhaps Bisa would not be here when she returned to Kamorga to fetch Gabriel.

Fatimah sent Hawa to look for Jelani and the two boys, and she came back with Jelani and Rahul. Rahul looked around the compound and turned to Anjali,

"Where's Gabriel?" he asked.

"What do you mean? He was with you."

"We were trying to get some mangoes from this tree. Gabriel was there and then he wasn't there," Rahul said.

Anjali stared disbelievingly at Rahul.

"I mean ... I thought he had come back here. To read or something," said Rahul, colouring up.

"I'm sure he is not far. On his way here he must have met someone and started chatting," Fatimah said.

An unlikely hypothesis, thought Anjali. Gabriel wasn't the type to start conversations with strangers. She recalled that he had been unusually subdued today.

"Maybe he is sitting under a tree somewhere, reading," she said.

"But he didn't have a book with him," Rahul said.

"Go look for him," Fatimah told Hawa and Jelani. "And call out his name. Loudly."

As they turned to go, Rahul started after them.

"You stay right here," Anjali said sharply.

Rahul sat down under the awning, looking sulky. He took his Game Boy out of his pocket and held it in his hand. Why was Anjali blaming him?

Suddenly Peter's words raced through Anjali's mind: "Funny things ... strong magic ... boy is good ... sick, very sick."

Maybe Peter's men had taken Gabriel away! They were not far, guarding the fenced land. The three hearths, framed against the outline of the Men's House, blurred before Anjali's eyes. She sat down heavily on the mat, her mouth dry, her palms sweaty. She should have left the country at once instead of putting Gabriel at risk! And Rahul too!

Rahul looked at her, concerned. Fatimah, who had been watching, called out to Arza to get a glass of water. She sat down beside Anjali and put her hand on her shoulder.

"We'll find him. Where could he have gone? Not far," she said, touching her *Tawiz*.

Anjali touched her own too. The blinding panic was passing; Anjali could clearly see Fatimah's face, lined with tiny beads of sweat. Her own armpits felt damp; her body limp. The kidnapping idea was ridiculous! Peter would know that they were leaving Kamorga soon. There was a farewell party at HELP on Wednesday. He had defeated Anjali. He knew that. He probably knew the exact flight they were going to take. And yet ... a snake circled her consciousness, looking for a hole through which it could enter, and strike. Wasn't Peter venomous enough to take revenge anyhow?

Ten minutes later Hawa and Jelani were back, without Gabriel.

Fatimah went immediately into action. She sent Jelani to call Amadu, Abubakar, Ebun and Ebun's sister from the compound next door. She asked Hawa to get her father who was resting in the Men's House. She told Arza that she was needed and that Feeza should stay behind in the compound. Three search teams had been organized in short order and they set off in different directions. Anjali went with Fatimah and Amadu, Rahul with Lahmey and Hawa.

Lahmey lead them past the granary and into a stretch of fields with a few plants and trees. Rahul noticed the stubbles of some crop that the Aanke had grown and harvested. The sun beat down, bleaching out most of the colour from the arid landscape. He lingered under the shade of a tree, feeling guilty for not keeping better track of Gabriel, and he was resentful: how could he have just gone off like that, without a word? It was so unlike Gabriel. Could he have ... been bitten by a snake, or something? Rahul shuddered. He could be lying somewhere, poisoned, dying!

He touched his Tawiz. Then he started running, unmindful

of the heat, not caring where Lahmey and Hawa were. Soon he was no longer on a path. He was moving fast, trying to rid himself of his mounting fear. The ground here was all scrub and bush, and he fell down.

He got up, rubbing his right knee. All the vegetation ahead was low to the ground expect for a hefty, baobab trunk a little way ahead. He paused. It was weird—a sawed off trunk with a tangle of branches that seemed to have fallen into it. He approached it silently. His heart beat faster as he peeped in. Yes, it was hollow, just as he had suspected.

Curled up uncomfortably at the bottom, half sitting, half lying on a knot gnarled roots, was Gabriel. He had not heard Rahul approach.

"Hi," said Rahul feebly.

Gabriel did not respond.

"It's me, Rahul," he continued louder, dropping to his knees, wincing.

Gabriel raised his head, slowly. He looked dazed.

Taking a small, crushed looking banana from the pocket of his baggy pants, Rahul held it out to Gabriel. "Didn't eat it at lunch. Was too full."

The gesture dislodged something in Gabriel. He did not take the fruit, but his eyes cleared and he started hoisting himself out of the hole. Rahul got out of the way as Gabriel emerged slowly, and stood beside Rahul, unsteady. Squinting at Rahul, Gabriel bent down and slapped the dust off his pants.

Rahul's fear had dissipated. It was so good to see Gabriel again!

"What a cool place to hide. Pity I don't have my camera," he said.

Gabriel straightened up and asked: "Was Anjali worried?"

"Yeah, she was. We were all worried. But I found you!" Rahul felt a little proud.

Gabriel shook his head. "I can't go to Canada," he said.

"Really? Why?" Rahul's voice came out all squeaky.

"Because my father is here," Gabriel said.

"I thought he was ... kinda lost."

"He is. I don't know where he is."

Rahul looked squarely at Gabriel; he sure wasn't making much sense today.

Gabriel paused for a moment before saying: "If I leave Kamorga I'll never meet him."

Rahul considered the idea. "Well, you need to find out where he is first. Mary will know. Why don't you ask her?"

Gabriel said nothing. Rahul was like that; everything was simple for him.

"I'll ask her if you like," Rahul said.

"No! I'll ask her."

"Good," Rahul said, looking relieved. "You can see him, and come to Canada after that."

"But what if ... what if he wants me to stay with him?" Gabriel whispered.

"If he wanted he'd have come and got you ages ago."

Suddenly Gabriel hated Rahul—what did he know? What did he know about his father?

Catching Gabriel's expression Rahul said more gently: "He may want you to stay with him, that's true. But when he hears you have a chance to live in Canada, I think he'll say yes."

Gabriel said nothing.

"Once you know him, you can write to him, or call him

from Canada," Rahul said. "And you can come back and visit him too." He desperately wanted Gabriel to come to Canada. It had all been so certain minutes ago!

After a few moments Gabriel asked: "Your father? Where is he?"

"In India. I see him every year. And I see my grandma and grandpa. I have two each."

Gabriel said nothing.

"Mom will take you to Bombay I think, to meet *aaji,* grandmother and *aajoba,* grandfather. They're nice, you'll like them."

Suddenly Gabriel wanted to go home. It was all too much. He started walking, looking straight ahead. Rahul had to hurry to keep pace.

After a few moments he found himself asking Rahul: "You think of your father?"

Rahul didn't reply at once. Then he said: "Sometimes. Jeremy doesn't live with us, but he takes me swimming on Sundays and stuff."

Gabriel had a strong urge to wrestle Rahul to the ground and punch him. Rahul had two fathers! Two fathers!

"And Jeremy will be my dad when we get back," Rahul said, blithely. "Like a real one. He and mom will get married and we'll all live together."

Gabriel came at him with full force. Rahul fell with Gabriel on top. Gabriel hit out blindly; Rahul rolled himself into a ball, knees up against his chest, arms crossed in front of his face. Suddenly, Gabriel stopped. He rolled off Rahul and lay in the dust, thistles pricking his back, looking up at the howling sky. Tears rolled down his face.

Rahul sat up, rubbing a tender spot on this neck. "What

the hell!" he yelled. "What the hell's going on?" Catching sight of Gabriel's face he looked away, letting Gabriel finish crying.

Rahul had thought a lot about Gabriel being in Canada. He had had moments of doubt and flashes of jealousy, but all his imaginings had ended in upbeat images: both of them together at the games, with Jeremy; Gabriel learning to skate, Rahul teaching him some tricks; Gabriel on his school hockey team, playing on his side; Gabriel sitting on the living room sofa, reading; Gabriel helping him with his math homework.

Now he wondered what it would be like for Gabriel, what it would really be like. How he had hated Venimeli when he first got here! And he had known all along that he would return to Canada. For Gabriel, there was no turning back.

After a couple of minutes, Gabriel sat up too.

They got up and shook the dust off themselves but they still looked like that had rolled on the ground.

"We'll say we fell," Rahul said.

Gabriel nodded. He wanted to say he was sorry, but no words came. He couldn't even look at Rahul.

They started walking back in silence.

"Jeremy will be your dad too," Rahul said, after a few moments. He just had to say something. "I like Jeremy, don't you? I think he likes you."

Now Gabriel looked at him and his lips parted in a sudden smile. How black his skin is, and how white his teeth, Rahul thought. Gabriel's smile was something special. He smiled back.

"Do you have oranges in Canada?" he asked.

He's really gone nuts, Rahul thought.

"For sure. Plenty of them. And all kinds of fruits—mangoes, pineapples, bananas, kiwis, grapefruit, berries, cherries, plums, peaches, apples." He was happy to boast about Canada in an uncontroversial way. He had to be careful; mom was always on and on about not making Gabriel feel small.

"Mangoes? They grow in the cold?" Gabriel asked.

"Oh no, only a few things grow there. We just get stuff from all over the place."

It seemed that they got people from all over the place as well, Gabriel thought. That's what Anjali had told him.

The vision of a snowman bearing a large tray with a pyramid of colourful fruit on it came to him. Right on top, of course, were oranges. Father Emmanuel gave them a Christmas card every year; last year it had featured a snowman, and Anjali had spoken a lot about winter and snow.

Suddenly he laughed aloud, and a cloud started to lift, shift, slowly, very slowly. It even looked as if it might gently drift away.

By telling him about her illness, his mother had unleashed a tornado and Gabriel spent countless hours trying to deal with the havoc that followed. Then she had told about the possibility of going to Canada. His first response had been a vehement no. But Mary had kept talking, every day, every night, her voice low but strong, and gradually he had been persuaded.

Kamorga without his mother lost its contours, becoming strangely hollow, insubstantial. At least he would be somewhere else. Yet the images of Canada, vague and blurred, brought no solace. Thoughts of one or the other opened an abyss that he could not, would not, face. So he had directed his energies into the present. Always attentive in class, he focussed even more keenly on what the teachers said. He plunged into books, allowing them to swallow him whole. But escaping into his studies wasn't that easy.

And he needed to ask his mother about his father. Time was flowing like a river in spate. Soon it would engulf his mother and carry her off. And then it would flow on from Kamorga to Canada, without remorse.

Earlier that day he had dashed off fearfully and hid in the baobab, scarcely knowing what he was doing. The hollow had been strangely comforting, holding him in, containing all his emotions. His mind had blanked and he had readily suspended himself into a comforting nothingness. Then Rahul had found him, and he had confessed. It was something like being in Father Emmanuel's presence, in church. Not that he went often to confession, but he had gone a few times.

He noticed that the sky was mostly clear. Around them were plants, open fields, insects, and light, a lot of light. Where there had been only darkness and dread, there was now a little opening.

They ran into Anjali and Fatimah well before they reached Fatimah's compound. Anjali's face lit up at once and Gabriel ran into her arms. Rahul watched, with a twinge of jealousy. Fatimah, noticing, caught his hand, and gave him a smile.

That night, in the room built a little away from the big house, where Gabriel and Mary lived, Gabriel asked his mother who his father was. She told him, readily enough, that his father's name was Atu Mwaka, though the last name Gabriel bore was Iwu, his mother's surname. His father lived in Mapaanji. He used to work for the municipality, and probably still did, because people did not give up good jobs like that.

"Aunt Edith knows him. His family is from Mapaanji so even if he moves she would be able to find him. Father Emmanuel knows about your father too."

His father wasn't a soldier! He hadn't died in war! He

lived! His name was Atu Mwaka! He worked for the municipality! He lived in Mapaanji! His father's family lived in Mapaanji! Gabriel looked at his mother in wonder.

"Does my father know about me?"

Mary nodded. "He has never seen you, but he knows." Then she grew serious. "Gabriel, listen carefully. You can meet your father someday, but only when you are full-grown. It is not the right time now. You must become a man first."

Gabriel nodded. He did not think to ask why she did not live with his father, or why she had not taken him to meet him. The sudden knowledge that he now had, after years of unknowing, filled him to the brim. The questions would come later, but by then it would be too late. He would never hear his mother tell her version of the story.

"Can you promise you'll wait?" Mary asked.

"I promise," Gabriel said solemnly.

Mary held him close and gently stroked his head. Soon after, he lay down on his little bed near the window, and after some tossing and turning, he fell asleep.

But there was no sleep for Mary that night. She sat in a chair near the window for a long time, looking out on the kitchen garden, poorly lit by a few moonbeams.

She thought about how she had met Atu Mwaka, 12 long, hard years ago. She needed to think about it once more, one last time, before her death. God had willed it so.

CHAPTER 29

Gifts

Anjali WAS FOLDING clothes and putting them in her massive suitcase, made expressly for transcontinental travel.

Saturday morning. Tomorrow they would fly to London and from there to Toronto. How unreal! She had some tepid bush tea sitting on the dresser. She traced the rim of the teacup with her finger.

She had carefully stowed the large batik they had given her at the HELP farewell lunch at the bottom of the bag. It portrayed a huge, old baobab, gnarled and twisted like life itself, and under the tree, the figure of an old man in a pointed, woven, reed hat of the sort Anjali had sometimes seen in the streets. A few people sat on the ground at his feet. Some had their backs to the viewer; others were shown in profile. From his expression and stance he seemed to be recounting a dramatic tale to a willing audience.

"This painting will be in my living room with me. *Mandi mana*," Anjali had said. Then she had presented her carefully prepared speech in Morga.

Instead of catering from the Women's Coop Elizabeth had ordered Thai vegetarian from the only Thai restaurant in Jamesville, and a frosted pink cake that read: "Best of Luck" in shiny, lime-green letters. Grace had spoken eloquently in Morga, all praise and thanks for Anjali's work. Later she had come over and thanked her personally.

"I wish I had learnt Morga better," Anjali responded.

"You didn't have time," Grace said.

There was an awkward pause; then Grace was called away by a colleague.

Looking at her retreating figure Anjali remembered how badly she had wanted to know about Grace's possible role in the land grab, and how it mattered much less now. Grace had probably blinded herself to many things because she loved Peter. That sort of misguided adoration was common enough; she had witnessed it often in India. At least Anne was going to speak with Grace, and she would tell Anjali how Grace responded.

Alima Samake had called from Mali to say goodbye. After the call, Anjali paused in the privacy of her office, looking out at the mangosteen. The crow had paid a visit the day before, when she was clearing the desk of her personal things. He had cawed and tilted his head just so, staring fixedly. How sleek and shiny he was. Pity he could not be stroked. "Goodbye Mr. Crow," she had said softly.

Last night Mary had come to Anjali and listed Gabriel's preferences—what food he liked, what colours, when was he most energetic during the day. When asked what hereditary diseases her family members suffered from, and if she had the same information about Gabriel's father and his family, Mary had given a vague, mumbled reply.

"I told him I'm at peace because I know he is going to be with you. I told him to look to the future," she said.

"I'll will try my best to see that Gabriel stays in touch with everyone here," Anjali responded. "He can go to church in Canada if he wants."

"It's okay. His life will be in Canada."

Mary never said Toronto. Perhaps she found the word hard to remember, or say. And she had her own particular pronunciation for "Canada."

"Anjali, someone to see you," Anne called out from downstairs.

Anjali was brought back to the present, her senses quickening. Maybe it was Hassan. After adjusting her hair in the mirror, she went downstairs.

It was Elizabeth. When they sat down together on the sofa, she pulled out a slim, spiral-bound volume from her large purse. "Mama Penda's Kitchen," the handmade cover read.

"All the vegetarian recipes I could think of," she said.

"How sweet!" Anjali embraced Elizabeth. She had already given Elizabeth a card and a gift.

Rahul, who had been observing from the corner, came forward and picked up the booklet.

"We'll start an African restaurant in Toronto!" he said.

Elizabeth smiled. Turning to Anjali she said: "I learnt so much from you. I can't thank you enough."

"Elizabeth, it was lovely working with you. That was the part I really enjoyed the most."

Elizabeth had to leave soon. As always, she had family obligations.

A special lunch followed. Mary had made a spread, and everyone ate at the table together. They now had a maid who came in part-time. Edith, Aissa and John had been invited as well. Anne led the conversation in her fluent, lightly accented Morga.

Anjali wasn't really listening; her mind in a daze. She

looked time and again at Mary, masking the turmoil she felt within with little smiles and nods. She was never going to see Mary again! Never! HELP had failed Mary, failed her badly. The regulars and the irregulars; the luck of the draw.

Despite a heavy heart, Anjali's taste buds were enjoying themselves. Mary's meal was a delight—garlicky, steamed greens, *gali* cooked with nuts, served with a thick, mildly spiced cabbage broth, plantains slow roasted over a charcoal fire, with a jaunty, home-made, tomato dip, and fried fish. She knew that a coconut cake with a caramel topping that the children adored was to follow.

Gabriel sat quietly at the table, his eyes on his plate, chewing slowly, methodically. Anjali dared not guess what he was thinking. Rahul, who sat at the other end, also remained unusually silent. She had seen them playing checkers that morning; it was unusual for them to stay indoors in the day. Perhaps they had talked about the departure and said goodbye.

She had sat down with Gabriel last night, met his solemn eyes and reiterated that she would call soon, write, keep him posted, come back and get him. He had nodded, unsmiling. But in the end he had given her a strong hug that had brought her comfort and relief.

After lunch the children went outdoors, Anne went upstairs and Mary and Edith made for the kitchen. Anjali sat down in the living room and started leafing through a magazine. Surely Hassan would come to see her one last time? But the day wore on with no sign of him.

Anne was going out after dinner, and Rahul asked her to drop him off at Martha's house. Anjali would bring him back in a couple of hours.

Hassan came soon after they had left. He had been at a

movie, he said, and started telling her about it. She felt he was talking to fill time.

"I have something for you," she said, though he had not quite finished.

"Oh?"

She opened a box that lay on the table and gave him a brass and silver bracelet. She had bought it in India for her brother-in-law but had ended up giving him something else.

"Why don't you try it on?" she asked.

He wore it, a trifle self-consciously. It suited him well.

"Thanks. You didn't have to," he said.

"It's nothing." *It's nothing compared to what we could have had together.*

"Maybe you're not disappearing forever," he said, keeping his eyes on the bracelet. Then he looked up. "Perhaps we'll meet at a conference somewhere."

She had thought of that too.

"I'll come back to get Gabriel."

His expression lightened. "Oh yes, of course! I was forgetting that somehow!"

They sat in silence for a few moments. Anjali fingered her *Tawiz*.

Then he showed her what he had brought—Frantz Fanon's *The Wretched of the Earth*, a cheap paperback version. It reminded her of the books she used to buy as a student, from the pavement sellers in downtown Bombay, books that were usually pirated. Fancy printing wasn't a priority in Kamorga either.

"Read it yet?" he asked laughingly.

"I haven't. It's not in the Jamesville expat library for some reason!"

"Hmmm, surprising! And not ideal plane reading either!"

She flipped through the first few pages, expecting that he had written something inside.

"You didn't write something? I mean ... like an autograph."

"Why? I didn't write that book. Unfortunately."

"Still."

He took the book from her and asked: "What should I say?"

"Say, Dear Anjali, I will miss our strange relationship."

"Good idea," he said. He took a pen from his pocket.

"No!" she tried to seize the pen.

"What now?"

"You won't write that!"

"But you just asked me."

"You're really terrible!"

"Okay." He made the peace sign.

When he had finished writing he handed her the book. *To Anjali, With all my love, Hassan*, she read silently.

A big smile brightened her face.

At the door, as he was leaving, they embraced briefly, a distance between them.

She watched him walk away until she could see him no more.

CHAPTER 30

Airborne

ANJALI LOOKED OUT of the plane window, her eyes meeting an endless stretch of undulating land, sand coloured, pockmarked with minute shrubs. A pencil thin line, grey and glinting, snaked through. A river: lifeblood, hope.

Beside her, Rahul dozed. He had pushed his seat back and was slumped to one side, his mouth slightly open. His hand lay in his lap, half covering his Game Boy. It looked like a mechanical but valid extension of his hand.

Outside the immensity of the sky pressed against the plane window. Blue. Would blue be still called blue if there was no sky? She watched the wonderful parade of clouds, wanting to reach out and touch them. The dusty land sets limits but the sky knows no boundaries, open to infinite possibility, she thought. So much possibility scares us humans. Our feet are rooted to the earth, even though our heads occupy space. When we look down we see earth, when we look up, sky. When we look around we see the world we have created. We tend to look down or around, less inclined to gaze at the sky, the stars and the moon. And if we do, we are called dreamers and pulled back to earth.

Yet there are people like the Aanke who believe that they are beings of light.

She wondered if the hopeful scenario that Fatimah had painted on her last visit to Madafi would come to fruition. Or would other barriers emerge? And what about Hassan's vision? She had *The Wretched of the Earth* in her purse; she did not feel inclined to read it just as yet. She was content "being," breathing in the hushed silence that fills planes, and the low, mechanical hum in the background that tells passengers that the great bird is in good flying form. It was nice to have something with her that Hassan had touched, and that had touched him.

She was going to miss the lakeshore at Jamesville and the baobab at the Alliance Française; the mangosteen at her window and the sleek, tar-black bird. And the garden! She would always miss the garden. Such beauty! Lost to her forever.

The room she had put to order at the field office had come to mean something as well.

But most of all she would miss Mary in her neat little kitchen. Martha in her untidy living room. Fatimah in her compound under the awning. Elizabeth's presence in the office even if she was out of sight. Hassan sitting across at her desk.

Suddenly it occurred to her that she would even miss Grace!

Perhaps she would grow a garden in Toronto. Moving into Jeremy's semi-suburban house would make that possible.

She would miss Morga as well. Maybe Gabriel would help her keep bits and pieces of it.

She had put down some roots in Kamorga after all.

Jeremy would be waiting for them at Pearson airport. She

imagined flying into his arms, snuggling against his chest and staying there for an eternity. And Vandana, Vandana was coming to Toronto the following weekend.

She would go back to her job at HELP, but could she commit to being there long term? What else could she do? It was time to reflect, long and deep, share her thoughts and hear what other people had to say.

She pictured talking to Jeremy, sitting by a cheerful fire in his living room, nursing a cup of hot chocolate, Rahul in bed upstairs. There would be chats with Rani as well, likely at her favourite Roti shop on Bloor Street. Francesca would divest herself from the demands of family life, her busy husband and her two young children, and they would take a walk in High Park, or through the Mount Pleasant Cemetery. In Toronto she was blessed with people she could communicate with, who cared deeply for her. That's why she called it home.

Looking down at the land far, far below, she imagined a red stain spreading slowly on the bleached brown surface—the promised revolution. Or would a lot of fences spring up, more and more land moving into private hands? Franz Fanon believed that extreme oppression and loss of freedom justified the use of violence. An armed struggle staged by the Mine Workers Front would be the right action as far as Hassan was concerned. So many predictions about the future went awry. What guarantees that the rebellion would bring a socialist state? And if the socialist state came about, would it really care for its people? Even the formidable, fearless Thomas Sankara, who had defied the West, spawned incredible ideas and wrought change in Burkina Faso, his tiny, West African nation, had gone the way of extrajudicial executions, arbitrary detentions, torture, and a ban on unions and press freedom.

Hassan and Indumati dwelt within ideological certain-
ties that Anjali lacked. Was her own more liberal stance so
wishy-washy after all, or did it have resilience, and some
quiet strength?

Whatever it was that would unfold in Kamorga, she was
no longer part of the equation, no longer someone who would
have a role to play. She had made her small contribution and
now it was Anne's game again. Anne, who had been at it for
10 long years. How much could she have accomplished in just
one year?

More! She had expected more; she had wanted more, for
herself, for Fatimah, for the Aanke, for HELP, for Mary, and for
Kamorga. What was human life after all without ambition,
without striving? They had lost the land, but they had tried.
There had been so much pain and misunderstanding at work.
But she had tried. They had all tried. Even Grace had tried.

And then, through a twist of fate, an event as dramatic
as something in a story, something that happened in someone else's life. Perhaps that was her greatest contribution. Not
what she had sought, but what had been offered to her—a
strange gift, precious and anxiety evoking.

She turned towards Rahul. Beyond him was the third
seat, empty. For a moment she saw Gabriel there, looking
steadily at her, trusting yet watchful. She would be back soon
to get him. She wanted so much to come back for him.

She fiddled with her *Tawiz*.

She had hopes for her boys, and dreams; big ones. What
mother did not? She didn't just carry her own, she shoul-
dered Mary's as well.

The plane would land in London in a few hours, anchor-
ing them again to a fixed territory where they would be

shorn of their feathers and asked for passports. Paperwork! But for now they were suspended, their thoughts no longer earth-bound, soaring, rising, light as butterfly wings, playful as snowflakes. She liked this in-between state.

Author's Notes

How are you? *Kabari ani?*
Good. *Hoori.*
Very Good. *Hoori mana.*
No. *Nigoya.*

I believe in using non-English words and phrases in my fiction to bring home to the reader, directly and tangibly, the fact that s/he is reading about a non-Anglo culture. Morga, is Kamorga's national language. Kamorga, an imaginary African country, has other languages like Fatimah's mother tongue, Bisseau, and Grace's mother-tongue, Kakwa.

Anjali's mother tongue is Marathi, a real language! This is my mother tongue as well. Marathi phrases appear in the text with a translation alongside. An occasional Hindi, Urdu or Arabic word can be found as well.

I used a slightly modified version of Kiswahili to evoke Morga. This may put off some readers; apologies in advance! I'm not a linguist and do not have the talent, interest or time to create an entirely new language. Reshaping Kiswahili a bit, which is widely spoken in East Africa, served my purpose. (Kamorga is also situated in East Africa.)

Long live the diverse languages of the world! They bring us unfathomable riches.

Acknowledgements

This book would not have been written without the support of all who contributed to it.

Merci Vivacité Montréal, Conseil des arts et des lettres, Quebec, for giving me a literary grant in 2011.

Many thanks to Parul Kapur Hinzen for early conversations about the novel, and Andra Tamburro and Sudha Ganapathy for letting me interview them. Shripad Dharmadhikary read a particular and important chapter. Andra Tamburro read the first, imperfect draft of the book and cheered me on. (Sadly she passed away in 2013.) Lynn O'Rouke also did the same and provided great feedback. An experienced editor, she helped me rethink and reshape it, all for free!

My partner Marc-Antoine Parent also commented on the first draft and was a wonderful support all through the writing of this book. A later draft was edited by my multi-talented friend, Clare Thorbes, who gave detailed feedback. Thanks to Vinay Kolhatkar, a novelist himself, on comments and feedback. Cathy Nobleman and Mike Heffernan read a particular chapter and came up with useful suggestions.

Further editorial feedback came from Isabelle Schumacher of Guernica Editions and Jyotsna, from Siyahi, India. Special thanks to Michael Mirolla of Guernica Editions for showing an interest at an early stage. It is always a pleasure to work with Michael. Ditto Connie McParland, co-publisher at Guernica. My mother-in-law, Geneviève Guy, my brother, Amar, and mother, Pramil anointed the final version!

Authors Anita Rao Badami and Mark Frutkin generously provided the names of their agents. H. Nigel Thomas took the time to read the manuscript and provided an author blurb, and additional feedback. The enthusiastic readers and promoters of my first book, *Bombay Wali and Other Stories,* egged me on as well.

Many thanks to David Moratto for consulting with me as he was doing the cover and book design. Thanks also to Paul Century and Brenda Cleary.

Many others engaged in different ways; I am truly touched by all this support.

About the Author

Veena Gokhale, an immigrant shape shifter, started her career as a journalist in Bombay. This "tough, tantalizing" city inspired *Bombay Wali and other stories*, published by Guernica in 2013. Veena came to Canada on a fellowship, returning to do a Masters. After immigrating, she worked for non-profits. *Land for Fatimah* is partly inspired by the two years she spent working in Tanzania. Veena has published fiction and poetry in anthologies and literary magazines and received writing grants. She continues to write freelance, and is currently marketing her book, *The Artichoke, Sensuous Stories*. She lives in Montreal.